MW01124723

The Ajax Protocol

By

Alex Lukeman

http://www.alexlukeman.com

https://www.facebook.com/alexlukeman

pro-to-col: noun
(prōtə ˌkôl,-ˌkäl)

An original note, draft or minute of an agreement, e.g., terms of a treaty agreed to in conference.

To the unsung heroes...

CHAPTER 1

The underground bunker smelled of human stress and old concrete. Half a dozen technicians watched a bank of monitors ranged along one side of the room. The walls and ceiling were of gray concrete, unfinished, without decoration. The main feature of the room was a large wall monitor displaying a world map in green against a black background. Rows of fluorescent lights bathed the room in cold, soulless light.

A man in uniform stood contemplating the screen, hands clasped behind his back. The creases in his pants were as sharp as the points of the four silver stars gleaming on his shoulders. His eyes were dark and intense, under a prominent brow topped off with gray hair cropped close to his skull. He seemed to fill the room with his presence.

His name was Louis Westlake. General Westlake was in charge of the US Army's secret satellite weapons program.

Standing next to Westlake was the US Senate Majority Leader, Edward Martinez. Martinez was the picture of a successful politician. His carefully tailored hair was streaked through with silver. An American flag was pinned on his lapel.

Martinez had risen to power as the strident voice of the average American. His supporters called him "Eddie" and thought he was one of them, someone in Washington who believed in their ideals and values. They could not have been more mistaken.

Martinez and Westlake were the point of a spear aimed at the heart of America.

"Put the satellite image on the big screen," Westlake said. His voice was resonant, authoritative. It was one of his strengths. When Westlake spoke, people listened. They tended to believe him. They did what he ordered, whether they believed him or not.

One of the technicians entered a rapid series of commands on his console. "Coming up now, General."

The map on the wall monitor was replaced by a live satellite picture of Russia and the Siberian plains.

"Bring Ajax on line."

More keystrokes. The word *ready* began flashing in green on the lower part of the big screen.

"Enter the co-ordinates for Novosibirsk," Westlake said.

The technician's fingers played across the keys. A series of numbers appeared on his screen.

"Target acquired," he said. "Alaska standing by."

Martinez turned toward General Westlake. "This is it, General. What we've been waiting for."

"In the end, people will thank us," Westlake said. "It's for their own good. Someone has to take action. The President's policies are turning us into a third world country."

"Rice has been a real problem," Martinez said.

"He won't be a problem much longer."

"You seem certain of that."

"Trust me," Westlake said, "he won't."

"This test will give us valuable data," Martinez said. "The UK will let us refine it. Then we can start here."

"Are the detention facilities ready? Homeland Security is ready to move?" Westlake said.

"Of course." There was a hint of exasperation in Martinez's voice. They'd been over this before. "The legislation has already been drafted. Everything's on schedule, as we planned."

"I just wanted to hear you say it." Westlake turned to the technician. "Activate."

The man on the console pressed a key. The screen changed and displayed a rapid scroll of numbers. The *ready* message changed to *transmit.*

On the other side of the world, people went mad.

CHAPTER 2

Nick Carter took one look at Director Elizabeth Harker and knew it was going to be a long day. Harker headed the Project, an intelligence agency few Americans knew existed. Nick ran the Project team in the field.

Nick tugged on his left ear, where a Chinese bullet had ripped off the earlobe a few years back.

"Director, why do I have the feeling you're about to tell me something I don't want to hear?"

Elizabeth swiveled toward him in the big executive chair she liked. The chair dwarfed her petite frame. She wore her favorite combination of a black pantsuit and simple white blouse. Nick thought her closet was probably a study in black and white. An emerald pin on her jacket picked up the color of her eyes.

"Take a look at this."

Harker touched her keyboard. A monitor on the wall of her office lit with a video of soldiers armed with assault rifles, hunched down behind concrete barricades stretched across a wide boulevard. Ominous columns of black smoke rose from a city in the background. A mob of people was running straight at the barriers, their faces distorted with rage and fear. Nick watched a young woman holding a baby trip and fall and vanish under the trampling feet of the mob. No one paid any attention.

The soldiers began firing as the mob clambered over the barriers. Then the soldiers disappeared under the sea of screaming people.

"Jesus," Nick said. "Where is this happening?"

"Novosibirsk. This is from Russian television, about a half hour ago. We picked it up before Moscow shut down the feed."

She touched another key. The picture switched to an overhead satellite. The cameras on the bird could read a newspaper from 80 miles up.

The center of Novosibirsk looked like a war zone. The streets were deserted. Hundreds of bodies lay where they had fallen. Wrecked cars littered the roads. It looked as though some of them had tried to ram each other. All the shop windows were smashed. The sidewalks and pavement were covered with broken glass.

"What happened?" Nick said.

"I don't know. Whatever it was, it happened fast. Everything was normal. Then it's as if someone flipped a switch. The time stamps on the sat transmissions show less than a half hour from normalcy to that." She gestured at the screen.

"That's impossible. It takes time for a riot to spread."

"Nonetheless, there it is. Something happened, and we need to know what it was."

"You don't think this is just a Russian problem?" Nick said.

"No. Anything that can turn a modern city into a lunatic asylum is a threat. Maybe it was something in the water. Maybe the Russians are experimenting with something and it got out of hand."

"Like what?"

"The Vector Institute is in Novosibirsk. Vector is Russia's bio warfare center. It's possible something got loose."

"A virus that makes people go nuts? It would have to be airborne to affect everyone at once."

"I have a bad feeling about this," Elizabeth said. "Go find Ronnie and Selena and get them up here."

Ronnie Peete and Selena Connor were two of the members of Nick's team. Lamont Cameron was the third. Lamont was in Bethesda Hospital, recovering from a bullet he'd taken in Jordan. He'd been shot through the lung and had almost died.

"They're downstairs on the range." Nick rubbed his chin, where he'd nicked himself shaving that morning.

Harker looked at him. "Well? What are you waiting for?"

CHAPTER 3

At the door to the lower level, Nick almost tripped over a huge orange cat lying on the floor next to a cat bed. Burps was as big as some dogs and tougher than most of them. His ears were tattered and torn. The carpet was damp where he'd drooled on it. It was typical of the cat to ignore the bed and sleep on the floor. Nick stepped over him and started down the spiral stair that led below.

Project headquarters was in the Virginia countryside, not far from the Capitol. Except for a wide cement helipad located at the end of the drive, it looked like a middle class American home, a ranch-style building surrounded by lawns and flower gardens. A low structure that might have been a garage was situated across from the house. A tool shed graced the far end of the lawn and gardens.

The appearance of normality was an illusion. The windows were proof against a .50 caliber round. The front door was made of steel and required a bio-scan and code for entry. Even the French doors leading off to the garden would resist anything short of a vehicle smashing through them.

Underneath the lawn and flowerbeds were three vaults of hardened concrete and steel that had housed a Nike squadron in the days of the Cold War. The missiles were long gone, replaced by the an operations center and emergency quarters, a large room for the computers and a fully equipped gym and firing range. There was an armory next to the range. There was even an underground swimming pool.

Nick opened the door to the range and winced at the echo of pistol fire. Ronnie and Selena stood at the firing line on the indoor range. A row of Plexiglas barriers separated each firing station. Down range, automated targets could be manipulated at will from the stations.

Selena was at the third station. She squeezed off the last round and the slide locked back on her pistol. Nick looked at her target, a man sized silhouette with a neat pattern of holes in the center. She'd put three in the forehead for good measure.

She looked up as he came in and smiled. They'd been lovers for the best part of two years but he never got tired of seeing that smile. Sometimes when Nick looked at her he wondered how someone like her had ended up with someone like him. The best anyone could say about the way Nick looked was that he was rugged. What they said about Selena was that she was beautiful. One of her cheekbones was higher than the other, keeping her face from the burden of perfect beauty. Her reddish blond hair shone under the overhead lights.

"Hey," she said.

"Nice shooting," he said.

She smiled again and took off her shooting glasses, revealing eyes the color of a field of violets.

Ronnie set his pistol down on the bench, took off his ear protectors and pressed a button to pull his target back. He studied the pattern of holes in the middle of the silhouette and then put it in a pile with the other targets he'd shot that day.

"The new vests are here," he said. "They came in this morning."

He walked down the firing line to an empty station. Lying on the bench were a half dozen dark armored vests designed to protect against anything except a neck or head shot or a bullet to one of the limbs. The vest wrapped around the sides and tucked under the groin.

Nick picked one up and hefted it. "Light," he said. "It feels a lot lighter than the ones we've been using."

Ronnie grinned at him. "It is, but it will stop everything short of a .50 with no trouble. It's made out of some kind of new nano ceramic technology that's supposed to minimize secondary damage."

"You mean like busted ribs? You ought to know about that."

"I'm still getting over the last two times," Ronnie said.

Getting hit wearing a vest was no fun. Usually you ended up with cracked ribs. Even though the vest might stop a round, the hydrostatic shock from the impact could kill you.

"I hope we don't have to test them out," Nick said. He put the armor back in the pile.

Ronnie went back to his station and began field stripping his pistol, a SIG-Sauer P229 chambered for .40 Smith and Wesson. Everyone in the project carried the Sig.

Ronnie was Navajo, born and raised, a solid, muscular man just two inches shy of Nick's six foot height. He lived alone in a small apartment on the outskirts of the city. As far as Nick knew, his only indulgence was an extensive collection of Hawaiian shirts.

"Harker wants us upstairs," Nick said.

"Where is it this time?" Ronnie said.

"I don't know. Maybe Russia."

"You don't know? How can we have a mission if you don't know where we're going?"

"I guess we'll find out. Are you two about done?"

"As soon I clean my weapon," Selena said.

"Same here," Ronnie said.

"Come up to Harker's office when you're done." He went back upstairs.

Stephanie Willits was talking with Harker when Nick walked into the office. Steph was Harker's deputy and computer guru. The project had a bank of maxed out Crays that rivaled Langley's and Steph could do things with them that bordered on magic. She wore a midnight blue skirt and blouse that set off her dark brown hair. Steph favored big, dangly earrings and gold bracelets on her left wrist. Nick liked her.

From where Elizabeth sat behind her desk, she could look out through a set of French doors at a wide patio paved with gray stone. Beyond the patio, a green lawn and flower beds blazing with summer colors stretched down a gentle slope until they met a line of trees that shielded the back of the property.

A long, leather couch flanked by two chairs faced Elizabeth's desk. Nick took a seat on one end of the couch. Stephanie took a chair. Selena and Ronnie came in and sat on the couch.

Harker began with the riots in Novosibirsk. Then she turned to Stephanie.

"Steph, what have you got for us?" Elizabeth asked.

"Langley doesn't know what happened," Stephanie said. "Moscow ordered a Spetsnaz division into the city. They're deploying through the city as we speak."

"An entire division?" Nick was surprised. "You don't send those guys in without a damn good reason. Things must be completely out of control. "

"There's something else," Stephanie said. "I decided to take a look at satellite activity over Russia and I found an anomaly. It almost slipped by me. It could be a coincidence, but I don't think so."

"I don't like coincidences. Or anomalies either," Elizabeth said. "What is it?"

"Just before the riots started, there was a very high frequency transmission centered on Novosibirsk. It may be connected to what happened. An attack of some kind."

"What sort of transmission?"

"A micro-burst of energy. A signal. It was right before things went south."

"Where did it come from?"

"Well, that's just it," Stephanie said. "There were only three satellites in range at the time. One of those was Russian. I don't think the Russians would attack their own city. One was Chinese, but it's supposed to be a communications satellite."

"You said three. What's the third?" Elizabeth asked.

"A new one of ours that went up six months ago, controlled by the Pentagon. I don't know it's purpose. Probably surveillance."

"Do you think the Pentagon zapped Russia from it?" Ronnie said.

"I didn't say that. As far as I know we don't have anything that could produce that kind of effect. But that electronic burst is a red flag," Stephanie said, "and our satellite was overhead."

"I don't believe we'd do something like this, even if we had the ability," Selena said. "It would mean war. No one wants that."

For a moment, the room was quiet as they thought about what war would mean.

Then Nick said, "No one in this room wants that. But if Steph is right, someone deliberately started those riots and somehow used a satellite to do it."

Harker sighed. "Steph, there had to be a command transmission from the ground to activate the satellite. See if you can pin down where that signal came from."

"As soon as we're done here. I'll get on the computers and see if I can track the source."

Nick said, "What do you want us to do, Director?"

"Be ready. Until we have more intel, there's not much else we can do."

CHAPTER 4

In the Yasenevo district on the outskirts of Moscow, the hot sun of a humid Russian summer beat down on a gray office building. On the top floor of the building, a tall, athletic man with close cropped blond hair walked toward the office of his boss, the heels of his shoes echoing from the linoleum floor of the hallway. His eyes were the clear blue of an Arctic sky. Two gold stars gleamed on the red and gold shoulder boards of his uniform. His chest bore ribbons honoring secret campaigns and battles that would never find their way into the history books.

Lieutenant Colonel Arkady Korov was Spetsnaz, part of Russia's elite special forces. He carried a thin folder in his left hand. He paused at the door of General Alexei Vysotsky's office to gather his thoughts, knocked twice, and went in.

Alexei Vysotsky commanded Department S of the *Sluzhba Vneshney Razvedki*, Russia's Foreign Intelligence Service. SVR was Moscow's equivalent of CIA, the latest in a long line of Russian secret police and intelligence organizations that had begun with the Czars. Department S included the secretive Spetsnaz unit called Zaslon. The Kremlin refused to admit that Zaslon existed, but it was Zaslon that took care of the black ops assignments, the ones that needed to be officially denied. Everyone in Zaslon had gone through the rigorous Spetsnaz training, had seen serious combat, and spoke at least three languages. Korov was one of Vysotsky's senior commanders in Zaslon.

Vysotsky sat behind an old-fashioned wooden desk rescued from a Kremlin storeroom. The desk had belonged to Lavrenti Beria, head of the secret police during the reign of Stalin. It amused Vysotsky to use Beria's desk. It appealed to his sense of history. Vysotsky even looked a bit like Beria. His black hair showed signs of gray and had started to recede from a large, rounded forehead. His eyes were unreadable, but they sent a message that it would not be wise to offend him.

The nature of Vysotsky's job meant that he dealt with rumors, stories, false leads, disinformation and lies. He had assigned Korov to sort out what was useful and what was not in the mass of conflicting data accumulating in the aftermath of the riots in Novosibirsk.

"Colonel. Tell me you have good news inside that folder."

Vysotsky leaned over and pulled open the bottom drawer of his desk. He took out a bottle of vodka and two glasses, fairly clean. He poured the drinks and pushed a glass across to Korov.

"Sit down, Arkady." He raised his glass. *"Na zdrovnya."*

"Na zdrovnya."

They downed the drinks. Vysotsky refilled the glasses. Five days had passed since the riots and he'd slept little during that time. Russia's domestic security agency, the FSB, had failed to produce anything except reams of useless paperwork that led nowhere. The Kremlin suspected that foreign sabotage had somehow caused the events in Siberia. The problem had been given to Vysotsky to solve, with the unspoken certainty that failure would terminate his chances of promotion.

"Tell me what you have learned," Vysotsky said.

"The riots have stopped and order has been imposed on the city," Korov said. "The sequence of events is clear but confusing."

"What do you mean? How can it be both?"

"Not long before the trouble started, a bomb exploded in the factory district on the edge of the city. It drew all available police and fire units. They were engaged when the riots started. The epicenter of the riot was near the city center. By the time police got to the scene, everything was out of control. The riot had already spread over a wide area."

"How could it spread so fast? What triggered it?" Vysotsky asked.

"At first glance there seems to be no specific cause for what happened. However, questioning of survivors reveals a consistent pattern."

"Go on."

Korov twirled his empty glass between his fingers.

"People report that before the trouble started they heard a high pitched sound, more like a vibration than an actual sound, and felt a sensation of heat. Immediately after that, most said they felt angry, enraged. In many cases they attacked anyone nearby."

"Most? What about the others?"

"Some became nauseous and vomited, followed by a blinding headache. They were incapacitated. All the survivors report headaches, to a greater or lesser degree."

"Continue."

"It appears that everyone within a radius of about eight square kilometers was severely affected, with lesser degrees of affect farther away from city center. The riots spread out from the center and people got caught up in them."

"Casualties?"

"Still unknown," Korov said. "Estimates are over 4000 dead and injured. People were murdering each other for no apparent reason. There are countless injuries, many severe. Property and infrastructure damage is extensive."

"What is your assessment?"

"Of the cause?"

Vysotsky nodded and downed his drink.

"I can't say. We don't know enough."

"Speculate."

Korov chose his words with care. "I think it's an attack. At first I thought perhaps the water supply had been poisoned or drugged. Analysis shows nothing. Besides, if the water was the problem there wouldn't be a sudden, simultaneous explosion of rage like that. Everyone would have to drink at the same time."

"Some kind of electronic weapon, then? We have beams that can make people sick or kill them with microwaves."

"Those weapons are narrow in their focus and limited in range," Korov said. "They couldn't affect a large area. We don't have anything that can produce an effect like this."

"I agree," Vysotsky said. "We should assume it was an attack. Why Novosibirsk? It doesn't make sense. Who would risk war for such an insignificant result?"

Vysotsky refilled the glasses. Korov didn't drink like his boss, but it would be insulting to refuse. The men drank.

Vysotsky continued. "There aren't many who would have the kind of technological resources to do something like this. The Americans, perhaps. Or Beijing."

"It doesn't make sense," Korov said. "Why would either the Chinese or the Americans do this? Why risk war for no strategic gain? The Chinese are preoccupied with their economy. They can't afford a war. The American President would never sanction such an attack. And how was it done?"

"If it is a beam weapon of some kind, it had to come from a satellite."

Korov nodded. "We can look for anything that was in range."

"Find out what was up there."

"Yes, sir."

CHAPTER 5

Phil Abingdon was bored. He reached into a large jar of jelly beans he kept on his desk and chose a green one, popped it in his mouth and chewed. Abingdon was the chief programmer at the underground command center that controlled Ajax. Part of his job was maintaining computer security. The system of firewalls and hacker traps he'd created on the Ajax computers was as good as it got, better than Langley's. Phil knew that was true because he was able to hack into the CIA servers with relative ease.

Hackers across the world formed a loosely knit internet community, the members known only by their screen names. Abingdon was one of the elite, a recognized master of the art.

He'd discovered his gift for programming as a teenager. He loved the challenge of hacking into places he wasn't supposed to go. One of those places had been the Pentagon and when the military cops showed up at his door seven years ago, he'd thought he was headed for Guantanamo. Instead, General Westlake had offered him a job.

Abingdon's screen handle was Apocalypse. He thought it had a nice ring to it. It conveyed his message: *You have no future. I bring the end of your world.*

When the computers signaled an intruder on the system, his first thought was that it was a false alarm. Someone would have to get through the outer rings of his defenses for the alert to go off. It had never happened. Routine probes were dismissed and answered with a malicious worm that corrupted the hacker's files. No one ever tried more than once.

The hacker had gotten past the automatic blocking programs, past the anti-virus and spyware programs, past the secondary defenses.

Phil smiled to himself in silent admiration of the skill of the attacker. *You're good, whoever you are.* Of course, it couldn't be tolerated. He activated a program that diverted the incoming code to a meaningless file that appeared important but contained nothing. He entered another command and the screen filled with lines of code the intruder was using to gain access. There was something familiar about it. He'd seen this style before, he was sure of it.

There were very few hackers at Phil's level. Each had a distinctive touch, what the old radio code operators had called a "fist", an identifying pattern as unique as a fingerprint. Then it clicked.

Butterfly.

It had been at least two years since he'd seen that signature style. He thought it was probably a woman, but he didn't know for sure. It was only a hunch, a feeling. He thought of Butterfly as her, not him.

Well, hello, Butterfly. I'm about to ruin your day.

Phil entered a new string of commands. The incoming code flickered, paused, then resumed.

Son of a bitch. She must be on something with a lot of horsepower. Maybe a Cray. She picked it up and countered.

He sent a vicious virus that would wipe out everything in her files. She went offline. Phil stared at the empty screen. *That ought to do it,* he thought. *I'd like to meet her someday.*

Where had the attack come from? He pulled up another program designed to trace unauthorized attempts to access the Ajax files. The screen showed that the attack had come from the Ukraine, after bouncing around the globe to various IP servers. Phil didn't believe that for a moment. Butterfly had been clever, but Phil had written a program that reverse engineered attempts to conceal the source by diverting the servers. In less than a minute, he had it. The server was in Virginia, outside of Washington.

This isn't good, he thought. *The General isn't going to like this.*

He picked up the secured line and called Westlake.

In his home outside Washington, Westlake had just poured himself a large measure of single malt whiskey. The blinking light on his secured phone told him the call was coming from the command center.

He picked up the phone.

"Yes."

"General, this is Phil Abingdon. We have a problem."

"What kind of problem?"

"We've been probed. I've identified the source and was able to trace it."

"Yes?"

"I wouldn't bother you with this but the attack came from a computer assigned to one of the intelligence agencies."

"Which one?"

"I've never heard of it. Something called the Presidential Official Joint Exercise in Counter Terrorism."

The Project, Westlake thought..

"I know who they are," he said. "Were they successful?"

"No, sir. I blocked them from getting anything important."

"How did they find us?"

"I don't know. They might have tracked us by the satellite transmission over Russia."

"You're sure they didn't get into the database?"

"Yes, sir."

"Good work, Abingdon. I'll take care of it. Keep me informed."

"Yes, sir." Abingdon put down the phone.

Westlake sipped from his drink and considered his options. He knew about the Project and he knew about Elizabeth Harker. She had a reputation for being relentless. Once she fastened onto something, she was like a dog that wouldn't let go. She'd probed his command server, it was possible she could discover the location of the bunker. He couldn't let that happen.

He'd have to do something about her and her group. Action against her was necessary.

How much did she know? Who had she told? The only way to find out was to ask her. He'd have to get her someplace where she could be questioned and if that wasn't possible, eliminate her. If he went after Harker, he'd have to take out her team as well.

Somehow his glass was empty. He got up and filled it again. Tomorrow evening, the next phase of the plan was set to unfold. It would provide a perfect opportunity to catch Harker off her guard.

Westlake picked up his phone and made the arrangements.

CHAPTER 6

It was almost 8 o'clock on the evening of the next day. President James Rice sipped from a glass of water as he waited for his cue to go on stage. He was about to make an important speech on national television about the struggling economy.

Rice was worried about more than the economy. A potential crisis was shaping up in Russia and no one knew for sure what had happened over there. The signs weren't good. Recent relations between the White House and the Kremlin were slipping toward cold war status. Earlier, a cable had come from his ambassador in Moscow warning that the Federation suspected the US could be involved with what had happened in Siberia.

Rice didn't know what had happened in Siberia. He was afraid it would turn into one of those terrorist incidents that threatened America. If the public knew how many times the country had come within a hair's breadth of total destruction because of the insane acts of suicidal terrorists, Rice was sure they would run screaming through the streets. He wanted to be back in the White House, working on a way to defuse the building tensions. Instead, he was about to make a speech aimed at convincing the American public that everything was fine while the world economy tottered on the brink of collapse.

At moments like this, he would think about his family and how fragile the illusion of security and safety that surrounded them and every other American family really was. Sometimes it wasn't much fun playing the role of leader of the free world.

He felt unwell, a little feverish. He took another sip of water. It had an odd taste, but at least it was wet and cold.

The Secret Service agent standing next to him said, "There's your cue, Mister President."

"Thank you, Sam. Everyone in place?"

"Yes, sir."

Rice straightened his tie. It was his favorite necktie, given to him by his daughter. That had been years ago, but he still liked to wear it. For some reason it felt unusually tight.

"Showtime," he said.

He strode onto stage to the strains of *Hail to the Chief*, flashing his traditional wide smile and waving to the expectant crowd. He reached the podium and looked out at the teleprompter. Sudden pain ran down his left arm like a bolt of fire. Then it was as if a giant hand reached out and grabbed his chest and squeezed. He couldn't breathe.

Rice staggered, clutched at the podium and pitched forward onto the stage. Shouts came from the crowd. The Secret Service detail ran forward and surrounded him.

At home in Virginia, General Westlake watched the confusion and chaos on his television and smiled. The cameras cut away to the network studio. He poured himself another drink.

That's one problem solved. One to go.

He eyed the amber liquid in his glass and decided it was the last of the evening. Alcohol helped him think, but lately he'd caught himself drinking more than usual. He'd come too far to make a mistake at this stage of the game. The last pieces were being moved into place.

Westlake came from a strong military tradition. His grandfather had been wounded in France during World War I. His father had won the Distinguished Service Cross and a Silver Star in World War II. When Westlake graduated from West Point he'd been a naïve young man who believed his country was led by those who wanted to make the world a better place.

Instead, he'd watched America become a country run by people who thought profit and compromise was a successful national strategy. He'd watched the military hamstrung by incompetent leaders and misguided policies, even as superior technology and a giant budget turned it into the most fearsome fighting force the world had ever seen.

He'd risen almost to the top of the military pyramid, but high rank was political in nature. He'd been passed over for the Joint Chiefs and high command in the field. His outspoken and public views that mistakes had been made and changes were needed had earned him enemies in Congress.

Westlake was not alone in his views. He had the support of powerful men in Congress and at the Pentagon. Men who made a difference, who believed as he did in the nation's destiny. Patriots and realists like himself, ready to do something about it.

Four years ago, he'd gotten an invitation to a quiet meeting that had altered his life. That meeting had led to more meetings, with men who had a plan to take control of the government, men of influence and wealth. They wanted him to lead a new America, an America that would claim its place as the one supreme power in the world.

Still, he'd hesitated. Then his son had been killed in Afghanistan. It had been the final argument that convinced him to join them.

Westlake looked over at the picture he kept on his desk and felt the pull of grief that never seemed to leave him. The photo had been taken on the day his boy graduated from West Point. Alan Westlake was smiling, proud and tall in his gray uniform. He had died for no good reason in a badly managed war that was bleeding America dry.

When the transition was over and he was in control, there would be no more wars fought without the political will to win.

Westlake raised his drink to the picture of his son.

CHAPTER 7

Elizabeth was working late. Everyone else had gone home.

She was debating with herself about working for a few more hours and spending the night downstairs. She leaned back in her chair and looked at the picture of her father she kept on her desk. She missed her father, his stable presence, his ability to see to the heart of any situation. More importantly, his ability to see to the heart of whatever situation was troubling her.

Her father had been a judge in western Colorado, in an era when judges still had wide discretion over their decisions. That had changed during his last years on the bench, as more and more political interference crept into the court system. The growing rigidity of the sentencing structure and the turnstile approach to sentencing and release was one of the few things she'd ever heard him complain about.

When her direct phone line signaled a call, she knew it was bad news. No one called at this time of night unless the news was bad.

"Harker," she answered.

"Director, this is Agent Price of the President's Secret Service detail. I'm calling you from Walter Reed. President Rice has had a heart attack. He's asking for you."

Her heart skipped a beat. She knew he'd been giving a major speech that night but she decided to watch it at home later. The voice on the other end of the line continued. "A helicopter is on the way. It will be there in 10 minutes. Please be ready."

"How is he?"

"Not good. Ten minutes, Director."

Elizabeth stood and put her phone in her purse. If they were sending a helicopter, it meant Rice was probably dying. She prayed it wouldn't happen. Rice was one of the very few people Elizabeth had ever admired. If he died, the world would become a more dangerous place.

She turned out the lights in her office, went outside and walked over by the helipad to wait. After a few moments she heard the distinctive *whop, whop* of rotors beating against the humid air. She watched the helicopter descend in a wide, sweeping turn. The pilot brought it in over the landing area and hovered before setting the craft down. The rotors continued to turn. The chopper was all black and unmarked.

Funny, she thought, *I don't think I've ever seen a model quite like that before. Usually they send a Marine unit.*

A man in a dark suit descended from the craft. He was about six feet tall, with a dark complexion and longish hair. He needed a shave. For some reason Elizabeth felt uneasy, but she couldn't quite put her finger on why.

"Director Harker? I'm Agent Williams. Let me help you in."

He started toward her. Elizabeth noticed an earpiece with a cord trailing behind it, something every Secret Service agent seemed to have. He wore the traditional garb of the service, a dark suit and tie. If it'd been daylight, he probably would've had sunglasses. All that was standard issue. She noticed his shoes. He was wearing brown loafers.

Her intuition sounded an alarm. No agent would have been caught dead with loafers, brown or any other color, especially someone from the White House detail. His hair was too long, and she had never seen a Secret Service agent who needed a shave.

Something in her face gave must have given her away. The man's expression hardened. He reached under his suit jacket. Behind the glass canopy of the helicopter the pilot watched the two of them.

Elizabeth had not gotten where she was by being stupid. Even as he moved, her mind had processed the details it was taking in. The hair, the need for a shave, the shoes. It all added up to trouble. She made a decision. Her pistol came out of the quick draw holster at her waist as Williams drew a gun from under his jacket. She fired three, fast rounds. He fired into the ground, the round ricocheting off the cement, and fell back onto the hard surface of the pad.

With a full throttle roar, the helicopter lifted off the pad and started to rise, turning as it climbed.

Elizabeth was angry. She raised her gun in both hands and emptied the rest of the magazine at the chopper. Sparks flew from the metal fuselage. Some of her hollow point bullets found the engine intake. The slide locked back on her empty pistol. The helicopter rose steadily away from her.

A sudden, strident sound of shrieking metal filled the night as the engine seized in mid-air. A thick plume of black, oily smoke poured from the rear of the bird. The helicopter tipped sideways and veered toward her. She could see the terrified face of the pilot through the canopy as the machine plummeted out of control. Elizabeth ran off the pad and dove onto the lawn. The helicopter passed over her and flew straight into the ground. The spinning rotors hit the dirt. The machine cart wheeled and exploded in a blossom of orange flame. The sound rolled across the Virginia countryside like thunder and faded away.

Elizabeth raised her head and looked at the burning wreckage. Then she looked over at the man she had killed. He lay on his back. Blood soaked his shirt and oozed under his body. The toes of his brown loafers pointed into the air. She got to her feet. Her hands were shaking.

She inserted a fresh magazine into her pistol, released the slide and de-cocked the hammer. She holstered the weapon.

The crash would have been noticed by someone. She couldn't afford to have the local cops and the NTSB and everyone else poking around the crash scene, not until she knew who had sent the helicopter. Not until she had more information. She would have to call in favors and invoke National Security. It would be messy, but she could keep things under wraps long enough to find out what the hell had just happened. She didn't have a choice, if she wanted to keep control of the situation.

She took out her phone and called Clarence Hood on his private, secure line. Hood was the current Director of Central Intelligence and an ally Elizabeth could rely on. There were good reasons for that. If it hadn't been for Elizabeth and her team, Hood would be in a federal prison instead of on the seventh floor of Langley.

"Clarence, it's Elizabeth. I need your help."

"Elizabeth. You've heard about the President?"

"Yes. What's his status?"

"Uncertain. He's in the ICU at Walter Reed."

"Something has happened here," Elizabeth said. She told him about the phone call and the helicopter. She looked over at the wreckage as she spoke.

"It still burning," she said. "Someone must've noticed. The state police and everyone else are going to be here in a few minutes. I need your help to head them off."

"The man who identified himself as a Secret Service agent said the President had sent him?"

"Yes. I'm wondering if somehow it's related to what happened to Rice."

"You think it may have been an assassination attempt?"

The only thing that gave away Hood's stress was a slight increase in his soft, southern accent.

"It seems like too much of a coincidence, and I don't believe in coincidences," Elizabeth said. "I think you should boost Rice's security."

"I'll have a team there in 15 minutes," Hood said. "If anyone shows up, stall them until they get there. Call me tomorrow. We'll talk. "

"I'll do that," Elizabeth said. She ended the call.

The flames from the burning helicopter lit up the night. Over on the patio by her office, she saw the cat watching the fire.

CHAPTER 8

The next morning Elizabeth briefed the team.

After his conversation with Elizabeth, Hood had ordered Rice's doctors to administer a specialized panel of tests designed to look for unusual results well outside the normal coronary event. Trace elements of a rare toxin had been discovered in his blood. The poison came from a plant that grew only on the upper slopes of the mountains in Haiti. The extract of the plant produced all the symptoms of a heart attack. It was usually fatal. Someone had tried to kill him.

Flowers and notes were piling up in heaps at the barriers in front of the White House. The information that Rice had been the target of an assassination attempt was being kept from the public. The Secret Service, the FBI and the others had no leads.

No one said a word as Elizabeth told them about the attempt to kill her. From where he sat, Nick could see the charred remains of the helicopter in the flower beds outside. Someone had just upped the ante, but they didn't know the name of the game or who was playing.

"No one called from Bethesda," Elizabeth said. "Rice wasn't asking to speak with me. It was a set up."

Nick said, "Remind me not to get you mad at me. Hard to believe you shot that down with a pistol." He gestured out the windows at the wreckage.

Everyone looked at the ruins of the helicopter. It wasn't something you saw every day.

"I was mad." Harker picked up her Mont Blanc and began tapping on the desk.

"That's my point."

"What happens to that wreck out there?" Ronnie asked.

"Hood will handle it."

"Any ID on the phony agent you killed?"

"Former FBI, kicked out a few years ago. He was suspected of compromising an important investigation. There was nothing they could charge him with at the time, but they let him go."

"Why send a chopper?"

"I think they wanted to kidnap me. If they couldn't do that, then kill me."

"What's the status of the president?" Selena asked. She wore a pale blue silk blouse that offset the violet of her eyes.

"He's alive, but he's out of commission for a while. Vice President Edmonds has taken over. He won't be sworn in unless Rice dies or is declared unable to perform."

"That could be a problem," Nick said. "Edmonds doesn't like us."

"I don't like him either, but we have to deal with it. Edmonds thinks we're a bunch of loose cannons. We're not going to get any cooperation from the White House as long as he's sitting in the big chair."

"Are we going to try and find out who went after Rice?" Selena asked.

"Plenty of people are looking at that. For now they can deal with it. I'm more concerned with why someone came after me. Why me? Whoever it is knew my private number and knew I'd have to respond to a summons from Rice. There aren't many who have that number. Which I'm changing, by the way."

Ronnie rubbed a knuckle across his nose. "Someone's playing hardball."

"They've got to be well financed and well organized," Nick said. He gestured out the window at the wreckage. "That's an expensive pile of junk out there."

Elizabeth set her pen down. "That doesn't narrow things down much.,"

Nick tugged on his ear. "Who knows how to reach you?"

"The Chairman of the Joint Chiefs. Hood. The President. The Director of National Intelligence. The Director of the NSA."

"Don't forget the Russians," Nick said. "Vysotsky has it."

"He's more subtle than that," Harker said. "It's not his style."

"What about Edmonds?" Selena asked.

Harker gave her an odd look. "That's an evil thought, Selena. He doesn't like me and he'd be happy if I was out of the picture, but I don't think he wants me dead."

"Somebody does."

"Well," Elizabeth said, "If they want it badly enough, they'll try again."

"What's next?" Nick asked.

"I'll try and track down the helicopter," Stephanie said. "We might be able to find out who owns it and where it came from." She twisted the gold bracelets around her wrist. She did that when she was tense.

Elizabeth looked at them. "All of us may be targets. I don't want to go into lockdown but everyone needs to be careful."

"What else is new?" Ronnie said.

CHAPTER 9

The kitchen of Nick's Washington apartment was a comfortable place, big enough for a table and four chairs. It was set off from the living area by a wide counter that did double duty as a bar. A Paul Klee reproduction hung over a Danish modern couch in the living room. Nick liked the clean, uncluttered look of European furniture, just as he really liked Klee's paintings. A genuine Klee hung in the bedroom, a gift from Selena. Selena sat at the table reading a magazine and humming to herself. Nick stood at the stove making them something to eat.

He looked over at her and thought about the file in his top dresser drawer, the one Adam had given him. He had decided that it was time to show it to her.

Nick knew Adam only as a disembodied electronic voice from the other side of a partition in the back seat of an armored Cadillac. He'd never seen what Adam looked like. He didn't even know if Adam was a man or a woman.

Nick would come out of his building and Adam's black Cadillac would be waiting by the curb. He'd get in the car, they'd drive around for a while, and Adam would talk about unpleasant things he thought Nick needed to know, about unpleasant people planning the kinds of things that started wars. The problem was that he was always right. Nick thought of him as a kind of personal messenger from the gods of conspiracy.

Just a week before, Adam had given him a classified CIA file from the days of the Cold War, when records and reports were printed on paper and kept in locked cabinets instead of computers. He'd told Nick it would affect his relationship with Selena. After he'd read it, he wished he'd never seen the damn thing. He'd been unable to make up his mind about when to tell her about it. The contents of that file were going to upset her and make her unhappy. It was about the deaths of Selena's family, killed when she'd been ten years old. Their car had gone over a cliff near Big Sur.

An accident, the police said. Except it hadn't been an accident. The file revealed that her family had been murdered by the KGB. Worse, it proved that Selena's father had been a spy. A traitor. How could he tell her that?

Nick stirred the vegetables and meat simmering on the stove and added a little cayenne, a dash of salt.

"You hungry?" he said.

Selena smiled. "Starving. Whatever you're making over there, it smells good."

"Just stir fry, nothing special."

Nick scooped the food out of the pan and put it in a bowl. He carried the steaming bowl over to the table, dished some onto Selena's plate and his own and sat down. They began eating.

"A lot of people are praying for Rice," Selena said.

"He's tough. He'll make it."

"Who do you think went after Elizabeth?" Selena took a sip of white wine and set her glass back down on the table.

"I don't know."

Nick pushed his food around on his plate.

"Something's bothering you, isn't it?"

After two years with Nick, Selena had gotten good at reading him.

Somewhere in his mind a quiet voice said *tell her*. He was tired of walking a mental tightrope about it. She'd handle it, or she wouldn't. It was time to come clean.

"The last time I saw Adam he gave me something."

Selena knew about Adam, everyone in the Project did. She waited.

"A file," he said.

"A file? What kind of file?"

"A classified file from Langley. From the 80s. Adam said it's the only copy."

"What's in it?"

Nick sighed. "It's about your father."

"Adam gave you a CIA file about my father? When were you planning on letting me know?"

"That's what I'm doing now."

"Why would he do that? Give it to you?"

"I suppose he wanted me to know what's in it."

She set her fork down "Where is it?"

"In the other room."

"Maybe you'd better show it to me."

Nick sighed again. He got up and went into the bedroom and took the folder from the drawer. He set the file down on the table in front of her and went over to the liquor cabinet. He was going to need something stronger than wine once she'd read the contents. Nick poured himself an Irish whiskey and went back to the table and sat down. He pushed away the remains of his meal. He'd lost his appetite.

Selena read in silence. He watched the impact of what she was reading sink in. She finished reading and went back to the beginning and began to go through the papers again. After a while she looked up. Her eyes were wet.

"Why didn't you show this to me before?"

"Because I didn't know how it would affect you. I knew I'd have to give it to you sooner or later."

"You didn't think I could handle it." Her voice was flat, emotionless.

"I didn't say that."

"This says that my father was a double agent, working for the KGB."

Nick felt helpless. What are you supposed to say when your lover finds out that her father was a traitor?

"I'm sorry, Selena."

"I don't believe this," she said. "My father wasn't a traitor."

"Adam has no reason to make it up."

"You don't know that."

"I know everything he's said in the past has turned out to be true. Why would he make something like this up? It's real," Nick said. "The paper is the right age. It even smells like the 80s."

"Maybe it's a false plant, a trick."

"Why would he do that?"

"I don't know."

She picked up the folder, set it down.

"This says it wasn't a car accident that killed them."

"No."

"The KGB killed him. And my mother and my brother."

"They would have killed you too, if you had been in that car."

"Bastards," she said.

"I'm sorry," he said again. He didn't know what else to say.

"BASTARDS!" she shouted. She stood and hurled her glass of wine across the room. It shattered against the wall. Then she put her hands over her face and began sobbing.

Nick went over and put his arms around her and held her close without speaking. He could smell the clean scent of her hair. After a few moments she calmed. She wiped her eyes, used a napkin to blow her nose and sat back down at the table.

"I want a drink," she said. "A strong one."

Nick poured a double whiskey for her and another for himself. He gave her the glass and sat down across from her. She took a long swallow.

"My uncle knew," she said. "He knew all along. His name was on those papers. He signed off on them. I knew he had ties to the CIA, but I didn't know he worked for them. He had friends at Langley. One of them set up the security at my loft in San Francisco."

"It must've been a hell of a shock when he found out about your father," Nick said.

"How could my father do that? How could he betray his country? He was a wonderful man, a wonderful father. What makes someone turn on the country that gave him everything?"

"I don't know. I don't think Langley knew for sure which side he was really on. It looks like he was feeding the Russians false information along with the real goods. That would give the KGB enough reason to eliminate him. He might have been under orders to give them bad info."

"But if he was passing false information and Langley knew about it, why do these reports make it look as though he was a traitor, another rotten double agent?"

"There could be a lot of reasons. Maybe someone higher up wanted to cover their ass. Or someone wanted to manipulate the truth for their own advantage. When you start looking at Langley during the 80s, it's all smoke and mirrors."

"Bastards," she said again.

Nick wasn't sure whether she meant the Russians or the CIA.

"What are you going to do?" she asked.

"About what?"

"Are you going to tell Harker?"

"I don't see any reason to," Nick said.

"You don't think this could affect my clearance? Whether she trusts me or not?'

"Are you getting biblical on me?"

"What do you mean?"

"The sins of the fathers being visited on the generations and all that. You're not your father."

"You don't think she ought to know?"

"What good would it do?"

"Selena held up the file folder. "I want to study this," she said. "There could be something in it to clear my father's name. A detail, a name. Something."

"Maybe." *Or maybe not,* Nick thought. But he kept his thoughts to himself.

"I'm going home," she said. "I need to think."

Nick wasn't sure what to say. He opted for neutral.

"We have a briefing at 0900 tomorrow," he said. "You want to pick me up and give me a ride in?"

"I'll meet you in front of the building at eight."

"Call me. If you want to talk."

"I need to think," she said again.
He watched the door close behind her.

CHAPTER 10

The next day, Nick and Selena were riding back to Washington after the morning briefing in Virginia. Traffic on 66 was heavy. Selena had been quiet ever since they'd left the Project.

"How are you doing?" he said.

"All right. I've been thinking a lot about that file." Selena stepped down on the gas and blew past a delivery truck.

"Whoa," Nick said.

"What's the matter?"

"You just missed taking off the side mirror." He glanced at the speedometer. They were doing a little over 80.

"It's still there, isn't it?" Her voice was tight.

Nick started to say something and thought better of it.

"The whole thing stinks," she said.

"What do you mean?"

"The file makes it look like dad was a traitor. He would never be a traitor. Not to his family or his country. Langley knew he was passing things to Moscow. Why didn't they stop him? You don't let someone give away secrets, once you know what they're doing. He had to be working with the blessing of the Director."

"You think he was a double?"

"Yes. I think Langley used him to pass disinformation to the Soviets."

"Why wouldn't the file say that?" Nick asked.

"I don't know. Maybe someone made a mistake and didn't want it known. Maybe there really was a traitor, someone who tipped off the Russians and covered it up by making my father look guilty. I may never know exactly what happened, but I know that the KGB killed him. If the person who did it is still alive, I want to make him pay. I want him to tell me what he knows."

"Whoever killed him was a KGB assassin. How would you find him?"

"I don't know, but I will."

Looking at her, Nick was certain of one thing. If whoever killed her family was still alive, Selena would track him down. He suspected that once she found him, his days were numbered.

"There's something I have to say," Nick said.

"What?"

"I need to know your judgment isn't being clouded by what you learned about your father."

"What do you mean?"

"It's understandable that you'd be pissed at the Russians. I don't blame you, but we may have to work with Vysotsky."

"He can't be trusted."

"The people who killed your father aren't the people we're dealing with now. "

"You don't know that," she said. "SVR is the successor to the old KGB. Some of the same people who worked for state security back then are still around. Vysotsky, for one."

"Yeah, but Vysotsky has helped us in the past."

"Are you done?" Her tone was cold.

They entered the morass of downtown traffic.

Nick felt himself getting angry. Maybe it was the sessions with the shrink. Things had been going a lot better with Selena since he'd started seeing someone to deal with his PTSD. The Afghanistan nightmare was coming less often but he still thrashed out during the night. It had made it hard to share the same bed. They'd been sleeping apart and the strain was taking its toll.

The nightmare had started after he'd been wounded by a grenade in Afghanistan. A child had thrown the grenade, a boy no more than ten or eleven years old. Nick hadn't wanted to kill him. He'd hesitated, not wanting to shoot. The hesitation had almost cost him his life.

The sessions seemed to stir up things that had nothing to do with what had happened in Afghanistan, things he didn't want to think about, like his childhood. Like thoughts about his father. His father had been a drunk, a womanizer and a bully. Carter Senior beat his wife and Nick with monotonous regularity, until the day Nick had been big enough to fight back. His sister had pulled him off before Nick killed him. His father had always left Shelley alone. She still defended him but she would never tell him why. It was one of the reasons Nick didn't get along with her.

It felt like Selena was shutting him out because she didn't want to hear what he had to say, just like his sister. It pissed him off when she did that. He took a deep breath.

"No, I'm not done. As long as I lead this team I have to know I can count 100 percent on everybody on it. If you can't separate out what happened to your father from what we have to do now, I have to worry about you. I know how you feel..."

She interrupted him. "No, you don't." Her voice rose. "You have no idea how I feel. Don't you dare presume to know how I feel."

They'd reached DuPont circle. She pulled to the curb and jammed on the brakes.

"Get out," she said.

He looked at her.

"Get out," she said again.

He started to say something and bit it back. He got out of the car and slammed the car door shut. She floored it and took off, tires smoking.

Sometimes he wondered what the hell he was doing with her in the first place. He began the long walk back to his building.

CHAPTER 11

The haunting voice of Sarah McLachlan filled the elegant rooms of Selena's luxury condo. Her drink sat untouched on the end table beside the couch. She'd been staring out the windows for the best part of an hour, trying to make sense of the conflicting thoughts and feelings swirling through her mind.

Selena's home was on the top floor of one of Washington's exclusive residential buildings. The wall of the living room was all windows from floor to ceiling. A wide, private balcony with an ornate, wrought iron fence ran outside the glass. The windows afforded a spectacular view of the Virginia countryside across the Potomac. Potted trees and a variety of colorful, flowering plants were spaced at random intervals along the balcony. It was the kind of city living space that inspired the covers of architectural magazines.

Usually the impressive view calmed her and reassured her that there was stability and order in her world. Not today. Today the foundation of that order had crumbled.

Her father was a traitor.

The word *traitor* echoed in her mind. She remembered the last time she'd seen her father. She'd been 10 years old. Her mother, her father and her older brother were going to Big Sur for the weekend. She'd been looking forward to the trip. But she'd caught a cold and had a fever and couldn't go. Her father had come into the bedroom. She'd been sitting propped up against the pillows, playing with her favorite doll. She remembered he'd smelled of aftershave and cigarettes.

"How's my girl feeling?"

"I'm much better, daddy. Can I go?"

"Not this time, pumpkin."

"Joe." Her mother had called up the stairs. "We need to get going."

"Uncle William will be here with you. We'll be back Sunday night, before you know it. You'll be all better by then. Next weekend we'll go to the beach."

He bent over and kissed her on the forehead.

"Bye, daddy."

"Bye, pumpkin."

He'd gone out the door. That was the last time she'd seen him.

It had taken more than a year and a lot of love from her Uncle William to bring her out of her shell after the death of her family.

The contents of the file Nick had given her had been a series of shocks, one after the other. The first shock was that her father had worked for the CIA. She'd never dreamed he was a spy. According to the file, he'd been under surveillance for almost 3 years before his death. That was a long time to let someone hand over important secrets. It reinforced her belief that the file was false, meant to cover somebody's tracks.

The file contained dates of clandestine meetings with enemy agents. Records of suspicious deposits into his bank account. Old black-and-white photographs showing drop points and meetings in San Francisco and Washington. Records of phone calls. A damning chain of evidence that led to what seemed an inevitable conclusion, that her father had been selling classified material to the enemy.

Langley knew her father was working with the Russians and had allowed him to continue. The only thing that made sense to her was that his involvement with the KGB was a sanctioned CIA operation. If that were the case, he wasn't a traitor, he was an unacknowledged hero. Just because the file accused Joseph Connor of treason didn't make it true.

Nick had said the file was the only record of her father's activities. If that were so, there was no way to prove her father's innocence or guilt, one way or another. Worse, there was no one she could ask to look into it. Except Nick.

Nick.

Selena picked up her drink. The ice had melted. She stood and went to the kitchen sink and threw away the old drink, got some ice from the refrigerator door and poured herself an Irish whiskey. It was a taste she had acquired since she'd met Nick. She walked over to the windows and stared out over the city and sipped from her glass.

Nick had kept the file from her. She didn't know if she should be mad at him or grateful. How had she ended up in love with a man who seemed unable to make up his mind about what kind of relationship he wanted from her? She knew he loved her, she was certain of that. At least most of the time she was certain of it.

She was in love with him, wasn't she? Maybe she should be asking herself what kind of relationship she wanted with him, rather than the other way around.

Lately she'd found herself thinking about children. If she wanted to have children, time was running out. At 35, it was already a little late to be having kids. Not so much because of physical reasons but because of personal ones. She was used to doing things pretty much as she wanted. It wouldn't be exactly right to say she loved her work with the Project, but there was no denying she loved the excitement the unpredictability of it. How could she give that up? Children would change all of that. It would change her entire life, really.

She had a hard time picturing Nick as a father. As far as that went, she could barely imagine herself as a mother. If she did decide to have children, it would mean leaving the Project. She wouldn't be able to accept the risk if she had a child to think about.

Her thoughts turned back to the file.

The KGB killed my family.

Her hand tightened around the glass. It wasn't that long ago, she thought. If the people who did this are still alive, I'm going to find them.

She downed the rest of her drink and poured another.

CHAPTER 12

The next morning Selena called Nick.

"I'm sorry." She sounded tired over the phone. "I lost it, I shouldn't have gotten mad. I know you worry about all of us, about making sure we get in and get out alive when we go in the field."

"Okay."

"I'm angry, I want to see the bastards that killed my father get what's coming to them. But I'm not going to let any of that get in the way of what we have to do."

"That's good enough for me. Maybe I could have been a little more diplomatic." He paused. "Sorry I slammed the door."

"So, we're okay?" Her tone was light but Nick knew it was serious.

"We're okay. Listen, Lamont is getting out of the hospital today. Let's have breakfast at that café near your place and then go pick him up. I'll call and let him know we're coming."

"Deal."

After breakfast, they headed for the hospital. Twice, Nick thought he saw a blue car following. He watched for it in the side mirror. When it didn't reappear, he relaxed. Sometimes a car was just a car.

They found Lamont in his room, reading a back issue of Sports Illustrated and looking bored. He was dressed for the street. His face broke into a big smile as they came into the room.

"The cavalry's here," Nick said. "Get your gear."

Lamont held up a red gym bag. "Boy am I glad to see you two."

"How you feeling, Shadow?"

"Ready to get out of here. I was waiting for the doctor to show up and sign me out."

"Let's go find him."

Lamont had been a Navy Seal before Nick brought him into the Project. Lamont's mother had been a big fan of the Shadow radio show and named her son for the hero, Lamont Cranston. His Seal team had dropped the nickname of Shadow on him. It had stuck.

There wasn't much of anything except muscle on Lamont's wiry frame. His skin was the color of fine coffee. He had unusual blue eyes, a gift from some forgotten Ethiopian ancestor. A thin ridge of pink tissue ran from over one eye down across his nose, a souvenir of Iraq.

He picked up large pill container from the side table and put it in the gym bag.

"You still on meds?" Nick said.

"Antibiotics. Some new version. They mess up my guts, but the medicos say I have to keep taking them. I don't like them much." He zipped up the bag.

They found the doctor. Ten minutes later they were in the hospital parking lot.

Selena's car was a Mercedes CLS 550, a sleek 4 door product of German engineering with a turbocharged V6 engine and over 400 horsepower. Selena liked the Benz cars. She'd had a burgundy red coupe with more horses for a while, but it kept ending up at the dealership for repairs. She'd given up on it and traded for this one. Before that, she'd had a silver Benz she'd owned when she'd first met Nick. That one had ended up full of bullet holes and riding on the rims. This one was a beautiful metallic gray with an undertone of blue, a color somewhere between gunpowder and midnight.

Lamont opened the rear door and tossed in his bag. At the edge of Nick's vision, something flashed. There are some things you never forget, like the reflection of light on a rifle scope aimed at you.

Nick was standing between Selena and Lamont. Without thinking he ducked and pushed out and knocked them aside as the dulled sound of a silenced rifle came from somewhere in the rows of cars parked in the lot. Nick felt the round go by. The rear passenger window of the next car over shattered into a thousand pieces. They scrambled away from the Mercedes and ducked behind a white Ford truck in the next space.

Lamont crouched down behind the rear tire. "Where is he?" he said.

Before Nick could answer, a rapid burst from the shooter peppered the Ford, blowing out windows and striking the truck body with flat, metallic sounds. The tires on the side away from them blew out. The truck settled heavily onto the asphalt, listing to one side.

Lamont began swearing. Nick risked a glance over the hood of the Ford. He caught a glimpse of the shooter behind a blue sedan.

"He's on the left near the exit road," Nick said, "behind a blue Caddy. Lamont, are you armed?"

"Nope. Hospital, remember?"

"He can't keep this up, it's too public. Selena, you and Lamont stay here. I'll work across the lot and try and get behind him. If you can spot him, take a shot to keep him busy."

Selena was about to answer when they heard the squeal of rubber on pavement. Nick looked in time to see the shooter's car speed away, headed out of the hospital parking complex. The car was moving fast, already beyond an easy shot. The angle was bad. Nick held the Sig in two hands and kept the white dots of his sights lined up on the driver's side window of the speeding vehicle. He let out half a breath and squeezed off three rounds. The big pistol rocked back in his hands.

One. Two. Three.

The window shattered. The car drifted to the right and crossed a curb at speed. It plowed into a row of parked cars with a sound as though someone had dropped ten tons of scrap metal from the sky. For a moment there was silence, then the gas tank exploded. Flame and black smoke billowed into the air over the parking lot.

Lamont and Selena stood and gazed at the destruction.

"Nice shooting," Lamont said.

"I think I saw him behind us earlier, when Selena and I drove over here," Nick said.

Selena raised an eyebrow. "You didn't say anything in the car."

"I thought I was just being paranoid."

Lamont gestured at the burning car. "Looks like you had a good reason."

Nick took out his phone. "The cops will be here soon. I'll call Harker."

CHAPTER 13

The morning after the parking lot attack, Ronnie came back from his daily run. He showered and went into his bedroom and looked in the closet, deciding which shirt to wear. It was summer, which meant one of his Hawaiian shirts. With over a hundred to choose from, it wasn't an easy decision. Not very many people had a closet like his. He'd been accumulating the shirts for years, ever since the first time he'd been in the islands, stationed at the Marine Corps barracks on Oahu. It didn't fit anymore but he still had it, hung in the place of honor as the first one on the left.

After some thought, he went for one with a scene of ukulele-strumming hula girls in grass skirts dancing beneath an unnaturally bright sky.

He finished dressing and went into the kitchen and fired up the stove. He put a half dozen pieces of bacon into a pan, took two slices of bread out of the pantry and put it in the toaster. He got a couple of eggs out of the refrigerator while the bacon was cooking. He threw some butter into the pan, turned up the flame and cracked the eggs in. He turned the bacon the couple of times, waiting for it to get dark enough so it would be crisp when he took it out. He flipped the eggs over. The toast popped up and he picked it out and put the pieces on his plate. He forked the bacon out of the pan onto a paper towel to drain the grease.

Multitasking.

Ronnie took the food over to a table and began eating. He lived in a one bedroom apartment on the outskirts of the city, where he had a place to park his car, a black Hummer. Aside from the shirts, the Hummer was the only thing Ronnie owned that he cared about.

He looked at his watch. It was time to head in for the morning briefing. He clipped the holster with his Sig onto his belt and let the shirt drape over it. He put on a pork pie hat and a pair of sunglasses and went out into the hall to the elevator.

He scanned the parking garage as he stepped out of the elevator but there was nothing out of the ordinary. He got into his car and began the drive to work. Traffic was heavy. It was always heavy, except in the early morning hours. Not like the long, empty stretches of desert highway back home.

It had been too long since he'd been home. His Auntie had done her best when she was bringing him up to pass on to him the traditions of the *Diné*, his people. She'd made him learn *Diné bizaad*, the Navajo language. She'd taught him respect for the healing ceremonies that traditional Navajos relied upon to restore their sense of harmony and oneness with the world.

Somehow life always managed to shatter one's sense of harmony. At the moment, about the only thing Ronnie felt at one with was the steering wheel under his hands. Lately he'd felt like he was being stalked by the *Chindi*, the evil ghosts of the enemies he'd killed. It wasn't that he really believed in ghosts, but it wouldn't hurt to undergo a healing ceremony. He decided that when this new mission was finished he would go back to Arizona for a while. Maybe he could get Lamont and Nick to go with him. He wasn't the only one who could use a little help with his ghosts.

When he got to Harker's office, he was late. Everyone was already there. Lamont pretended that the glare from Ronnie's shirt was hurting his eyes. He put on a pair of Ray Bans and leaned over to stare at one of the hula dancers.

"Nice shirt, Ronnie."

"One of these days you're going to hurt my feelings," Ronnie said. "It's not my fault you can't appreciate true art."

Harker said. "I'm glad you're back, Lamont. Now, can we focus here?"

"Sorry, Director."

She turned to Nick. "What happened yesterday?" she said.

"Someone followed us on the way to the hospital," he said. "When we came out, they began shooting. Usually the shooting doesn't start until we're in the middle of a mission."

"Looks like the mission has already started," Elizabeth said. "We need to brainstorm this. Make some assumptions."

"What do we know?" Selena said.

"We know someone considers us a threat," Nick said, "but not much else."

Harker said, "First me, then the rest of you. Coming after us is a preemptive strike. Do we all agree on that?"

She looked around the room. The others nodded.

"The question is why?"

Nick said, "It could be the same people that tried to kill Rice."

"My intuition says it is," Elizabeth said, "but I can't prove it yet."

"If it is the same people," Selena said, "they could be worried we'll find out who they are."

Stephanie was sitting apart from the others at her computer console, near Harker's desk. Now she said, "I think it has to be more than that. What do they gain by poisoning Rice?"

"It's like a regime change," Lamont said. "With Edmonds running things, it's a whole different ballgame."

"You think someone is planning a coup?" Nick said.

"Not planning it, starting it," Lamont said. "Edmonds could be in on it."

"He's not the President yet. Rice is still alive. It takes more than a failed assassination attempt to take over the government."

"What else would they need to do?" Ronnie said.

"They have to create fear," Selena said. "Enough to get everyone so upset they'll accept harsh government controls, like martial law."

"They'd need an excuse like massive riots," Stephanie said, "like what happened in Russia."

Harker said, "You think what happened in Russia is related to what's happening here?"

Stephanie frowned. "It could be. If a riot like that happened in New York or Chicago or LA, the government would have to send in troops, like they did in Russia. Impose a curfew. Take over services, all of that."

"That's a real leap, Steph," Nick said.

"I don't think so." Stephanie twisted the bracelets on her wrist, first one way than the other. "Look what happened in Novosibirsk. If that happened here, it would provide an excuse to bring down the hammer."

"That's a Presidential call," Selena said.

"And who's the acting President?" Nick looked at her. "Do you trust Edmonds to defend personal freedom?"

No one had anything to say about that.

Stephanie cleared her throat. "Speaking of Edmonds, I tracked down that helicopter that came after Elizabeth. It was manufactured in France and sold to a company called Global Enterprise Solutions."

"I've heard of them," Nick said. "Aren't they a big construction firm?"

"Construction, engineering, oil and more," Stephanie said. "It's a huge company doing billions of dollars worth of business a year. Guess who was the former CEO before he got elected to office?"

"Edmonds?"

Stephanie nodded. "It doesn't prove he's involved, but it's another one of those coincidences."

Ronnie scratched the top of his head. "Sometimes I don't like what we find when we do the assumption thing," he said.

"Do you really think a coup could happen here?" Selena said.

"If people thought we were under attack, it might be possible," Elizabeth said. "The Patriot Act suspends the Bill of Rights. It's never been hard to get most people in line when they think they're being threatened. Any new regulations would be presented as necessary and temporary."

"So what do we do now?" Lamont said.

Harker picked up her black pen. Nick waited for her to begin tapping. She set it down again.

"We have no proof at all that someone wants to overthrow our government. The key to this is that satellite weapon, or whatever it is. We need to find out what it is and who's behind it. There has to be someplace they're using as a headquarters or communication center, a place to control it.

Something this sophisticated can't be called up on a cell phone."

"Once we find it, then what?" Lamont asked.

"Then we destroy it."

"Sure," Nick said, "but we have to find it first."

Stephanie said, "I have a lead. It's not much, but it's better than nothing. You remember I said I detected a micro-burst of high frequency energy when Russia got hit?"

"Yes?" Harker said.

"I traced the signal to the Western US and started to hack into the computer that sent it. It had very sophisticated firewalls and security, something I'd never seen before. Actually, it was quite a challenge. You know sometimes I miss the game, back when I was just hacking into things for the fun of it."

Harker said, "Stephanie. Would you please stick to the point?"

"Oh. Sorry."

Ronnie looked over at Nick and raised his eyebrows.

Stephanie said, "I got part way in, then someone diverted me and tried to fry our computers with his own attack. I blocked it and dropped off."

"You said out West. Where, exactly?"

"I don't know. Somewhere on the other side of the Mississippi."

"That's a lot of country," Nick said. "Doesn't help a lot."

Stephanie looked annoyed. "I said the lead wasn't much."

"Actually, it does help," Harker said. "It tells us the nerve center is here in the US."

"Unless they're using some kind of transparent system to re-route the signal," Stephanie said. "If that's the case, that computer could be anywhere."

"What's our next move, Director?" Nick asked.

Harker tapped her pen on her desk. "Normally, I'd go to the White House and talk to Rice. But I can't do that, can I? Instead I've got to do something outside the bounds."

They waited for her to finish her thought.

"I'm going to have to talk with General Vysotsky. Sooner or later, the Russians will discover that a signal was sent from American territory. I don't want them drawing the wrong conclusions and he's our best channel to the Kremlin."

"Do you think he'll be straight with you?" Out of the corner of his eye Nick saw Selena frown.

"Probably not, at least not entirely. But it's worth a try. It's to his advantage to cooperate. That's the key with him, he's an opportunist. Besides, he's smart and he may know something we don't."

"How come we always end up bailing out the Russians?" Nick asked.

"Self interest," Harker said. "We can't let them think the US is behind this. Plus if Russia goes down, they'll take everyone else with them. We can't let it happen. We have a common enemy in whoever has that weapon. That makes Russia our friend, at least for the moment."

"The enemy of my enemy is my friend?" Lamont said. "Give me a break."

"Some friend," Ronnie said.

CHAPTER 14

Alexei Vysotsky saw that Elizabeth Harker was calling on his secured line. Circumstances had forced them into an unlikely alliance in the past. At first he'd been suspicious of her. After all, she was American, in the same business as he was. Russia had benefited from the alliance, but he had to be careful. The Cold War was back, if not as frigid as it had been in the days of Stalin and Khrushchev.

She had earned his respect. He hoped he never had to take her on as an enemy. In Alexei's inner world, that thought constituted high praise.

His curiosity was aroused. He'd met her face to face once in Denmark, and he liked her. It was too bad she was on the opposite side. He picked up his phone and allowed his considerable charm to color his voice.

"Director. To what do I owe the pleasure?"

"Good morning, Alexei. Or I should say afternoon, where you are. You sound well. Something's come up we need to discuss."

"Oh?"

"It concerns Novosibirsk."

"That is an internal affair, Director. We'll find the terrorists responsible."

Harker knew that the best way to work with Vysotsky was to be truthful, at least when it wasn't in conflict with security concerns.

"It's gone beyond that, General. I believe that whoever is responsible is planning something here in America as well. They are a threat to both of us."

"Go on."

"We think a satellite weapon has been developed that uses targeted radio frequencies to disrupt mental behavior and that someone used it on Novosibirsk."

"You are certain?"

"Almost certain."

Vysotsky debated with himself. Should he pretend to be surprised, or respond with the truth? He decided on truth.

"We have arrived at a similar conclusion. We couldn't believe terrorists would have such technology available. Frankly, we thought it might be a hostile move on the part of your government. Or Beijing. There are several in the Kremlin who believe this."

"Our government did not do this," Harker said. "If the situation were reversed, I am sure I would have thought Moscow or Beijing was behind it." A thought occurred to her. "Have you discovered anyone who was involved?"

How did she know that? he thought.

She seemed to read his mind. "I can hear you thinking, General. I'm right, aren't I?"

He sighed. "We have someone in custody. We are, ah, questioning him. What you would call a person of interest, yes?"

"Have you been watching American television again, Alexei?"

He laughed. "You have so many crime shows. America must be a very dangerous place, with all those persons of interest wandering around."

"Don't believe everything you see on television," she said. She paused.

Vysotsky waited. Now we're getting to it, he thought.

"We worked well together in the past, " she said. "I propose that we cooperate again. You and I both want to prevent another incident."

"What do you have in mind?"

"You have full access to whatever your people discover and I do not."

"You wish to share information?"

"If we work together, we'll be more effective than if we work alone."

"What have you discovered?"

"Nothing concrete, yet. A suspicion, only. It may lead to something or not. If it proves accurate, I'll tell you."

More than a suspicion, Vysotsky thought. "Are you thinking of sending your team here?"

"I have no plans to do so, but it could be necessary in the future. That is one reason I'm calling. I don't want there to be any misunderstandings if it becomes necessary."

Vysotsky ran through the options in his mind. The riots had shaken the Kremlin. Whoever discovered the cause would be rewarded. He had nothing to lose by cooperating with her. Harker was offering an opportunity he couldn't pass up.

"I also would like to avoid misunderstandings. If you keep me informed, I think we have an agreement. Who else knows about your suspicions? Your FBI? Langley?"

"For the time being, no one else. You know we have serious security leaks."

Not long before, there had been a rash of publicity about a high profile American defector who had ended up in Russia.

Vysotsky smiled to himself. "Yes, you do. How do you want to proceed?"

"I'll pursue this on my end. If I discover something, I'll pass it on to you. I would like you to do the same." Harker paused. "Do you have any leads yet from your person of interest?"

"Not yet. But I don't think it will be very long until I do."

Thousands of miles away on the other side of the world, Elizabeth could hear a ruthless certainty in his voice. She was glad she wasn't the one Vysotsky was questioning.

CHAPTER 15

Nick had always thought counseling was an admission of weakness. *A man ought to handle things on his own* had been his dominant thought almost as long as he could remember. Even so, it had finally come home to him that he had to do something about his PTSD. It gave him nightmares and headaches. It was driving a wedge between him and Selena. It interfered when he was in the field.

He'd chosen Dave Milton from a short list recommended by other vets. Milton had made Major in Special Forces, no mean feat. He'd lost an arm in Afghanistan. Those two things gave him a lot of credibility with Nick. Now he was back in Milton's office.

The doctors he'd talked to when he'd come back from the war had told him his guilt about the child was misplaced and that it wasn't his fault. That feeling guilty just made the stress worse. That was like telling him the sky was blue. Intellectually, he already knew that. But they didn't really understand. They hadn't been there. They didn't know what it felt like, but Milton did. That was the difference. Nick trusted him.

Milton was a black man, about Nick's height but a little heavier. Today he had on a blue shirt and a tie. The left sleeve of the shirt was attached with a gold safety pin against his shoulder. Milton was the kind of man who seemed at ease with himself, a man who knew who he was.

They'd been talking for a half hour. Nick told Milton what had happened at Bethesda, in a general way. Milton's clearance was good, but it only went so far.

"You're keeping something back," Milton said.

"What do you mean?"

"You just got through telling me someone tried to kill you. Again. In a parking lot here in the US, where those kinds of things aren't supposed to happen."

"You know I can't go into all the details."

"That's not what I mean."

"Then what are you talking about?"

"You haven't said one word about how you feel. You told me what happened. You didn't tell me anything else."

"How do you think I feel? How would you feel if someone started shooting at you?" Nick could feel himself tensing up.

"If you don't want to tell me how you felt in that parking lot, why not tell me how you're doing with the dreams?"

"Better," Nick said, "but the headaches are starting again."

"You remember what you discovered the last time you were here?"

"Yeah. I can get killed like anybody else. But I already knew that. I'm not sure it has much to do with the dreams or PTSD."

"It was more than that. What was the word you used, to describe how you felt? Do you remember? It's important."

"Why?"

"Why do you think?"

"Damn it, you're doing that shrink thing."

"What shrink thing?"

"Throwing questions back at me. Answering a question with a question."

"Would it do any good if I told you what I thought?"

"That's why I'm here."

"No it isn't," Milton said. "You're here because you want to stop the nightmares and the rest of it. Me telling you what I think isn't going to help you solve anything. You have to figure it out yourself."

Every time he'd been here, Nick had wanted to get up and walk out. Now he wanted to do it again. He thought about the last time he'd been in this office. He'd been talking about Afghanistan, about the day he'd almost died. About the grenade. About the child he'd killed who was trying to kill him. The scars on his body began throbbing as he thought about it. What was the word he'd used?

Helpless.

Milton saw it register on Nick's face. "Stay with it," he said. "Stay with the feeling."

"Helpless," Nick said. "Helpless is the word."

Milton was silent.

...the grenade comes toward him, a dark, green shape tumbling through the air...everything goes white....

"How the hell do I deal with that?"

"How do you usually deal with it?"

Nick laughed. "More firepower."

Milton smiled. "Okay, but what else?"

Nick thought. "I get headaches," he said. "Nightmares."

Milton nodded. "Because...?"

"I don't know."

"When we have a nightmare over and over again, it's because our unconscious mind is trying to get our attention. It's a way to get a message through to the outer mind."

"What message?" Nick asked.

"What do you think?"

"There you go again," Nick said.

Milton waited.

"The only message I get is that I almost died."

"That's right. You almost died. How do you feel when you have the dream?"

"Damn it, you know how I feel." Nick was getting angry. "Helpless. Frightened. That good enough?"

"So why do you have the dream?"

Nick took a deep breath. He wanted to punch Milton. He wanted to leave the room. He felt like he was on the verge of something, some discovery. "All it does is remind me."

"Of what?"

"That I feel unprotected. That I could die."

"Yup. Does it work?"

"What do you mean?"

"Do the nightmares keep you safe? Protect you?"

"Of course not."

"Right. It's a failed strategy. Now you know what the issue really is."

Nick felt a surge of adrenaline. "Survival?"

Milton nodded, pleased. "At the most basic level. Life and death. Now that you know that, you don't have to get headaches and nightmares to remind you."

"It can't be that simple."

"Maybe it's a little more complicated than that but that's the foundation," Milton said. "Think about it some more and we'll do something a little different next time to defuse whatever is left."

When he walked out of the office, Nick felt that something had changed. What had Milton said? That since Nick knew what the issue really was, he didn't need the dreams to remind him. He remembered the feeling, like an electric jolt running through his body, when he realized the issue was survival. It was more than knowing it. He'd felt the rightness of it, felt the energy and truth of it ripple through his body, like touching a live wire.

It wasn't the first time he'd thought about getting killed. It wasn't the first time he'd thought about personal survival either. Hell, he had years of practice surviving in situations where others died. Where he could have died. Knowing that survival was the big issue couldn't make any difference.

It couldn't be that simple.

Could it?

CHAPTER 16

"I've pinned down the location of the signal that triggered the satellite," Stephanie said. "You're not going to like what I found."

Elizabeth had made fresh coffee. "It's nice out. Let's have coffee on the patio," she said. The coffee break had become a regular habit, something Elizabeth and Stephanie tried to do every morning about this time.

They sat down at a painted wicker table. The sun felt good on Stephanie's face.

"What did you discover?" Elizabeth asked.

Stephanie said. "The signal that triggered the satellite came from Alaska."

"Alaska? Where in Alaska?"

"The middle of nowhere. The Yukon Flats National Wildlife Refuge."

"Okay. You have my attention. What is a high frequency radio signal doing coming from a wildlife refuge? What's there that could do something like that?"

"SATWEP."

"The Satellite Weapons Program?"

"That's right. The Army runs it in conjunction with DARPA, the Defense Agency Research Projects Agency," Stephanie said. "The Pentagon does love their acronyms, don't they?"

"But that's the government." There was disbelief in Elizabeth's voice.

"I said you wouldn't like it," Stephanie said.

"Are you sure?"

"Positive. The signal definitely came from there. The signature is unmistakable. There's nothing like it anywhere else on the planet."

"Steph, you just said someone used a defense agency installation to attack Russia. If Moscow finds out, it's going to make a lot of trouble. It's an act of war."

"Then this probably isn't something you want to share with Vysotsky," Stephanie said.

Elizabeth snorted and choked on her coffee.

"You shouldn't make me laugh when I'm drinking."

Stephanie said, "I'm glad you think it's funny."

"It's the way you said it." Elizabeth blotted her lips with a napkin. "I don't think you realize how funny you can be sometimes."

Stephanie started to say something then changed her mind. Instead she said, "The main SATWEP facility is located near Anchorage, but there's a classified program that uses the same technology in smaller installations and research facilities. They aren't always manned. The signal came from one of those. I've got the GPS coordinates."

"Where is it?"

"It's remote. The nearest town is just a wide spot at the end of the road called Circle, around fifty miles south of the Arctic circle. They run a big dog sled race out of there every year. Beyond that, it's all wilderness. The only way in is on foot or by air. "

Elizabeth sipped her coffee.

"What do you want to do?" Stephanie asked.

"I'll send the team in. There could be something on site to give us a lead."

Stephanie said, "There's bound to be some kind of security, even if it's an unmanned station."

"We'll treat it as if it were a hostile installation," Elizabeth said.

Stephanie waited.

"Normally I would go to the White House on something like this," Elizabeth said, "but I don't trust Edmonds. I don't want to tip our hand or let anyone know what we're doing. We'll use the Gulfstream to transport the team and supplies to Alaska."

"When do you want them to go?"

"Right away. I don't think we have a lot of time to stop this. Taking Rice down is a bad sign. We need more intelligence and we need it now. We need evidence. Once we have that, I'll decide the next step. Get the team together and we'll plan the mission."

"What about the Russians? Are you going to tell them what we've discovered? "

"Let's see what Nick finds in Alaska before we talk to them," Elizabeth said.

CHAPTER 17

Vysotsky's investigators had uncovered the scorched remains of a device in the ruins of the Central Bank of Novosibirsk, a receiver for the signal that had driven the city mad. There was no way to know who had made it. On the other hand, it hadn't taken long to identify and arrest the person who had placed it. He was a bank teller with financial problems.

Korov had come to interrogate him. The prisoner was being held in a military prison built in the days of the Czar. It wasn't far from the old Lubyanka prison in central Moscow. Like the Lubyanka, it was not a place anyone wanted to find themselves. The massive building was made out of stone. The walls were cold and rough and sweated during the hot days of a Moscow summer. In winter, the cells were freezing.

The prison was run by the GRU, the *Glavnoye Razvedyvatel'noye Upravleniye,* Military Intelligence. SVR and GRU had a long standing relationship of mutual cooperation. No one asked any unnecessary questions. No one was very concerned with the welfare of the prisoner. You didn't come to this place because someone was looking out for your welfare.

"This way, Colonel."

Korov's escort was a brutish Senior Sergeant named Grigorev. He smelled of garlic and looked like a man who spent too much time in places with no sunlight. His skin was pale and he needed a shave. His face was dark with shadow, even though it was early in the afternoon.

To reach the cells, everyone went through a passage guarded by iron gates that had served the same purpose before the October revolution. Korov and his escort waited as each one clanked open in turn and closed behind them. They descended worn steps to the lower level. The steps opened onto a hallway lined with dozens of faceless iron doors with numbers.

Grigorev stopped in front of number 17. The door had been painted green, long ago. The paint was chipped and scarred. A narrow slot allowed the passage of food into the cell. A circular viewport covered with a movable shield let the jailer observe the prisoner.

Korov slid the metal covering aside and peered in. There was no window in the stone room. Light came from one dim bulb hung somewhere high above. The floor was of stone. In the far corner of the room a foul hole lined with dried excrement served as a toilet. A thin mattress marred by dark stains was laid on the floor. It was the only thing in the room except for the man lying on it.

The prisoner's hair was matted with blood. His arm rested at an odd angle where it lay across his chest. His mouth was open as his breath rasped in and out. The mouth was bloody. Several teeth were missing. His eyes were blackened, swollen and closed.

"What happened to him?" Korov said.

Grigorev shrugged. "He was unruly. We had to teach him the rules."

"Ah."

Korov concealed his distaste and reminded himself that this prisoner was a traitor.

"Open the door."

Grigorev placed an old fashioned key made of heavy metal into the lock and turned. The door swung open.

"Prisoner! Stand!" Grigorev shouted at the man.

The man's name was Litvenenko. He tried to raise himself on one arm and fell back against the mattress.

Grigorev moved toward him but Korov laid a hand on his arm.

"It's alright. I don't think he can stand up. I'll talk to him there."

"As you wish, Colonel."

Korov stepped into the cell. The prisoner had soiled himself. Korov held his finger under his nose as the stench of the man and the filth hit him.

Korov squatted down beside Litvenenko. "I am Colonel Korov. I am your only hope. Do you understand?"

Litvenenko opened an eye.

"Do you understand?" Korov said again.

"Da. Understand." The voice was hoarse, choked with phlegm.

"Good. I will only ask a question once. If you lie, I'll know it. If you lie, I'll leave you in the care of Sergeant Grigorev. Do you understand?"

Korov saw the fear in the man's eyes. He hated this, but it had to be done. He had to know who had bribed this man. Someone had given him that device. Someone had told him to place it exactly where it had been placed. Korov needed to know who it was.

"Yes, understand."

"You placed a package in the central bank."

"No, it wasn't me."

"No? Then why are you here?"

"I swear, it wasn't me. I gave the package to Yevchenko."

Korov looked at the Sergeant. "Why wasn't I told about this?"

"I don't know, Colonel. I was only told to bring you to the prisoner."

Korov turned back to Litvenenko. "Who is Yevchenko?"

"The janitor. He cleans up after everyone is gone."

Dimitri Yevchenko was on a list of people still missing after the riots. Korov had an almost photographic memory. He remembered seeing the name. The man was listed as an employee of the bank.

"Why did you have to give it to someone else? Why couldn't you place it yourself?"

"The manager, Kaminsky. He was always the last out. He always made everyone else leave before he locked up. Only Yevchenko could stay."

"Who gave you the package?"

"A man, I don't know, I swear. Just a man. He told me to give it to Yevchenko."

"What did he look like, this man?"

Litvenenko squinted through his swollen eyelids at Korov. "Like you. He looked like you."

"Swine," Grigorev said. "You are talking to an officer." He stepped forward and kicked the man in his ribs. Litvenenko screamed.

Korov raised his hand. "Enough, Sergeant. Wait outside. "

"Sir..."

"Wait outside."

Grigorev moved back to the door, scowling.

Korov said, "What do you mean, he looked like me?"

"Blond, like you, tall. Short hair, like a soldier. He paid me a hundred rubles. I was afraid, I thought maybe he was FSB. He said to give it to the janitor and tell him to leave it in Kaminsky's office after the bank closed. He said it was a surprise for Kaminsky and I shouldn't say anything about it because it would spoil the surprise."

Litvenenko coughed and spit blood onto the floor.

Korov shook his head at the man's stupidity and greed. "You didn't think that was a lot of money to give a package to a janitor?"

"I needed the money. Please, I didn't know. Please..."

He clawed at Arkady's sleeve. Korov pulled his arm back in disgust and stood. He thought about what the prisoner had said. It would be necessary to question him further, but Korov didn't think there was much more to be learned. The man was terrified, as he should be. Arkady had taken part in enough interrogations to know when someone was lying. Litvenenko was guilty of greed and poor judgement, but nothing more. He was an expendable part of someone's plan. Unfortunately for him, his greed would cost him his life. The Russian justice system was not noted for compassion and understanding.

Back outside the prison, Korov took a deep breath of the smog-filled Moscow air. A bus rumbled by, trailing black smoke and diesel fumes. After the stink of the cell it seemed like pure oxygen.

Time to report in. He wondered if his boss was going to share what he'd learned with the Americans.

Korov thought about the Americans, about Nick and Selena and the others. Especially Selena. He'd never met a woman like her. Women in combat roles were nothing new in Russia, but they didn't have Selena's combination of beauty, skills and courage. She even spoke Russian like a native.

Twice, now, he'd seen her in action under fire. Once in America, in Texas. Once here in the Motherland. He wondered if he was going to see her again.

He'd like that.

CHAPTER 18

It had been two days since the firefight in the hospital parking lot. Harker was briefing the team in the ops center below Harker's office.

"You're sending us to Alaska?" Nick said.

"As soon as we plan out the mission," Harker said. "Lamont stays here. He's still on meds and recovering from his wound."

"Director..." Lamont said.

"You're not going."

Lamont settled back in his chair. He looked unhappy.

"What's our objective?" Nick asked.

"Are you familiar with SATWEP?"

"Isn't that the Army's secret satellite program? The one no one wants to talk about?"

"That's the one. The signal that triggered the riots in Novosibirsk came from a substation that's part of the program."

"Isn't the installation on an Army base near Fairbanks?" Ronnie said.

"The main facility is. The signal came from farther north, near the Arctic Circle."

"How certain are you that it came from there, Director?" Nick said.

"Completely certain."

"What are we looking for?"

"Anything that can help us figure out what's going on or who is behind it."

"That's pretty vague. Do we at least know where to look?" Nick asked.

"I can show you," Stephanie said.

Stephanie's laptop was linked into the Crays in the other room. She entered a series of keystrokes, humming to herself as her fingers danced across the keyboard. The Ops Center had a large wall monitor identical to the one in Elizabeth's office. The picture that appeared on screen was a satellite shot over the Alaskan wilderness. Steph zoomed in on a white dot in the middle of a forest. The dot became two low buildings, set next to each other and connected by a short passage. Nearby, rows of tall antenna towers were laid out in a grid.

There was no road to the site. The land around the facility consisted of old growth forest that had been cleared back about a hundred feet. There was a helipad and hangar.

"Way out in the boonies," Ronnie said.

"Out of sight, out of mind," Nick said. "I wonder what they're doing out there?"

"Probably playing talk radio for the grizzly bears," Lamont said.

"I don't think they'd do that," Ronnie said. "You don't want to piss off grizzly bears."

Harker rolled her eyes. "Steph, show the nearest town."

"That would be Circle. It's not just the nearest town, it's the only town." She brought it up on the monitor.

They studied the picture. A wide river snaked past a cluster of low buildings laid out on the river bank. West of the town was a single, straight airstrip. There were no planes or hangars, only a cracked strip of pavement. A narrow access road ran like a tee from the center of the strip to a cleared area that was probably a parking lot and then to the town. A highway entered the picture from the lower left corner and ended at the town. A single main street ran through the settlement.

From miles above the Earth's surface, Circle looked like a one horse town without the horse.

"Is that the Yukon River?" Ronnie asked.

"It is." Stephanie adjusted the picture. "The highway you see is Route 6, if you can call it a highway. Circle is literally the end of the road in Alaska."

"How many people live up there?" Selena asked.

"Around 80, year round. More in the summer, when they get a few tourists."

"Not much going on," Lamont said.

"The nearest big city is Fairbanks," Stephanie said. "It's about a hundred and fifty miles from Circle."

"We can fly to Fairbanks and drive to Circle from there," Nick said.

"That might not be so easy, " Ronnie said. "I've been to Fairbanks. That road going North is unpaved gravel and in rough shape. No one will risk renting a car to go to Circle. We'd have to hire someone to drive us."

"There's that airstrip. We could hire a plane in Fairbanks to take us to Circle and hike in from there," Nick said, "but it's days on foot over rough country to the objective."

"There's a helipad right on site," Selena said. "Why not use that?"

Ronnie shook his head. "If anyone's there, we'd be sitting ducks coming in."

"A chopper is a good idea, though. We could land somewhere nearby and hike the rest," Nick said. "Call for extraction when we're done and have the chopper pick us up."

"I can't requisition a helicopter without someone asking why," Elizabeth said.

"I know a guy who lives in Fairbanks," Ronnie said. "He flew choppers in RECON. Now he's got a charter service that takes hunters into the backcountry. We can trust him."

Elizabeth nodded. "Good, Ronnie. We'll use him."

"I'll call and have him meet us at the airport."

Elizabeth looked at Nick. "You have to be careful, Nick. Get in and get out. Don't get caught and please, don't blow anything up."

"Mm," Nick said.

CHAPTER 19

It was after midnight when Ronnie, Nick and Selena landed at the private terminal in Fairbanks. Ronnie's friend was waiting for them. Sam Newhouse was a wiry, short man who looked like he'd been carved out of beef jerky.

"Hey, Gunny. Long time. How they hanging?"

The two men hugged and clapped each other on the back.

"Sam, these are my friends. This is Nick and this is Selena."

"Pleasure," Newhouse said. They shook hands. He looked at Nick. "Afghanistan, right? Recon? I remember you from Bagram. I was flying the bird that pulled you out. You were hit pretty bad. Glad you made it."

He's in the market, ramshackle bins and ragged cloth walls. Clouds of flies swarm around the butcher's stall. He hears a baby cry. The street is deserted.

The rooftops erupt with men firing AK-47s. The market stalls shatter in a firestorm of splinters and plaster and rock exploding from the sides of the buildings.

A child runs toward him, screaming about Allah. Nick hesitates, a second too long. The boy cocks his arm back and throws a grenade as Nick shoots him.

The child's head dissolves in a red fountain of blood and bone. The grenade drifts through the air in slow motion...everything goes white...

"Nick?" It was Selena. Newhouse was looking at him. Nick realized he'd been gone for a moment.

"Sorry, yeah, that's right. Bagram. You have a good memory. I never got a chance to thank you."

"No thanks needed. Follow me," Newhouse said.

He led them outside to the parking lot and a red Toyota Highlander spattered with mud. They stowed the bags with their gear and weapons and got in. Newhouse pulled out of the lot. Ronnie sat next to him in front.

Newhouse said, "You said on the phone you wanted to fly up past Circle. We have to wait for daylight. There's a motel near here that's clean. I figured you might want to rest up a little. The only had two rooms available. I hope that's okay." He turned onto the highway.

"Sounds good," Ronnie said.

"You want to fill me in? You don't look like you're going fishing and there's nothing up there except bears and black flies."

Nick had checked out Newhouse. He'd talked it over with Harker and they'd decided the pilot would need to know something about why they were in Alaska.

"There's something we want to take a look at," Nick said from the back seat. "It's a government installation. We don't exactly have permission to visit it."

Newhouse said nothing.

"I can't tell you everything but you need to know that we all work for the President."

"Rice? He's a good man, not like that jerk he picked for a VP. It's too bad he had that heart attack."

"Rice didn't have a heart attack," Nick said.

Newhouse looked at him, surprised. "What do you mean, he didn't have a heart attack?"

"Someone tried to poison him. We don't know who did it but this place we're going may have something to do with it. We need you to set us down about a day's hike away and then come get us when we call you. The whole thing needs to be kept quiet."

"You're spooks, aren't you?"

"No, we're not Agency."

Newhouse was quiet as he drove. Then he said, "I guess not, or you wouldn't need my bird."

"It's complicated," Ronnie said. "We need to stay below the radar. Literally."

"Like the old days," Newhouse said. "Hell, I thought I left all that behind over there."

"At least no one's going to be firing missiles at you," Nick said.

"You sure about that?"

"Pretty sure."

"Well, hell, that makes me feel a lot better."

"We need you, Sam." Ronnie looked at him. "Are you in?"

"Makes a nice change from ferrying tourists around, I guess. Yeah, I'm in."

Newhouse turned into the parking lot of the motel, a low one story building with a row of rooms facing out toward the highway. A red neon sign read NO VACANCY. The V was out on the sign.

"Not fancy, but like I said, it's clean." Newhouse parked. They got out and unloaded the duffle bags with their gear.

"What time you want me to pick you up?"

"0600," Nick said.

"Works for me. Good to see you, Ronnie."

Newhouse got back in his truck and drove off. The night air was cool but not cold. This time of the year, temperatures didn't drop much below 50 at night. It would be warm during the day. Winter didn't move in here until September. It would be colder farther north, but the temperatures would still be bearable.

They checked in. Newhouse had reserved two rooms next to each other. Nick and Selena took one, Ronnie the other.

"Get some sleep," Nick said to Ronnie. "We'll need it."

The room was like a time trip from the 60s. It had two beds with quilted covers. A cheap print of red and yellow flowers in a brown vase hung over the headboard. A table lamp and night stand sat between the beds. A small TV was bolted to the wall. The narrow bathroom featured a toilet, a stand up shower stall and curtain. The rings on the curtain were rusty. The sink stood on thin chrome legs and was square and small. A small, wrapped bar of soap, a spotted water glass and two thin towels completed the amenities.

The outside wall was made of cinder blocks painted white. A heater and A/C unit sat in the front wall under a wide picture window. Nick pulled the drapes closed and turned on the heat. The unit rattled. Lukewarm air rushed out.

"Not the Taj Mahal," Nick said. He sat on one of the beds. The mattress sagged.

"I've never been to Alaska," Selena said. "I'm looking forward to hiking into the forest."

"I did a survival course here when I was in Recon," Nick said. "It's beautiful but it can kill you if you're not careful. Where we're going, it might as well be 1898."

"This was gold rush country, wasn't it?"

"Yep. Circle was an important town, back then."

"I suppose if you want to hide a secret installation this is as good a place as any to do it."

"Secret from the public, anyway. Any enemy worth his salt has to know exactly where it is."

"It doesn't seem like anyone can hide much of anything these days," Selena said. "Not with the kind of technology governments have now."

"Yeah. A brave new world." Nick stood up. "Better lay our gear out for the morning so we don't have to fumble around with it."

They spent the next minutes sorting out what they'd need. Woodland camouflage uniforms with no markings. Hiking boots, soft brimmed hats. Knives, their pistols and MP-5s. A GPS and compass. Nick hoped they wouldn't need the guns. The knives were handy for many things.

Each back pack held rations, extra ammo, first aid kit and a survival pack. They could live off the land for weeks if they had to. Nick didn't think that was going to happen. It was old habit to be prepared.

"I'm going to take a shower," Selena said. She undressed and walked naked into the bathroom. Nick watched her and felt himself getting aroused. False modesty wasn't one of Selena's faults. He heard the water running and thought about how he missed holding her at night.

After a while she came out, pink and clean, toweling her hair. A cloud of steam followed her into the room.

"Your turn," she said. She smiled at him. "It's small, but the water's hot."

He used the toilet and stepped into the stall. She was right, it was small. The water felt good. Some of the tension went out of his shoulders as the hot stream beat down on him.

He dried off and went back into the room with a towel wrapped around his waist. Selena was already in one of the beds. They hadn't spent a night together in the same bed for months.

Nick walked over and sat down on the edge of her bed. The mattress sagged under his weight.

"I've been thinking," he said.

Selena lay back against her pillow and rested her head on her arm.

"About what?"

"About us."

"It hasn't been easy," she said, "has it?"

"It seems like things keep getting in the way," he said. "The nightmares. The work we do. Every time we start getting close, something happens."

She reached out and took his hand. "How close do you want to get?"

"All I know is that when you're not around I feel like something's missing."

He reached out and touched her cheek. Her skin was smooth under his fingers.

"I love you," he said. "I don't want any distance between us. That's how close. "

"I like close," she said. Then she said, "Aren't you getting cold out there?"

Nick stood up and dropped the towel he'd wrapped around himself. He slipped under the covers and put his arms around her. "I don't like sleeping by myself."

"Me neither," Selena said. She ran her fingers through his hair. She reached down for him.

"Oh," she said. "Miss me?"

"You talk too much," Nick said. They kissed.

Later, they slept. Nick didn't dream.

CHAPTER 20

Newhouse was waiting for them outside the motel at 0600. They climbed into his red Toyota and fifteen minutes later stood looking at the helicopter. It was red and silver with blue stripes. The tail rotor was enclosed in a circular part of the fuselage under the vertical stabilizer.

"Slick bird," Ronnie said. "Sure beats the ones we used in the 'Stan."

"This is an Eco-Star 130," Newhouse said. "Seats seven, including me. It's got great visibility and good range We can average about 150 for cruising speed. It's quick and it's quiet. The tourists and hunters love it. So do I. Hop in."

There were four seats in the back. Ronnie loaded the packs and climbed in. Nick and Selena sat in front. Newhouse had the leftmost seat in front of a wide instrument panel.

The seats were covered in tan leather, padded and comfortable. The cabin was completely encased in Plexiglas, giving everyone a broad view. Newhouse fired up. The vibration was minimal as the blades began turning, the sound levels bearable.

"Buckle up," Newhouse said. "You've got individual headsets. Go ahead and put them on." He adjusted his and began talking to the tower while he flipped switches and watched his gauges.

They lifted away from the pad and swept out over Fairbanks. The raw beauty of Alaska stretched away in all directions. Nick looked south.

"What's that river?" he asked.

"The Tanana. It's a tributary of the Yukon."

The helicopter banked and headed north. A snow-capped mountain range dominated the distance. Newhouse pointed.

"Those are the White Mountains, right by the Yukon. That's where we're headed."

"Is that the Pipeline?" Selena said. She pointed down at a silver-gray line snaking over the landscape.

"Yep. Pumps around six or seven hundred thousand barrels a day. It keeps springing leaks, idiots shoot at it, the environmentalists want to shut it down, terrorists want to sabotage it. I guess you know how controversial the project was. It's still a big deal years after they built it."

The panorama of wild Alaska passed below, a natural paradise. Meadows dotted with lakes, wildflowers and streams mixed with thick forests of spruce and hemlock. In the distance, the sun reflected from snow covered peaks lining the horizon. There was wildlife everywhere. Once, the sound of the rotors sent a herd of moose scattering across a meadow. They saw a bear and her cubs.

A little less than an hour later they were over Circle. It didn't look any different than the satellite photo. The airstrip looked old and neglected.

"Used to be a wild place in the old days," Newhouse said. "Supplies for the mining camps came up the river and got unloaded here. All gone, now."

Nick consulted his GPS. "You know where you want to set us down?"

"Yeah, there's a flat meadow about a day from where you want to go. I bring hunters there sometimes. It's a good base camp."

"What do they hunt?" Selena said.

"Grizzly, mostly. Moose. You need a permit and you'd better know what you're doing. This isn't the season, right now. You won't run into any hunters."

"I'm not worried about running into hunters. It's the bears I worry about."

"Don't bother them and they probably won't bother you," Newhouse said. "They keep to themselves and they don't like people much."

"That's comforting," Selena said. "Especially the part about probably not bothering us."

Newhouse laughed. Five minutes later, the clearing appeared below. He brought the helicopter in with practiced ease and set it down in the field. He sat and watched them unload while the engine idled. Nick came over to him.

"We shouldn't be more than a couple of days. I'll call you when we're ready to go back." He held up his sat phone. "We'll meet you here or where we're going. Either way, I'll let you know."

"Keep your head down. Don't let the bears eat your lady friend."

"I think they probably ought to be afraid of her," Nick said, "not the other way around. Have a good flight back."

He stepped away from the helicopter. The turbine wound up and the bird rose into the air. They watched it go. The sounds of the Alaskan wilderness replaced the whine of the turbine and the beat of the rotors. There was a rustle of wind in the trees. The air was clean and smelled of the forest.

They were alone.

"Spray for bugs," Nick said. "They'll be on us soon." They sprayed the exposed parts of their bodies.

"Better give Selena a heads up," Ronnie said. "About the wilderness."

"What about the wilderness?"

"It looks like we're just walking through a park but it's not what it appears to be. Sam wasn't kidding about the bears. Most of the animals won't bother us but the bears are no joke. A big grizzly can go over 1000 pounds and twice as high as a man when he stands on his hind legs. When they get going, they're hard to stop. This time of year there's plenty of food, so I don't think we'll have any trouble unless we surprise one. The rangers want you to make a lot of noise as you walk to warn off the wildlife but we can't do that. So keep an eye out. Stick close."

Nick turned on his GPS. "That way," he said. "As much as possible, we'll stay under the trees, just in case someone's looking."

They shouldered the packs and set off.

Once inside the forest, there was little movement of air. It was hot. Selena was sweating within minutes. She walked behind Nick while Ronnie brought up the rear. She was wearing one of the new armored vests over her shirt. It was hot and uncomfortable and rubbed against her skin. She could see a dark patch of moisture spreading out from under Nick's vest as he sweated. The ground underfoot was uneven and treacherous. Sometimes they seemed to climb, sometimes move downhill. She knew her legs would let her know about it later.

Tiny black flies found them. The bug spray helped but it didn't keep them away. The insects swarmed around her. When they bit, it was a sharp pain like a needle stick. Afterward, the bite itched.

"Beautiful from the air," Selena said, "but this is something Dante might have dreamed up."

"Can't be helped," Nick said. "At least no one is shooting at us."

Selena almost said *not yet* but held her tongue. It wasn't something to joke about. She'd never been on a mission yet when someone didn't shoot at her. The MP-5 chafing her shoulder and the heavy pistol on her thigh were reminders she wasn't here to take in the scenery.

By the time they made camp that night in a hollow of rocks, Selena ached all over. With the darkness came cold that hinted of the Arctic ice not far away. She wished they could start a fire, but they couldn't risk being spotted. They ate a cold meal.

"Selena, you take first watch. I don't think anyone knows we're out here except the animals, but I don't believe in taking chances. Ronnie, you next. I'll do the last one. I figure we're about an hour from the objective," Nick said. "We'll leave at first light."

"Look," Selena said.

A green curtain of light swept and shimmered and filled the northern sky.

"Aurora Borealis. The Northern Lights," Nick said. "That's something."

They watched the display. After about twenty minutes, it faded.

"Get some sleep," Nick said. "Long day at the office tomorrow."

CHAPTER 21

While Nick and the others were making their way through the Alaskan forest, General Louis Westlake was having dinner at his club with Senator Martinez. They sat at a table in the corner, away from the rest of the diners. They could talk without being overheard.

"We had good results in Novosibirsk," Westlake said, "but Thorpe wants some modifications before we move to the next part of the plan."

Alistair Thorpe was the research engineer who had developed Ajax. He'd based Ajax on designs developed by Nazi scientists in World War II as part of Hitler's *Wunderwaffe* secret weapons program. The Germans had built an electron accelerator called the Rheotron. It projected hard x-ray beams to disrupt the engines of enemy planes. From there it wasn't much of a leap to target the pilot and a prototype of a radio transmitter that disrupted brain function had been designed. In April of 1945, the Americans captured the Rheotron and the designs for the transmitter near Hamburg.

The German scientists had found a new home in America and a patron in the Pentagon. Their research had continued. 70 some years later, it had borne fruit in Ajax.

Martinez sipped his martini. "What did you have in mind?"

"I want to repeat the test."

"Where?"

"Riyadh. It will give the Saudis something to think about."

Martinez nodded. "I like it. We can give them a taste of what's to come if they don't cooperate once we've taken over. "

"A receiving unit's already in place," Westlake said. "Thorpe is on his way to Alaska to install the new circuit boards. He says it should improve intensity by twelve percent or better."

"Twelve percent? Excellent. When do they arrive on site?"

"Tomorrow morning. It shouldn't take long to upgrade the system. Then we can reprogram the satellite and give the sheiks a lesson."

Martinez toyed with his glass. "Riyadh should be enough. After that we could go ahead and implement here."

"We've already discussed this, Senator. London is the best test. We have to see how a Western democracy reacts when the population of a major city starts trashing everything in sight. How will the government respond? Whatever they do, it will provide on the spot, real-time data for what's going to happen here. We can anticipate and influence the course of events, but the more data we have, the more certain we are of success. Besides, it diverts attention."

"It does make sense," Martinez said. He speared the olive in his glass with a toothpick and ate it.

"We have to be patient," Westlake said. "We've waited this long, another week or two isn't going to make much difference."

"What about Prometheus?"

Prometheus was another, different kind of satellite, named for the Greek god who defied Zeus and brought fire to humans.

"What about it?"

"Those in the Pentagon who oppose the new order could use it against us."

Westlake smiled. For some reason, that smile made the Senate Majority Leader uneasy.

"You don't need to worry about Prometheus," Westlake said. "I've already taken steps to ensure that can't happen."

Martinez picked up the heavy menu.

"Try the duck," Westlake said. "It's very good here."

CHAPTER 22

Breakfast the next morning was more cold rations. Nick, Selena and Ronnie set off through the woods. They'd been walking through the trees for about an hour when the sound of a helicopter passing overhead shattered the peace of the forest.

"That can't be Sam," Ronnie said. "He wouldn't show up unless we called him."

The sound of the rotors changed pitch. The helicopter was out of sight but it sounded to Nick as though the pilot was hovering. A moment later the engine shut down.

"They landed," Ronnie said.

"Only one place they could do that around here," Nick said. "Right where we're going. We must be right on top of it. Go slow. Make sure no one sees us."

A few minutes later they reached the tree line bordering the clearing surrounding the installation. A black helicopter was parked on the landing pad. The door to the cabin was open. The pilot sat inside, writing something in his log book.

A large area had been cleared out of the forest. Two low, white buildings connected by a passageway took up the Southwest corner of the lot. There was a big satellite dish on the roof of one of the buildings, painted white. Six rows of tall antenna towers connected by an orderly grid of wires marched across the rest of the lot.

The building was about a hundred feet from where they lay concealed in the trees. Ronnie had his binoculars trained on the site. He kept his voice low.

"Four men with M-16s in civilian clothes. They look like ex-military. There's a fifth guy, looks kind of geeky. He's carrying a box of something. Geeky's going into the building and the others are taking up position outside."

A generator started up. Lights went on in the building.

"Looks like they only use this place when they need to," Nick said.

"Those people are mercenaries or private security," Ronnie said.

"The helicopter looks civilian," Selena said. "If this was a government operation, wouldn't they use a military helicopter?"

"Not necessarily," Nick said. "But Ronnie's right. These sites are part of a top secret military program. Any military security would be in uniform. Something stinks about this."

"Maybe they're getting set for a repeat of Novosibirsk," Ronnie said.

Nick looked at the scene below.

"I don't like it. Those guys look like they know what they're doing."

"I thought this was too easy." Ronnie waved his hand through a cloud of black flies buzzing around his face."

"Party time," Nick said. "Lock and load."

Selena looked grim. They charged their weapons.

"How do you want to do it?" Ronnie said.

Two of the guards were standing by the side of the building, smoking and talking. One man was out of sight. Nick had seen him going toward the rear of the compound. Nick was about to answer when the fourth man began walking toward the tree line. His face looked strained. He reached the trees, zipped down his fly and began to relieve himself. The stream of urine spattered on the pine needles and landed a few feet from where Nick lay concealed in the undergrowth.

A glance passed between Nick and Ronnie. The guard redid his fly and turned to go back to the building. Ronnie stood, silent as a wraith. With one, fast move he wrapped his forearm around the man's throat, covered his mouth and pulled him back before he left the shelter of the trees. The guard struggled and went limp. Ronnie set him down on the ground.

"One down. Gag him and wrap him up," Nick said.

The men at the building were laughing. They hadn't noticed what had happened to their comrade.

"It won't be long before they figure out he's missing," Selena said.

"We'd never make it across that open space," Nick said. His voice was quiet. "We'll work around to the side, get over to the building and then come around the front and get the drop on them. If they're smart, they'll quit. If they don't quit, take them out."

Keeping low, they moved through the branches to the other side of the building. Now the open space they'd have to cover was only about 30 feet. Nick heard someone calling the name of the missing man. They crossed the gap and started down the wall toward the front of the building.

"Hey!"

The shout came from behind them. The fourth security guard, the one who had walked away earlier, stood at the far end of the building. He raised his M-16. The ripping sound of Ronnie's MP-5 cut short his motion. The man collapsed on the ground.

After that, everything seemed to happen at once.

One of the guards came around the side of the building and fired. The bullets punched holes in the building over Selena's head. Nick fired and brought him down.

They heard the door of the building slam shut.

"Sounds like he went inside," Ronnie said. He risked a quick look. There was no one there. He started around the corner. A burst of automatic fire knocked him down onto the ground.

"The helicopter," Selena said.

They reached around the building and opened up with their MP5s. The pilot was leaning out of the cabin, an M-16 in his hand. The spray of bullets peppered the helicopter and starred the glass. The man yelled and twisted back in his seat. His M-16 went flying. Fuel began leaking underneath the machine. There was a brief flicker of flame, then a sound as though someone had struck the earth with a giant hammer. The craft blew up in a brilliant ball of fire. Debris hurtled into the sky and fell back in flaming bits and pieces. The shock wave from the explosion rocked them with a blast of warm air.

"Whoa," Selena said.

"Keep the door covered," Nick said to Selena. He ran to where Ronnie lay gasping for air. He was wearing one of the new vests. It had stopped the bullets but he'd been hit more than once and an M16 packed a lot of punch. Nick figured him for cracked ribs.

"Can you get up?"

"Yeah. Uhh."

Nick helped him to his feet.

"There's one more guard inside," Nick said. "Plus the geek. Selena and I will go in after him. You cover us as best you can."

"I'm good."

"You scared me for a moment there."

"Yeah. Me too."

Selena stood by the closed door into the building, her MP-5 ready. Nick and Ronnie walked over to her. They were safe for the moment. There were no windows in the front of the building, only the one door.

"Are you okay, Ronnie?" she said.

"Yeah. Not going to be able to move fast, though."

"This could get tricky," Nick said. "We don't know what's inside. This building connects to the next one. The two men left could be in either one."

"You can bet your ass they're waiting for us to come through this door," Ronnie said.

"There have to be other ways to get in," Selena said. "Another door."

A sudden noise made them look up.

"What's that?" Ronnie said.

Nick backed away from the building, keeping his eye on the door. On the roof, the big satellite antenna was starting to turn. He hurried back to where the others were waiting.

"The satellite dish is moving," he said. "They're getting ready to do something. We're out of time. I'll open the door. Selena and Ronnie, you cover me."

Nick stood away from the door and put his hand on the knob. "Ready?"

Selena nodded. Her lips were dry, her heart pumping hard. Nick turned the knob and thrust against the door and ducked back. It flew open.

Nothing happened.

Nick stood on the opposite side of the door from Selena. "Can you see anything from where you are?" he asked.

"Not much. It looks like storage of some kind. A few big crates and some boxes pushed up against the wall. It might give us cover if we got behind them."

"On three, you make a dash for the boxes," Nick said. "Get behind them and I'll give you covering fire. You see anything move in there, you shoot it."

She nodded. Her heart was trying to pound out through her ribs. She gripped the MP-5 tight. Nick saw the tension. Adrenaline was good, but adrenaline could get you killed.

"Take a deep breath," Nick said. "Another."

"Better," she said.

Nick held up three fingers and counted down. On three, Selena sprinted into the building toward the big crate she'd seen from outside. Nick reached around the doorway and began firing into the space beyond. Answering fire came from somewhere inside the building. The bullets splintered the doorframe and thudded into the wall.

"I'm there," Selena yelled.

Nick heard her MP-5 open up. Ronnie reached around the door frame and fired toward the back of the building. Nick ran across the floor to where Selena crouched behind a wooden crate. He got down beside her.

The box was marked FRAGILE ELECTRONIC EQUIPMENT in red and black block letters. Another burst of automatic fire came from the back and smashed into the wooden slats. Nick heard things breaking inside the crate.

"From what I could see there's nothing in here but more boxes and a door to the other building."

"And whoever is shooting at us," Selena said.

"He's trying to keep us pinned down. We have to get into that other building before his buddy does whatever he's trying to do."

"To hell with this," Selena said. Before Nick could react, she stood and began firing. She let out a wild yell and began running and shooting toward the back of the building.

"Damn it," Nick said.

He jumped up and ran after her. He saw movement in the back corner. He flicked the selector switch to full auto and pulled the trigger. The 30 round magazine emptied with a sound like ripping cloth. The rounds tore into the last security guard.

Selena saw him go down. She veered toward the door to the other building and kicked it open. She ran down a short passage. The door at the other end was open. Nick was right behind her. She could hear him swearing as he ran.

The room was filled with electronic equipment. The man Ronnie had described as geeky sat before a computer screen and keyboard. He stared at her as if she were an apparition from hell.

"Don't move," she yelled.

He made a sudden grab for something on the desk, his eyes desperate. Selena couldn't see what he was reaching for. She opened fire.

The rounds stitched a bloody pattern across his chest and smashed into the computer and monitor behind him. The body fell back out of the chair onto the floor, legs splayed at an awkward angle. Sparks and smoke came from the computer. The monitor was shattered.

Selena walked over to the computer. The dead man had been reaching for a phone. She looked at him, at the sparking equipment on the bench. Nick came up beside her. Her face was chalk white.

"It's over," he said.

"I told him not to move," she said. "I told him. I thought he had a gun."

Nick rested his hand on her shoulder. "It's all right," he said. "You did the right thing. Don't worry about it."

Ronnie came into the room, one arm held tight across his chest.

"You all right, Ronnie?"

"Yeah. It hurts less if I hold everything tight."

Nick turned to Selena. The color had come back in her face. "That was a stupid move," he said, "jumping up like that. What the hell were you thinking?"

"It worked, didn't it? I don't know what I was thinking. Something came over me."

"You could have been killed."

"Well," she said, "it's not like it's the first time."

"All the same...aahh, never mind."

"What were they doing here?" Selena said.

"I'm not sure," Nick said. "That dish on the roof is a directional antenna. They were going to send a signal."

Nick looked around the room. It was a utilitarian space, the walls lined with workbenches and pieces of electronic equipment. The man Selena had killed had been sitting in front of what was obviously the main control console. It was in pretty bad shape. A burst from an MP-5 tended to wreak havoc wherever it went. The computers and monitors were no exception. Bits of shattered glass and jagged shards of metal covered the work table. The computer case was full of holes.

"Maybe the hard drive is still intact," Nick said. He reached behind the computer and pulled the plug.

"Selena, help me get this open."

With the inside of the computer exposed, Nick saw the hard drive. He found a screwdriver lying on the bench, undid the screws holding the drive in place and slipped it out of the smashed computer.

"We'll see what Stephanie can make out of this," he said.

"Here's a logbook of some sort," Ronnie said. He held up a black binder notebook and flipped through the pages. "Looks like our friend on the floor was running tests. It doesn't make much sense to me."

"Something else for Steph to look at," Nick said.

"I'd better call Sam for pickup," Ronnie said.

"Right. By the time he gets here we should have found anything else worth checking out."

"What about the guy we tied up in the woods?" Selena said.

"I forgot about him." Nick ran his fingers through his hair. "We can't just leave him here. I guess we have to take him back with us. Harker will know how to handle it. Ronnie, you and Selena go get him while I look around in here."

They left the room. Five minutes later they were back.

"He's dead," Ronnie said. "Looks like he threw up and choked on the gag."

"Bad luck. I wouldn't wish that on anyone," Nick said.

"I went through his pockets. He had a wallet and civilian ID. There wasn't anything else."

"We need to check the others," Nick said. "Call your friend and tell him to come get us."

"Already did it. He should be here in a little over an hour."

CHAPTER 23

It was Thursday night in Alexandria, Virginia, not far from the Capitol. General Westlake sat at home in his favorite chair, reading the *Iliad,* the epic poem about the war between Greece and Troy. It was Homer who had inspired him with the name for the operation that was about to begin.

Westlake sighed. He had been denied the opportunity to lead vast armies. His enemies in the Pentagon had made sure of that. They would soon discover the mistake they'd made by shutting him out from important command in the field.

His secured phone signaled a call.

"Westlake."

"We have a problem." The caller was Senator Martinez. Westlake felt his good mood begin to dissolve.

"What kind of problem?"

"There was a raid on the Alaska facility. We were unable to complete the test. "

"What happened?"

"Thorpe was about to activate when some kind of special ops force showed up. We ran a satellite pass. The helicopter that brought in Thorpe and the security team was destroyed. There are bodies outside the buildings and I can't reach anyone on-site. We have to assume the equipment was taken off-line by whoever hit the site."

"CIA?"

"My sources say no. I can't find any official operation, covert or otherwise. My guess is we're dealing with Rice's group, the Project. They have the balls to pull off something like this."

Westlake could feel his blood pressure rising, an instant band tightening around his forehead. The failure of his attempt to eliminate the Project had come back to haunt him.

"Those people have more lives than a cat," he said. "It's a setback, but that's all."

On the other end of the connection, Martinez said, "We've lost Thorpe."

"We don't need him. Everything he did is documented. Hell, any college sophomore could follow his directions and program the satellite."

"If he's a prisoner, that could be a problem," Martinez said. "He knows too much."

"Send someone up there and check it out. We need to know for certain."

"All right."

Westlake said, "We'll use Colorado for the rest of the transmissions. I wanted to reserve that for the final phase, but it will give us a chance to work out any glitches in managing the operation. "

"Have you chosen the London location yet?"

"Yes. We'll place the diversion in the financial district. The amplifier will go in an entertainment complex called the O2. There's a concert scheduled a week from Saturday. Some British rock star. It's sold out. There will be 20,000 people packed together and screaming their heads off. I thought that would be a good place to put our little gift box. The device will activate fifteen minutes after the bomb, while emergency services are responding to the explosion."

"There will be real panic in a crowd like that. A lot of people are going to get killed."

"You're not getting squeamish on me, are you Senator?"

"No, but are you sure it's necessary? After all, if we put it somewhere else it will serve our purpose just as well and there will be fewer casualties."

"Provocation has to be severe. We want to encourage the strongest possible response on the part of the British government. You can't make omelettes without breaking eggs."

"Please, Louis, spare me the clichés."

"Then spare me your false humanitarian concerns. I didn't hear you commenting on the numbers of dead in Russia."

Martinez thought about it. "I see your point. You're right."

"Of course I am."

"What shall we do about the Project?"

"The damage is done," Westlake said. "They screwed up the test but things are too far along for them to do much else. They don't know what we plan. By the time they figure it out, it will be too late. They won't be able to stop it."

"Still..."

"I'll talk with Edmonds and convince him the Project is interfering with a classified military operation. I should've done it before. He'll be so happy a four-star general is taking him seriously that he'll jump on the chance to do something he thinks is presidential."

"He could be useful. You think we should leave him in office afterward? He's familiar to the public. It might lend an air of legitimacy to the new government."

"I haven't decided that yet. Let's see if he'll cooperate."

CHAPTER 24

In Virginia, Stephanie waited until Elizabeth finished talking with Nick.

"Well?" Stephanie said.

"They're on the way back. Ronnie has cracked ribs and a bruised ego but everybody else is all right. They're bringing a hard drive and a logbook for you to look at. They didn't find anything of consequence on the bodies. Nothing to tell us where they came from. Whoever sent them won't be using that site anymore."

"How did they gain access to a secret defense facility?" Stephanie asked.

"I don't know. They had to know where it was and how to get into it. Not many people would have that information."

"That should make it a little easier to narrow down," Stephanie said. "The hard drive Nick found could help."

"If you can read it, it might."

Harker picked up her pen and began tapping on her desktop.

"We've reached the limit of what we can do on our own," she said. "This is getting complicated and there are too many implications for national security. It's been compromised. We can't risk making a mistake. I'm going to bring in Langley. We can't trust the White House to help while Edmonds is running things but we can trust Hood."

"Lucas likes him. He's a pretty good judge of character."

Lucas Monroe and Stephanie had been lovers for the better part of a year. He was on the fast track to become Director of National Clandestine Services. If he made it, he'd be the first black man to ever hold down one of the four top directorates at Langley.

"See? That's a powerful endorsement, coming from him. How are you two getting along?"

Stephanie twisted the bracelets on her wrist and took a deep breath. "We're going to move in together."

"Steph, that's wonderful."

"We thought we'd try it out." The words came out in a hurry. "Living together. If it works, we'll make it permanent."

"You're the first person I've told," Stephanie said.

"That's wonderful," Elizabeth said again. "Are you keeping your apartment?"

"No, it's too small. So is his. We've begun looking for a place with more room."

Harker set her pen back down. "It's good to talk about something normal for a change."

"Isn't that why we do this?" Stephanie said.

"What do you mean?"

Stephanie gestured around the room, at the monitor on the wall, the files on Harker's desk. "So we can have normal lives. Our job is all about stopping people who think normal means doing whatever they want. People who start wars because they're rich, sociopathic assholes who want to get richer, or religious lunatics who think God is on their side."

"I never thought of it quite like that," Elizabeth said, "but that sounds about right."

"What are you going to tell Hood?" Stephanie asked.

"Everything. That we're on the track of something that relates to Novosibirsk and that I'm waiting for more information. I want you to look at that hard drive Nick recovered before I talk with him. The more I know, the better."

CHAPTER 25

Stephanie was waiting for them when they got back to Washington. Nick handed over the salvaged hard drive and logbook.

"Meeting tomorrow with Elizabeth at 0900," she said. "Ronnie, you come with me and we'll get those ribs checked out."

Nick turned to Selena. "Do you want to stay at my place tonight?"

"It's better if I go home. All I want is a hot bath and a good night's sleep."

He pushed his disappointment away.

"I'll see you in the morning," he said.

Back at his apartment, Nick poured himself a whiskey. He thought about Selena. What was it between them, anyway? Sometimes it seemed like they were on the same wavelength, as close to each other as a person could get to someone else. Other times, it was as if they lived on two different planets.

The whiskey warmed his stomach. He poured another. What did he really want from her? He realized he had never thought it through. He loved her, but did he want to marry her? What did people usually want from a marriage? He knew what he didn't want, he didn't want all the complications that went with having children. As far as he knew, that wasn't an issue for Selena. She had never given any indication that she wanted kids. So what was it?

He knew that most men would envy a situation like his. He had his own place and she had hers. They could get away from each other when they needed to. The sex was great. They worked well together. She could hold her own in the unusual and dangerous world they shared and he could rely on her when the chips were down. What more could anyone want?

Nick thought about Megan, the fiancée he'd lost years ago, the only woman he'd ever loved before Selena walked into his life. It was getting hard to remember how she'd looked. He used to dream about her but there had been a dream where she said goodbye and she hadn't appeared since.

Megan had been so different from Selena. He'd wanted different things with her and he'd been a lot younger then. With Megan, Nick had looked forward to a life pretty much like other people had. A civilian life with a couple of kids, a house somewhere, a job doing something where nobody was shooting at him.

Then all that disappeared in a fireball of burning jet fuel and twisted metal. The image of her plane arcing into the ground as he watched was seared into his memory.

The hell with it, he thought.

Nick finished his whiskey and went to bed.

CHAPTER 26

The next morning they were gathered in Elizabeth's office. Lamont had the cat in his lap. Burps was drooling onto his leg and purring, a low rumble beneath the conversation. Ronnie sat next to Lamont on the couch. He wore one of his Hawaiian shirts, this one with a gaudy picture of a volcano erupting in a bed of exotic flowers.

"It feels like we're running out of time," Elizabeth said. "It's nothing I can put my finger on, just a feeling."

Stephanie said. "I was able to recover some files from that hard drive, but most of it was corrupted."

Elizabeth sipped from a cup of coffee. "Before you get into that, Vysotsky called me. The Russians found something at Ground Zero in Novosibirsk. It's a receiver and amplifier. The weapon sends a beam from a satellite, the device picks it up, amplifies it and broadcasts it out over a wide area."

"Any way to trace where it came from?" Nick asked.

Harker shook her head. "Not much was left."

"What about the explosion before everybody went nuts? What did Vysotsky say about that? Does he think it's related?"

"Yes, he does. The explosion was caused by a bomb. Vysotsky thinks it was a diversion to add to the confusion and pull rescue services away from the center of the riot. He has his forensic people working on what's left of the device but he's not hopeful. At least he's keeping me informed of what he discovers."

There was a sudden silence in the room, broken only by the erratic purring of the cat, one of those spontaneous moments when no one knew what to say. Stephanie broke it.

"What Vysotsky told you fits with what I picked up on the hard drive," she said. "I found a program that tells the computer to broadcast a specific frequency to a satellite and have it relay back to the surface. There's nothing particularly unique about it. It's common practice."

"So there isn't anything to indicate who sent it?" Elizabeth asked.

"No. Anyone with a reasonable amount of computer knowledge and satellite communications could have done it."

"Then it's another dead end," Nick said.

"Not quite. The disc was in bad shape, but I salvaged part of it. The drive contained instructions that triggered the attack on Novosibirsk. The attack you stopped when you hit the facility was against Riyadh. There are more targets."

"How many more?" Selena said.

"I don't know, most of the data was corrupted. But I know one of them," Steph said. "It's in London. The GPS coordinates tell us where the receiver will be. Do you know the O2 in London?"

"The big arena that looks like a flying saucer with sticks coming out of it? The one that sits in the middle of the Thames?"

"That's the one," Steph said. "It's an indoor arena where they put on shows and sporting events, one of the biggest in Europe."

Everyone sat up a little bit straighter. Knowing where the next attack was scheduled meant they had a chance to stop it.

"When?" Selena asked. "When do they plan to target it?"

Stephanie said, "I don't know. All I have is the location, not the timing."

"Why would they target an arena?" Selena wondered. "It's not a strategic target."

"Neither was the center of Novosibirsk," Nick said.

"People," Lamont said. "If there was a big event, the place would be packed with people. This weapon makes people crazy. There would be a massive riot."

"Like in Novosibirsk," Ronnie said. "Only it would be worse. All those people crammed in together. They would tear each other apart."

"It would be worse than Novosibirsk," Selena said. "London is much more crowded. The government would have to come down hard to stop it."

"They would declare a state of emergency and suspend civil liberties," Elizabeth said.

"But when the riots were over, the restrictions would be lifted. Wouldn't they?" Selena brushed a strand of hair away from her forehead.

"That depends on who is in control," Elizabeth said. "It's a lot easier to keep the lid on once the troops have been called out. You just keep the rhetoric going. You know, terrorist attack, threat to the nation, more attacks planned."

"That's cynical, Elizabeth."

"I prefer to think of it as being realistic," she said.

"What are we going to do about it?" Nick asked.

"We need to know what's happening at that arena. Stephanie, can you call up a schedule for the O2 on the monitor?"

Stephanie entered a few commands and a webpage came up with a list of events that were scheduled.

"Busy," Steph said.

"How many does the arena seat for one of the events?" Selena said.

"According to this, around 20,000," Steph said.

"I don't even want to think about 20,000 people going mad all at once," Nick said. "How do we know which event they're going to target?"

"We don't," Harker said. "We have to assume it could be any of them."

"They'd want to affect as many people as possible," Nick said. "Is anything coming up that's sold out?"

Steph scrolled through the list. "Yes, one. There's a concert this Saturday night featuring a British rock singer. I've seen him on television. He's got that same kind of electric energy Springsteen had when he did *Born to Run*."

"We have to let the Brits know there's a terrorist attack coming," Elizabeth said. "I know the Director of MI5. I'll talk with him. He'll get you inside the arena."

"We need to plan out the mission," Nick said. "I want Lamont in on this one."

Elizabeth looked at Lamont. Burps was still on his lap, with his paws in the air. Lamont was busy scratching his stomach.

"How are you feeling, Lamont?" she said.

"I'm fine, Director."

"You're up for a mission?"

"I'm going nuts sitting around here, Director. I'm okay, really."

"All right. Nick, you'd better get to it. You only have a few days before the concert. I'll book you on a commercial flight to London."

"The people behind this don't like us much," Nick said. "They could be waiting for us to show up."

"They could. I suggest you stay alert."

"That's it? Stay alert?"

"What do you expect me to say? This isn't a deep cover mission. MI5 will meet you in England."

"What about weapons?"

"Leave them here. The Brits have been sticky about Americans carrying guns lately. You'll have to get something from them." Harker paused. "Try not to step on any toes while you're there."

As they were walking out to the parking lot, Nick took Lamont aside.

"You really feeling okay, Shadow?"

"Yeah, I'm good Nick. I threw away those pills and I feel a lot better."

"Pretty soon to come back after a hit like that."

"Really Nick, I'm fine."

Nick looked at his friend and hoped it was true.

CHAPTER 27

The next morning, Nick and Selena sat next to each other on the flight to England. The Atlantic Ocean was a monotonous gray seascape far below. The first class seats were wide and comfortable, covered with cool, gray leather. Selena had upgraded their tickets. She didn't flout her wealth, but she saw no reason why she shouldn't make life easier with it. Lamont and Ronnie were two rows back.

Nick leaned back and closed his eyes. *Beats a C130,* Nick thought. He couldn't remember how many hours he'd spent inside the cold aluminum belly of some droning transport, sitting on a strap bench, weighted down with gear and heading for some godforsaken place where people wanted to kill him.

"Nick," Selena said.

Nick opened his eyes.

Selena said, "I need to tell Elizabeth about that file."

"What brought this on?"

"At first I thought that if Elizabeth knew about my father she'd want me off the team. But the more I thought about it, the more I realized you were right."

"About what?"

"When you said that I wasn't my father and that I was being biblical if I thought she would judge me because of what he was supposed to have done."

"So why do you want to tell her about it now?" Nick asked.

"I want to know who killed my family, if he's still alive. There isn't any way I can find that out on my own. I need help to get into the KGB files. Elizabeth has to okay that. Besides, it doesn't feel right to keep hiding this from her. What if someone discovers that my father is supposed to have sold secrets to the Russians? It could all come back on her."

"Adam told me that file is the only copy," Nick said.

"It may be the only copy Langley had but there must be something in the Russian files. They're even more obsessive about paperwork than we are. Even if it is the only copy, someone else may know what's in it."

Nick considered what she had said. "I suppose it's possible. It would be difficult to prove without hard evidence."

"All it would take is the accusation," Selena said. "It could make a lot of trouble for Elizabeth."

"What will you do if you find out that the assassin is still around?" Nick asked.

"I don't know. I'll figure that out when I need to."

Three hours later they landed at Heathrow.

Harker's MI5 contact was waiting for them. He was about 40 years old and looked like something out of a TV series made for PBS. He was dressed in a tailored blue suit with pinstripes. His white shirt gleamed. His tie was made of silk and probably told someone who understood the pattern what exclusive school he had attended.

"George Wigland," he said. "I'm your minder while you're visiting, Mister Carter. Let's hope your journey here is uneventful. Did you bring weapons?"

"No."

"Good. Then that's not a problem. We really don't want you going around armed, do we? I'm sure they won't be necessary."

"We were told you would provide them," Nick said. "We've had authorization to carry weapons in England before."

"It's not negotiable, I'm afraid. You won't need them. We'll take care of that."

"I hope you're right, Mister Wigland."

Ronnie lifted an eyebrow. Nick decided to keep his thoughts to himself. If Wigland thought this was going to be a walk in the park that was his business.

"Why don't you fill me in on the way to your hotel?" Wigland said. "We have a car waiting."

Nick briefed him during the ride in from the airport. Wigland didn't seem very interested in what Nick had to say. It was early evening. They agreed to meet in the morning. Wigland dropped them in front of the hotel and drove away. They watched him go.

"He doesn't seem too concerned about someone turning London into a kill zone," Lamont said.

"No," Nick said, "he doesn't."

"No weapons?" Ronnie said. "I know someone here who could help us out."

"I don't want to piss off the Brits. It would get Harker in trouble and she has enough on her plate right now. Maybe Wigland is right and we won't need them."

"Yeah, maybe. Maybe I'll win the lotto next time I buy a ticket."

"I'll talk to Harker. She might be able to get him to change his mind. Let's check in."

The hotel was a famous, exclusive landmark in the heart of London, overlooking Trafalgar Square. Selena had reserved a suite on the top floor.

The door to their room closed behind the bellhop. Nick eyed the perfect carpet and cream-colored furniture. No one could accuse the management of cutting corners when it came to providing for the luxury of its guests. The room was like something out of a designer magazine.

Nick gestured at the carpet. "Are we allowed to walk on this? And look at that furniture. I'm almost afraid to sit down."

Selena laughed. "Nice, isn't it? It would be hard to live with, though. You can't take care of something like this without an army of maids."

Five minutes later there was a light knock on the door. Nick opened it for Ronnie and Lamont. Ronnie took one look and whistled.

"Nice digs. And I thought my room was something." He looked out the window at the square and a tall column with a statue on top. "Who's the guy on the pillar?"

"Admiral Lord Nelson," Selena said. "England's greatest naval hero. He defeated a superior French fleet at the Battle of Trafalgar and saved England. He was killed in the battle."

"The heroes always are," Lamont said. "Most of them don't get statues."

"Let's get down to business," Nick said. He sat on the couch with Selena. Ronnie and Lamont took chairs. Nick spread out plans of the O2 arena on a low table in front of the couch.

"Big," Ronnie said.

Nick nodded. "Besides the arena, there are restaurants, shops and a movie theater. There are a million places where someone could hide something."

"Bad odds," Lamont said.

"Best we've got."

"We can't search that whole complex," Lamont said.

"We don't have to. Wigland and his boys will have a team going through the place looking for anything suspicious. Our job is to watch the crowd, in case someone brings it in with them."

"You don't think they'd plant it ahead of time?" Ronnie said.

"They might, but the opposition probably knows we're on to them. If they place it ahead of time, it could be found. I think they'll wait until the last minute."

Selena said, "If this weapon makes people crazy, why would they have their agent in place when it goes off?"

"He won't know what he's carrying," Nick said. "The man who placed the receiver in Russia is dead. He was just a patsy."

Everyone had seen the video of the murderous riots in Novosibirsk, the images of rage and fear. No one mentioned the fact that if they failed to stop the attack, they would be affected like everyone else.

"How big is this thing?" Ronnie asked.

"Hard to tell from what the Russians found. Maybe the size of a camera or a portable radio."

"You don't see those anymore," Lamont said. "Now everybody listens to their phone."

"Nobody is going to be listening to a radio at a rock concert," Selena said. "Or their phone either."

"Yeah, but they'll all be taking pictures with their phones." Ronnie scratched his nose. "We'd better hope this thing doesn't look like one of those."

"How do we pick one person out of 20,000?" Selena said. "The more we look at this, the more impossible it seems."

Nick tugged on his ear. "Let's narrow things down. Brainstorm it with a few assumptions."

"Where do you want to start?" Ronnie said.

"Think like the opposition. How do I get the maximum effect I want?"

"Well," Selena said, "if I'm sending someone in and I don't want them to know that they're about to get killed, I need them to feel comfortable. Safe. I need to distract them until I activate the device."

"Okay," Nick said. "It's a rock concert. How does anyone get comfortable at a rock concert?"

"You need a really good seat," Ronnie said. "Somewhere near the band, where you can see everything. If you're up in the bleachers, it's like watching ants from a distance. If I wanted someone to be thinking about anything except the package they were carrying, I'd get them the best seat in the house."

"That would be right up near the stage. Do they have seats there?"

Selena pointed at the seating diagram. "There's stadium seating on three sides of the arena and the stage on the fourth, then this big flat space in front of the stage. They probably fill that up with people standing. They might run a walkway out from the stage into the crowd."

"You see that a lot at a big concert," Lamont said.

"So," Nick said, "no seats right in front of the stage but they do have them on the sides. Big standing crowd in front. "

"The floor will be a mob scene," Ronnie said. "I don't want to be in the middle of that if that thing goes off."

"Then I guess we'd better make damn sure it doesn't," Nick said, "since there's a good chance that's exactly where we'll be."

"How is our patsy going to get a package through security?" Selena asked. "There's bound to be security. There always is at a big event. Don't they have metal detectors?"

"I don't know what their security looks like. I'll ask Wigland."

Later, they went down to the hotel restaurant. The room gleamed with Italian marble. Glittering crystal chandeliers hung from a ceiling far above. Nick wondered how they reached all those dangling facets to keep them dust free. The lighting was subdued. The tables were covered with white linen. The diners were elegantly dressed, some in formal evening clothes. It was if he had stepped back into an earlier time, into an England that no longer existed.

Later, Selena and Nick left Ronnie and Lamont at their floor and continued up another two stories in the elevator. The bed had been turned down. Mints had been left on the pillow.

Selena showered first. When Nick came out of the bathroom, she was already under the covers. He got in and turned toward her.

"This bed is too good to pass up," he said. "I'm not tossing around like I did. I don't think I'm likely to hit you in my sleep."

"I don't care if you toss around," she said. "But if you hit me while you're asleep I'm going to hit you back, so don't say I didn't give you fair warning."

Nick reached across and touched her face.
It was a long time before they slept.

CHAPTER 28

"Thank you for seeing me, Mister Vice President." General Westlake shook hands with Edmonds.

"My pleasure, General, my pleasure. Please, sit down." Edmonds gestured at a comfortable chair covered in a green and white striped fabric.

They were in the Vice President's office in the West Wing. The room was an odd combination of old and modern. Draped hangings on the tops of the windows could have been in style in Lincoln's time. The furniture was an expensive mix of modern reproduction and genuine American antique. The carpet was a deep blue, thick and soft underfoot.

Edmonds was a heavy man, with bushy eyebrows and dark eyes. Cartoonists had a field day drawing him in ways that made him look like a comical bowling ball. His feet were dainty for such a big man. His carefully tailored suits failed to conceal his enormous gut.

The Vice President liked sailing, as long as someone else was doing the work. The walls sported museum quality paintings of sailing ships from the early days of the U.S. Navy. The fact that he was not a very good sailor wasn't mentioned by those who knew him, at least not in his presence.

Edmonds had not made the transition to the heights of American politics by virtue of being stupid. He'd been CEO of one of the largest companies in the world, a man driven by self interest. Westlake did not make the mistake of underestimating him. He could be manipulated by fanning the flames of his ambition, but it would require subtlety.

His position a heartbeat away from the Oval Office gave him far more importance than he deserved. Rice had picked Edmonds for his running mate as a political move, garnering the support of big money in the business community. In terms of the leadership of the country, it had been a mistake.

Edmonds folded his hands. "I can give you 10 minutes, General. As you might expect, things have been a little chaotic around here since the assassination attempt."

Westlake put on a suitable expression of concern. "Yes, a terrible thing. I appreciate your taking time out of your busy schedule, Mister Vice President. The burden of running the country is now upon your shoulders. May I say that we at the Pentagon feel quite comfortable with you in charge during this difficult time."

Edmonds visibly preened. "Yes, well, I do what I can. Hopefully the President will return to office soon."

Westlake looked at this puffed up man and knew he was lying. *Not likely,* Westlake thought. *I'll bet you can't wait to get your fat ass in that chair down the hall in the Oval Office. Play along, and it might be sooner than you think.*

"Sir, as you know there are important military programs out of the public eye. There are several on a strictly need to know basis which do not include the President on the distribution list. It has always been felt that plausible deniability takes precedence over knowledge of programs that might be misunderstood by the electorate."

Edmonds' eyes narrowed. "Go on."

"One of those programs is called Ajax. It concerns development of a weapon which can be used with minimal cost and great efficiency against our enemies."

"What does this weapon do?"

"It causes great confusion and dispersion in the enemy ranks without destroying important infrastructure. We are at a sensitive stage in the testing and development of Ajax. Unfortunately, one of our own intelligence units is interfering with this highly classified program."

"One of our units? That borders on treason. Which one?"

"The Project."

"Ah. Rice's pet spies. I know who they are, a bunch of undisciplined troublemakers. They're led by that woman who created a lot of problems for the 9/11 commission."

"That's them," Westlake said. "They seem to be operating under some false assumption about this research. In time, I'm certain any misconceptions they have can be cleared up. But the fact remains, they are causing serious delays in the development of this important piece of our national security. This is a time critical program. We can't afford any more delays."

That ought to be enough, Westlake thought. *Don't lay it on too thick..*

"I appreciate your coming to me with this, General. And I appreciate your filling me in on this program."

You have no idea what this program is, Westlake thought.

Edmonds continued. "What do you think should be done?"

"That's up to you, sir. You are the only person who can tell them what to do. But I do think they should be prevented from further interference."

"Mm." Edmonds got up from his chair. Westlake stood at the same time. He came to attention.

"Interference with our classified military programs cannot be tolerated," Edmonds said. "I'll look into it. I am a believer in a strong military."

"We know that, sir. It's good to have someone in the White House who feels that way. The Pentagon would be grateful for anything you can do about this problem."

Westlake paused.

"Is there something else, General?"

"May I be candid, sir?"

Edmonds gave Westlake a careful look. "Please go on, General."

"Frankly, sir, many of us at the Pentagon feel that President Rice has undermined the country's interests by his insistence on negotiations with people who will never keep their agreements. Of course we hope that the President will recover but if circumstance elevates you to the presidency, I can assure you of our support."

Edmonds held out his hand and the two men shook. Their eyes met in unspoken agreement.

As he left the White House, Westlake was satisfied Edmonds was hooked. The man was self-important and ambitious and he wanted to be President. The thought of active support from the military probably had him fantasizing about redecorating the Oval Office. It would be interesting to see what he did to call off Harker's dogs.

His driver was waiting for him when he emerged from a side entrance of the White House. Westlake got into the back seat.

"The Pentagon," he said.

The car exited the White House grounds. Westlake watched the flow of cars and pedestrians through the windows of the car as it threaded through Washington traffic. He thought about when he had first come here. He'd only been a lieutenant then, wet behind the ears, proud to be part of a great military tradition. Over the years that pride had turned to confusion and then anger.

He'd watched politicians refuse to make the right decisions because of popular opinion or misguided notions of political correctness. Politicians like Rice, who backed away from victory even when they held it in the palm of their hand. Politicians who had sacrificed his son for nothing.

Westlake had been immensely proud of his boy. His death had been meaningless. Alan Westlake had died because he'd been ordered into an insurgent stronghold without adequate support. There had been no military or strategic value in the assignment. It had been a political gesture, meant to satisfy the arbitrary whims of a puppet president Washington claimed was an ally.

Westlake's wife had never been the same after that. She had gone into a deep depression. A year after George's death, she'd killed herself.

Westlake became known in military circles as an unrelenting hawk, an advocate of massive response with token concern for collateral damage. He'd been on the short list for a seat on the Joint Chiefs but as his views hardened and the political climate changed, he'd been shunted aside. He was given the satellite program, a poor substitute for the command of legions.

It was clear to him that political expediency had placed the security of the nation in danger. Washington's policies of appeasement and negotiation dishonored his son and every American. It was enough to make any patriot weep.

He would change that. America would reclaim her rightful place. At the end of World War II, the stars and stripes had flown in every corner of the globe. There was no reason why it shouldn't again. All that was needed was the right leader.

It was America's destiny.

His destiny.

CHAPTER 29

Nick and the others stood outside the entrance to the O2 arena, waiting for their MI5 escort. They wore earpieces so they could stay in radio contact once they were inside. Streams of people filed past. Wigland had been adamant: wait for him before they did anything.

Posters outside the stadium headlined a singer with long blonde hair, tattooed arms and the look of the streets.

"Guy has a lot of ink," Nick said.

"I wonder if he's any good?" Selena said.

"Must be, to book this joint solid," Ronnie said. "I looked it up on the net. Only the top acts play here."

"I don't like this waiting around for our minder to decide if we can be useful," Nick said.

Lamont coughed. "I don't think he likes us much," he said.

"Speak of the devil," Ronnie said.

Wigland came up to them. He was immaculately dressed. He looked as if he was on his way to the theater instead of hunting someone who planned to trigger a riot. "Well then," he said. "Here we are."

"What's the plan?" Nick asked. "Have your people turned anything up?"

"Not yet, but if something's there we'll find it. Not really your concern."

Nick controlled himself. It was obvious that Wigland had no intention of giving Nick and his team any operational responsibility. He decided to confront Wigland about it.

"I'd like to point out that you and your government would have no idea there was any possibility of an incident if my director hadn't called your boss and given him a heads up. Now you're marginalizing us. It's a mistake."

Wigland's face was closed. "You are only here as a courtesy, Carter. We do things our own way on this side of the pond. We don't need you cowboy types screwing things up, do we?" His voice was dismissive.

He handed Nick tickets. "Enjoy the show and stay out of the way. If you interfere in my operation, I'll have you on a plane back to Washington tonight. This whole exercise is a waste of time. If there does turn out to be anything to it, we'll sort it out."

Nick felt a headache start. He resisted the urge to punch the man.

"Remember," Wigland said. He pointed his finger at Nick. "Stay out of the way." He turned and walked into the arena, leaving them standing there.

"I know where he got his old school tie," Ronnie said. "Asshole University."

Selena laughed.

Nick smiled in spite of himself. His ear itched. He reached up and scratched it. Selena and Ronnie looked at each other.

"I'll never understand why people like him end up in charge of things," Nick said.

Lamont said, "What do you want to do?"

"What we were going to do before. Wigland may think this is all a waste of time, but we know better."

They walked through two huge O symbols and passed into the complex. To the right, a wide hallway curved away between rows of shops and restaurants. Civilian guards dressed in dark slacks and blue jackets with the name of their security service embroidered over the breast pocket stood about, looking bored. They appeared to be unarmed.

"I don't see any metal detectors," Selena said.

"Maybe they're out of sight," Lamont said.

"I don't think so. Anyone could walk in here with something nasty. Look around. People have handbags, camera bags, lots of places to conceal something. Nobody's checking them. "

"MI5 could have brought some in if they'd wanted to. I don't understand why they're not taking this seriously," Nick said.

Ronnie looked around. "This is a perfect setup for a terrorist attack."

The faces of the crowd were expectant, happy, in a mood for something exciting to happen. Nick hoped they didn't get more than they'd paid for.

"We have to assume Wigland is competent enough to lead a reasonable search," he said. "Even if he is, it doesn't mean he'll find anything."

Selena said, "If the attack is like the one in Novosibirsk, it will start with a diversion out in the city. Something to draw away the police and fire services. The Russians told Harker that a bomb went off before the riots started."

Nick said, "What are you thinking?"

"We need to know if something happens out there in the city. It would tell us that the device was about to be activated. Elizabeth can see London on the satellite. She can monitor it for us."

"Good point," Nick said. "I'll call her."

He took out his satellite phone and punched in Harker's number.

"Yes, Nick."

"Director, we're inside the arena. We've been shut out of the search. No one is giving us any help. I need to know if a diversion starts in the city, like the explosion in Novosibirsk. I thought you could keep track and tell us if something happens. We would have some warning that way."

"We have a satellite over the UK right now. I can watch London from here and if I see something, I'll call."

"Roger that." Nick ended the call.

They showed their tickets and walked into the arena.

The place was filling up. Seats rose in tiers on three sides around a central floor full of people milling about. The seating was arranged around the floor like a giant horseshoe. The ends of the horseshoe bordered two aisles angling down on either side of the stage. The stage itself was flat and wide, lit with a huge bank of overhead spotlights.

The edge of the stage was at eye level for the crowd standing on the main floor below. Instruments and microphone stands waited on stage. Someone was adjusting one of the microphones, making a sound check. Someone else was plugging in connections in a wall of amplifiers and speakers at the back.

The show was about to begin.

CHAPTER 30

Half an hour into the concert, the floor in front of the stage was filled with people jammed together, swaying in time to the music. The crowd was like an alien, giant organism with thousands of tentacles, people waving their arms back and forth in time with the music.

The band was all movement and high octane energy as the lead singer strode back and forth across the stage. Nick was in the fourth row at one end of the horseshoe of seats surrounding the arena floor. Higher up, Selena was slowly making her way along the aisles, eyeballing the crowd. Ronnie and Lamont were somewhere on the fringes of the swaying mob.

It seemed hopeless.

There were so many people. Everyone was focused on the spectacle taking place on stage. Lights, lasers, smoke and sound bombarded the crowd with an overwhelming spectacle that blotted out everything else.

"Nick, I can't see anything unusual up here." Selena's voice sounded in his earpiece.

"Me neither," Ronnie said. "All I can see are people bouncing around and waving their arms."

"Roger that." That was Lamont.

Nick said, "Ronnie, Lamont, get out of there. Work your way toward the stage and then up the aisle on the left. I'll meet you there. Selena, you too. This isn't working. Let's find Wigland."

The aisle on the left ran up from the arena floor past the stage, below the end of the horseshoe tier of seats were Nick stood. From the first two or three rows, the drop from the seating to the aisle wasn't far.

Nick started down toward the arena floor. Then something caught his eye, something that didn't fit. At first he couldn't put his finger on exactly what he had seen. *What was it?* He'd been looking at the aisle, the seats, estimating the distance to the floor. *What did I see?* He scanned the rows of concert goers. They were excited, smiling, rocking in rhythm to the music. There was movement everywhere.

Except for one man, sitting in the second row, three seats away from the railing at the end of the tier.

The man stared down at the stage. He looked worried. He wasn't tapping his feet. He wore a blue shirt and had a camera bag slung over his shoulder.

Who sits still at a rock concert?

"I've got him." Nick spoke into his microphone. "Second row up, three seats in. Over the left-hand aisle by the stage. Blue shirt, camera bag."

"I see him," Selena said.

"Roger," Ronnie said. "On my way."

Nick began to work his way toward the man with the bag. People complained as he brushed past their feet and bumped their legs.

"Oy," one man said in a loud voice. "Where d'ya think you're going?"

"Sorry." Nick pushed past him. Blue Shirt looked over and saw Nick coming. Nick was still a few seats away when Blue Shirt stood up, forced his way past a large man sitting next to him and climbed up on the railing over the aisle.

"Stop him," Nick yelled.

Blue Shirt went over the railing and dropped out of sight. Heads turned as Nick pushed past and leapt over the railing. He landed on his feet. The shock from the floor sent electric shocks up his spine. His back had bothered him ever since the jump injury he'd picked up in the Himalayas.

Blue Shirt should have turned to his left, toward the area backstage, or into the crowd in front. Instead he made for the stage itself. He knocked aside a security man and leapt up onto the stage. Nick scrambled up after him.

The band had just finished a number and the blond singer stood center stage, holding his guitar in one hand and a microphone in the other. He turned to look at the two men who had climbed onto his stage. On the floor, the crowd clapped and cheered at this new twist. The noise was deafening.

"Stop him!" Nick yelled.

Blondie's eyes widened. Blue Shirt ran straight toward him. Blondie dropped the microphone, grabbed the neck of his guitar with both hands and swung it like a baseball bat. The flat of the guitar caught Blue Shirt square in the chest. A discordant crash came through the amplifiers as the neck broke away from the body of the guitar and the strings came loose.

It was like being hit by a truck. Blue Shirt went down, hard. The audience screamed in excitement.

Nick reached the center of the stage. He looked down at the man lying dazed at his feet.

"Nice work," Nick said. He looked at the guitar. The body dangled from the broken neck, hanging by the strings. Nick gestured at it.

"Kind of messed up your guitar."

"Yeh, well." The singer didn't seem bothered by what had happened. He vibrated with nervous energy. The pupils of his eyes were black and wide. He looked at Nick. "I break these up as part of the show but I never thought I'd hit someone with one. I've got three more backstage. Who are you?"

"I can't tell you that. But you solved a big problem." He looked out at the audience. They were yelling and jumping up and down, waiting for whatever was going to happen next.

"Maybe you should take an intermission," Nick said.

"Nah." He gestured at the shouting audience. "They think it's part of the show. But can you get this bloke out of the way?"

"No problem," Nick said.

He grabbed Blue Shirt by his legs and dragged him away. The crowd cheered.

One of the singer's crew ran on stage with another guitar and handed it to him. Blondie turned to his audience. "All right!" he yelled. He launched into the next number.

Wigland was waiting for him in the wings. "I told you to stay out of this," he said. "What do you think you're doing? You're under arrest."

"On what charge?"

"You assaulted a British citizen."

"Actually, I didn't. It was the guy with the guitar who did that."

"Because you chased this poor man onto the stage."

The rest of the team joined them. Lamont was breathing hard. The man in the blue shirt lay on the floor, groaning. He coughed and blood trickled from his mouth. Out front, the concert was going full blast.

"Before you start feeling too sorry for him, you might want to check that bag he's carrying," Nick said. He hoped there was more inside it than a camera. He had acted on instinct and intuition. He was about to find out if he had been right.

One of Wigland's men opened the bag. "Sir, you'd better look at this." He eased a rectangular aluminum box from the camera bag onto the floor. A red LED blinked on the top of it.

"Doesn't look much like a camera," Ronnie said.

Wigland looked angry and surprised.

Nick's earpiece sounded. It was Harker. "Nick, there's been an explosion near Parliament. There can't be much time before they activate that weapon."

"Wigland," Nick said, "it's starting. Someone set off a bomb by your Parliament building. This thing is the next piece of it. You have to destroy it."

Wigland said, "It's evidence, and besides it could be a bomb. I'm calling in the explosives squad."

"It's not a bomb, it's a receiver and amplifier."

"You don't know that, Carter. Leave this to someone who knows what he's doing. I'm calling in the squad. "

"Damn it," Nick said. "I've had enough of your bullshit. There's no time for this."

Before Wigland could stop him, Nick turned and stomped on the box as hard as he could. The thin aluminum crumpled under the blow. The seams came apart. Sparks and a wisp of smoke shot out. The red LED stopped flashing.

Harker's voice sounded in his earpiece. "Nick, what's happening?"

"We found the device. It's been destroyed." He looked at Wigland. "I need you to call MI5 and clear us out of here," he said. "We've been getting flak from one of their people. His name is Wigland."

"I'll handle it," Harker said. "Good work. Come home." Nick heard her break the connection.

Nick turned to Wigland. "We're leaving now. We're going to our hotel and then we're going home tomorrow. I can't say it's been a pleasure working with you."

Wigland looked like he was ready to have a stroke. "You bloody Yank. You're not going anywhere..." His phone signaled a call. He picked it up and listened.

"Yes, sir," he said. His back straightened. He looked at Nick. "Yes, sir. Yes, sir, I understand."

Wigland put his phone away. He looked like he was choking. "I've been told to give you my full cooperation." His face was red. "I've also been told to offer you an apology."

Nick decided he didn't want to make it easy. He waited.

"I apologize for any problems I may have caused you," Wigland said. He sounded like he was strangling on something as he said it.

"Accepted," Nick said.

"One of my men will drive you back to your hotel."

"That would be appreciated."

As they headed back through the city, they could see a thick column of black smoke rising into the air where the bomb had exploded. A convoy of fire trucks and ambulances roared by. But there were no trucks full of soldiers, no police in riot gear.

"We were lucky," Selena said.

"Yeah." Nick looked out the window at the smoke. "Not so lucky for whoever was there when that bomb went off."

"Can you imagine what would have happened if that thing had gone off in there?" she said. "All those people."

"It didn't, that's what counts."

"They'll try again," Ronnie said.

Nick tugged on his ear. "That's a safe bet."

CHAPTER 31

The call from the White House caught Elizabeth by surprise.

"I've been summoned to the White House," she said to Stephanie. "Edmonds has something on his mind."

"What do you think he wants?"

"I have no idea, but I doubt that it's good news. The man has never liked me."

"I wonder if it has anything to do with Alaska?" Stephanie said.

"Only one way to find out."

An hour later Elizabeth was at the White House. A Secret Service agent escorted her to the Vice President's office. Edmonds was behind his desk, reading something. He didn't bother standing when she came into the room.

"Mister Vice President," she said.

"Take a seat, Director." Edmonds didn't look at her. He gestured at a chair in front of the desk.

She sat down and noticed that the chair seemed slightly lower than normal. It had the effect of putting anyone who sat in it lower than the desk. Already a small woman, Elizabeth was forced to look up toward Edmonds behind his desk.

So it's going to be like that, is it? Elizabeth thought. She controlled her anger. *What a cheap trick. That son of a bitch put this chair here on purpose.*

Edmonds continued reading for another minute. He set the document down and looked at her for the first time.

"I'll get right to the point, Harker. It's come to my attention that you have been interfering in a classified military operation code-named Ajax."

Elizabeth's expression revealed nothing. Without meaning to, Edmonds had told her something she hadn't known. Now that she had the name of the program, she'd be able to find out everything about it. She would get Stephanie on it as soon as she got back to Virginia.

"I'm not sure that I follow you, sir," Elizabeth said.

"Oh, I think you do. The President has seen fit to overlook your indiscretions in the past. This meeting is to clear up any misconceptions you may have about the way I view your unit and your methods of operation."

"I'm sure your observations will be helpful, sir."

"Are you trying to be funny, Director?"

"Of course not, sir." *Asshole.*

"Your meddling may have seriously compromised our security. I cannot allow you to continue. The undisciplined way in which you and your team approach issues affecting our nation's well being is unacceptable. As of this moment, you will immediately cease any activity associated with Ajax. I'm putting a hold on your unrestricted security clearance pending review."

"With all due respect, Mister Vice President, only President Rice has the authority to do that."

"Well, Harker, President Rice isn't here right now. You're on notice. Any more interference and there will be serious consequences."

Elizabeth wanted to throw something at him.

"That's all," Edmonds said. "You know the way out."

Sometimes when she felt stressed or angry, Elizabeth would remember something her father had said. A memory surfaced now.

Judge Harker had been sitting in his favorite green chair, a glass of aged Kentucky bourbon in his hand. A crackling fire balanced the cold of a Colorado winter outside the windows of his den. Elizabeth had been 20 years old, home on a winter break from college. They'd been talking about the cultural gender gap.

"There will always be men who don't respect women," her father had said. *"You can't change them, but you don't have to put up with it. Sometimes you can walk away. Sometimes you have to demand respect."*

Looking at this pompous man sitting across from her, Elizabeth knew she should keep quiet, but this was one of those times when her personal sense of integrity demanded more than walking away. She stood.

"Mister Vice President, you have no conception of what my unit does or how it acts to safeguard our nation's security. I find your implications insulting. I don't know who has been feeding you misinformation, but I'll find out. When I do, I will take whatever steps I feel are necessary to protect the national interest. In the meantime, I will continue to act with the authority of the President."

Edmonds pursed his lips and frowned. He looked as if he had eaten something unpleasant. Elizabeth looked down at the chair she'd been sitting in and back up at Edmonds.

"By the way," she said, "you might want to get a carpenter in here to fix this chair."

She turned her back on him and walked away.

CHAPTER 32

Stephanie's fingers sped over her keyboard, entering commands. She was hacking into the main server at the Pentagon. Elizabeth had come back from the White House, told her what Edmonds had said and set her on a search for anything about Ajax.

Stephanie entered a final command and the screen cleared. She was in, with full access to the Pentagon's servers.

The SATWEP substation in Alaska was a military asset. Stephanie decided to start there. Once she had isolated the proper location, the first thing she found was a damage report on the aftermath of the team's action. There was nothing in the report about any kind of unusual equipment or installation, much less a planned attack on Riyadh. The raid was being treated by the Pentagon as a domestic terrorist attack by an unknown group, possibly carried out by eco-terrorists.

Stephanie entered a new search using Ajax as a keyword, along with the facility location. A warning screen appeared with the seal of the Pentagon and a security level Steph had never encountered before. It requested a password.

Interesting, she thought. *What's this?* She activated a program she'd written to unravel encrypted and password-protected files. A progress bar appeared on the screen and began to fill with a solid blue stripe. She sat back in her chair and waited.

As she waited, Steph thought about Lucas. A few years ago, she never would have dreamed that she would be in a relationship with a rising star in the CIA. Langley and the Project had often been at odds in the past, although now that Clarence Hood was director things were good between the two organizations. Sometimes she felt uncomfortable with Lucas and she knew he felt the same. There were things they simply could not tell each other.

Elizabeth had been wonderful. She'd never given so much as a hint that she thought the cross agency relationship was inappropriate, or that Stephanie might somehow compromise a Project operation because she was so intimately linked to Langley. As for Lucas, he had appeared like a rescuing angel at the worst moment of her life. Since then, the two of them had been skirting the edges of deeper commitment. Now they were about to take the next step.

Stephanie smiled to herself. She reached up and absently touched a gold hoop earring dangling from her right ear.

The computer beeped and the screen cleared. Stephanie saw a neat row of icons that represented file folders. She opened one at random. It was an inventory of small arms pistol and rifle ammunition being stored by the Department of Homeland Security. *Why is this here?* she thought.

Steph looked at the total. DHS had stockpiled over 500 million rounds in .40 Smith and Wesson. It was the cartridge of choice for the pistols and MP5s favored by SWAT and military units. Another 900 million rifle and machine gun rounds were listed.

That's a lot of ammunition. Why does homeland security need so much ammo?

Steph opened another file. This one detailed supply logistics for the FEMA center near

Oklahoma City. *What's any of this doing in the Pentagon computers?* she thought. *FEMA is Homeland Security's turf.*

A third folder discussed the advantages and performance of specialist AFVs in an urban environment. AFV's were Armored Fighting Vehicles equipped with active protection systems and composite armor. They were designed to resist landmines, IEDs and attacks by rifle and machine gun fire. It took serious firepower to stop one. The Department of Homeland Security had contracted for a large number of new AFVs and had begun taking delivery the year before. Thousands of military versions had been brought back from Iraq and Afghanistan and classified as surplus. Those were in the process of being delivered to police departments all over the country. Why was this discussion here, in this encrypted file?

The fourth folder contained a memorandum. There was nothing to indicate who had composed it or how it had been distributed. It contained directives to be followed under something called the Ajax Protocol. The document was divided into sections. Stephanie started reading.

The Protocol began with a general discussion of legal issues surrounding enforcement of the plan presented in the memorandum. It noted that various Executive Orders already on the books permitted enforcement of the Protocol under direction of the White House.

Section 1 was an overview of the current media climate regarding terrorism. It discussed the American public's perception of how the government should respond in the event of a terrorist attack. It proposed several possible critical incident scenarios which would provide an excuse for implementation of the protocol. They all involved events taking place on a nationwide scale.

Section 2 presented a brief overview of detention facilities located throughout the country. These included existing federal and state prisons and the numerous FEMA centers that had been built since the disaster of Hurricane Katrina. All of those centers were currently empty. Steph remembered seeing pictures of them.

Most were located next to railroad tracks, many laid down to service a particular installation. The centers had state-of-the-art controlled entries manned by guard stations. Each center was surrounded by a high, chain-link fence topped with barbed wire. Steph had been struck by the fact that the wire on top was angled inward, as if to keep anyone inside the fence from climbing out. It had seemed to her that it should be the other way around, if you were going to have barbed wire at all.

Section 3 provided guidelines and listed available resources to help senior officers prepare their subordinates and troops for the psychological impact of armed resistance from their own countrymen. It acknowledged that deadly force would be required to suppress resistance and that there would be psychological consequences as a result of civilian casualties.

Resistance to what? Stephanie thought. *They're talking about Americans killing Americans. The way this is written, they might as well be talking about going to the dentist.*

Section 4 discussed disposal of civilian casualties. Preparations were extensive. There was an inventory of earth moving equipment and related items, including 150,000 stackable, individual burying units of plastic.

Burying units, Stephanie thought. *This is bureaucrat speak for coffins.* The coffins were stored at the empty FEMA centers.

Stephanie felt goose bumps. She shivered.

Section 5 discussed rules of engagement and the arrest and detention of Americans deemed undesirable or unfriendly to the government. Armed resistance was to be met with deadly force. Citizens would be given a grace period of one week to turn in all firearms. Anyone found with a gun after that time would be considered an enemy of the state and treated accordingly. The Violent Crime Act of 1991 was cited as the legal justification for seizing all privately owned firearms.

Section 6 proposed creating an intermediate judicial system modeled on the Universal Code of Military Justice, with absolute powers. It would supersede the existing civilian courts until something more permanent could be established. It would ultimately be administered jointly with the DOJ under authority of Executive Order 11310.

Section 7 pointed out the need to inventory and seize food supplies and any properties deemed useful. Food and fuel stockpiles would be established at central distribution points and then rationed out according to regulations yet to be established.

Section 8 listed key military installations and their roles in the plan. There were references to other documents that spelled out military involvement in detail.

Section 9 outlined a centralized system to identify and track all citizens, using existing technology and current databases. An RFID chip would be implanted in every man, woman and child under the guise of medical vaccinations against biological warfare.

The final paragraph acknowledged that it would be necessary to modify procedures as needed.

Stephanie sat in shock, trying to comprehend what she had read. She printed the memorandum and disconnected from the Pentagon. She sat in her chair and stared at the monitor screen. Phrases from the secret document stuck in her mind.

Psychological consequences.

Inventory and seize food supplies.

Disposal of civilian casualties.

Identify and track all citizens.

Enemy of the state.

150,000 coffins.

Stephanie rose from her chair and walked to Elizabeth's office. Elizabeth looked up at her as she came in the door.

"Stephanie, what's the matter? You look like someone just died."

"I know what Ajax is," she said.

Elizabeth waited.

"It's a secret plan to take over the government and establish a police state. It's filled with legal rationalizations to justify the take over."

"You can't be serious."

Stephanie handed the printed pages to Elizabeth and sat down. She waited while Harker read them.

Elizabeth looked up at her. Her voice was quiet. "Where did you find this?" she asked.

"On the Pentagon servers. It's buried behind heavy encryption. No one who didn't know about it could ever find it. I was looking for something about Ajax and got lucky."

"Someone told Edmonds we were interfering with a classified military operation," Harker said. She tapped the papers with her finger. "I'd say this qualifies"

"Remember what we were talking about right after Rice was shot? We were speculating that someone could be getting ready for a coup."

"I remember."

"I think it's started and this is the plan. A lot of thinking has gone into it and years of preparation. It has to be more than a cadre of senior officers behind this. They couldn't do it alone. The infrastructure like the FEMA camps couldn't have been put in place without support from senior government officials. They must be part of the plot as well."

"It would explain the assassination attempt on Rice," Harker said. "He would never be part of something like this."

"According to this memorandum, they want to impose martial law on the whole country. It would look like a legitimate response to a terrorist attack or a breakdown in civil order. Congress couldn't do anything about it once martial law was declared, not for a minimum of six months. The main authority is Executive Order 11615, signed by Nixon back in 1971."

"That order has never been rescinded?"

"No."

"Riots like the one in Russia would provide a perfect excuse," Harker said.

Stephanie nodded. "What happened in Novosibirsk could have been a test to see how well their weapon worked. They were going to do the same thing in Riyadh and London before we stopped them."

Elizabeth picked up her pen and began tapping it on the desk.

"I'm going to have to tell Vysotsky what we've learned," Elizabeth said. "Sooner or later he'll discover that the signal came from an American satellite. Maybe I can soften the bad news and convince him that we're dealing with it."

"What are you going to say? That someone in the Pentagon wanted to test an American weapon so they decided to use it on Russia? I don't think that's going to go over very well."

"I'll get him involved in the investigation, like we did before. That should buy us some time."

"He may think it's a trick," Stephanie said.

"He may. But I have some credibility with him. He's an intelligent man. It's to his advantage to let us do the heavy lifting, as long as he feels confident we're telling him the truth."

"And if he stops feeling confident?"

"I'll deal with that if I have to. Let me think about this."

Elizabeth set down her pen and looked across her desk at Stephanie. "What have we got ourselves into?"

"I don't know," Stephanie said, "but I know one thing."

"What's that?"

"We're running out of time to stop it."

CHAPTER 33

Alexei Vysotsky was in a foul mood. He was under heavy pressure from Red Square to find out what had happened in Novosibirsk. The Kremlin wanted a scapegoat. Alexei had no intention of playing that role.

His encrypted, private phone signaled a call. Vysotsky looked at the caller ID.

Harker. What now?

He pressed a button under his desk that blanketed the room with electronic interference. In Russia, some things never changed. Though his office was regularly swept for listening devices, Vysotsky assumed it was bugged by the FSB, Russia's internal security apparatus. Even someone in his high position of trust was not beyond suspicion. If FSB suspected he was collaborating with the Americans on his own initiative, his head would be on the block.

"Director Harker," Vysotsky said. "To what do I owe the pleasure of your call? Tell me that you have something interesting to share with me."

"Hello, Alexei. I can guarantee your interest but before I continue, I need your word that this conversation will remain between us for the present."

"I'm not sure I can do that, Director."

"Nonetheless, I must insist. I need to discuss a difficult subject that requires the greatest discretion. A mistake on your part or on mine could create serious problems between our countries. Even war."

Vysotsky's dark mood had vanished. All his senses were on alert. He respected Harker, even admired her. She would not make such a request without good reason. She had aroused his professional curiosity, knowing he would be unable to refuse.

Vysotsky was under no illusions about himself. No one achieved his position of power without sacrificing some of his humanity. He was a ruthless man, but he tried to balance that by being an honorable man, within his definition of honor. If he gave his word, he would keep it. It was clear Harker had learned that about him. His estimation of her went up another notch.

"Very well, Director. You have my word."

Elizabeth took a deep breath and plunged in. "I am certain that the events in Novosibirsk were a test run for the deployment of a new weapon."

"An American weapon?"

"Yes. Now you know why your discretion is required."

"We suspected this," Vysotsky said. He felt his blood pressure rising. A tight band seemed to be squeezing his head. With an effort, he controlled himself.

"You tell me it was an American weapon and ask me to keep quiet about it. That is too much, Director. Even from you."

"Hear me out, Alexei. It was not a sanctioned operation. I have discovered a conspiracy against our government. There is a plan to establish a police state here in America. Novosibirsk was a trial run in anticipation of using that weapon on our own people. You need to know about this. Our government is not behind the attack."

For the next 10 minutes, Elizabeth briefed Vysotsky on the raid in Alaska and on what had happened in London. She told him about the Ajax Protocol. When she was done, Vysotsky was silent.

Maybe I should go ahead and let that plot develop, he thought. Let the Americans destroy themselves.

"Still there, Alexei?"

"What are you going to do about it?" he said.

"Track down the conspirators and stop them," Elizabeth said. "I don't know who can be trusted. Someone got Vice President Edmonds to tell me to back off. I don't know if he's involved or not, but I've got no support from the White House until Rice recovers. Once I find out who talked to him, I'll have a better idea of who is behind it."

Vysotsky said, "Others are looking at what happened at Novosibirsk. They are certain to discover that your satellite sent that signal. Once that happens, there's nothing I can do unless I can show significant progress against the fascists who committed this crime."

"Understood. Alexei, I'm only asking for a little time. I understand that you need to protect yourself and that the interests of your country comes first. A militaristic take over in our country would be very bad news for everyone, especially Russia. It cannot be allowed to happen. We have a mutual interest in preventing it."

Vysotsky considered what she had just told him. She was right. Russia and the US did have an interest in common.

"Very well, Director. I'll keep this to myself as long as I can."

"I may need your assistance."

"What kind of assistance?"

"I was thinking of one of your special units," Elizabeth said. "It depends on what I find."

"Zaslon? You contemplate a joint operation?"

"I know it's unorthodox, but yes."

Vysotsky could hardly believe what he was hearing. Harker was director of one of America's most secretive intelligence agencies and she was asking him if he would be willing to deploy Russian special forces on American soil. He would mull over the implications later.

"If you have need of assistance..." Vysotsky said.

"Thank you. When this is over, perhaps you and I can meet again, like we did in Denmark."

"You are not worried that you will be considered a traitor?"

"No more than you."

Vysotsky laughed. "If I did not know better, Director, I would think you were proposing an assignation."

"Purely an exchange of views, Alexei. In the interests of international cooperation."

After he had hung up, Vysotsky thought about the conversation. Had she been flirting with him, at the end? In his mind's eye he conjured up a picture of Harker, her petite form and milk white skin.

She's a lovely woman, he thought. Attractive. I wonder what will happen if we meet again?

Vysotsky dismissed the thought and considered what he had learned. He didn't doubt that Harker's information was correct. She would never have called him if she was not certain of what she had learned. If the American plotters succeeded, it would almost certainly mean war. Harker wanted help. The act of sending a Zaslon unit into the United States could be construed as an act of war. If he did it without authorization from higher up, he would either end up against a wall or making ice cubes in Siberia.

Vysotsky lived for these moments when the great game took on urgency. Sometimes he missed the old days, when he'd been a field operative in the KGB. Now he had power, but with the power came the need to deal with the endless bureaucratic nonsense of the Kremlin bureaucracy. Elizabeth Harker was like a breath of fresh air.

Not for the first time, Vysotsky regretted that she was American.

CHAPTER 34

The next morning, Nick, Selena and Ronnie had landed in Washington and were on their way back to Project headquarters. Elizabeth, Lamont and Stephanie were in Harker's office. Elizabeth phone signaled a call. She looked at the display.

"It's Hood," she said. "Hello, Clarence..." she began, then stopped. "What? You're sure?"

The others watched her. "You're certain. All right. Yes. Thank you." She ended the call. She looked at the others, her face tight.

"Edmonds is sending a security team to shut down our operation. Hood thinks he intends to take us into custody with some excuse about national security."

"What?" Lamont said. "Are you kidding? He can't do that. Why would he do that? I thought only Rice could shut us down."

"Only Rice can," Harker said. "But it looks as though Edmonds thinks he has the authority. Until it gets sorted out he can create a lot of trouble for us."

"I guess you really pissed him off," Lamont said.

"It's more than that," Elizabeth said. "Something else is going on here."

"What do we do?" Stephanie asked.

Lamont was about to say something when the klaxon hammering of the security alarm drowned him out.

"What the hell..." he said.

Elizabeth flipped a switch on her desk. The monitor on her wall came alive. Three white Suburbans with Department of Homeland Security markings were coming down the drive toward the building.

"What are they doing here?" Lamont said.

"Edmonds must've sent them," Elizabeth said. "I don't think we'll wait and see what they want. It will take them time to get in here. Let's go."

They got up and headed for the spiral stairs leading down to the lower level. Stephanie grabbed her laptop from the desk. The cat was lying on the couch. Lamont scooped him up and held him against his body. Burps had been getting fat and lazy. He looked up at Lamont as if to ask what he was doing, but made no effort to escape.

Their footsteps rang on the metal steps as they hurried down the stairs.

Elizabeth had always been a believer in overkill when it came to security. She had installed an emergency escape tunnel from the computer room. It ran under the lawn and flower gardens and emerged a hundred yards away from the house in a tool shed. The entrance to the tunnel was out of sight behind one of the Crays, the only clue to its existence a thin outline in the wall. Stephanie pressed on a wall panel and the door slid open with a quiet, pneumatic hiss.

Lights came on in the tunnel. The door closed behind them. They walked quickly to the far end and climbed up into the tool shed. Lamont looked out through the screened window. From here they could see men in dark suits standing outside the building, arguing with one another.

There was a door in the back of the tool shed, out of sight from the house. Close by, a thick stand of oaks bordered the building. They slipped in single file from the back of the shed and into the woods. From there, a faint path ran through the western part of the property until it came up against the security fence. There was a gate here, electronically locked. Harker entered a code on a keypad mounted by the gate. It opened with a soft click.

Beyond the fence, camouflaged under the trees, was a single car garage. Another electronic keypad gave access to the interior. Inside was a dark blue Chevy SUV. It looked like any other SUV. There was nothing to make it stand out, but a close observer might have noticed that the glass seemed thicker than usual, the bumpers heavier.

"Slick," Lamont said. "I didn't know this was here. Will it start?"

"There's a solar feed to keep the battery charged," Elizabeth said. "It will start. The tires are a little low, but they'll do. You drive. I'll signal the others."

They climbed into the car and Lamont started the engine.

"Where to?"

"The Marine Corps Memorial," Elizabeth said. "Follow the track through the woods. In half a mile we'll come out on paved road."

Lamont put the car in gear and headed for the highway. Elizabeth looked at her watch. It was 9:30 in the morning. She took out her phone and punched in a series of letters and numbers.

Alpha Red. MCM. 10:00 AM. MAX.

She pressed send. "I gave them a half hour," she said.

"What do you think is happening?" Steph asked.

"What's the plan, Director?" Lamont reached the road. They bumped onto the pavement and headed for Washington.

"I don't know yet. We'll talk it over at the Memorial."

CHAPTER 35

Nick, Selena and Ronnie showed up about 10 minutes after Elizabeth and the others arrived at the monument. When they saw Lamont behind the wheel of the Chevy, they came over to the SUV and climbed in.

Nick looked wired. Selena and Ronnie didn't look happy. It was only the second time Elizabeth had used the emergency signal. She described the raid on Project headquarters. Stephanie briefed them about the Ajax protocol.

Through the windshield, Nick could see the Memorial and the flag that flew for all of the Marines who had died in the service of their country. The Ajax protocol was a betrayal of everything that flag stood for.

"Those sons of bitches," he said. "What are we going to do about it?"

"Before we can do anything, we need a new base of operations," Elizabeth said. "We have to assume all Project resources are either unavailable or monitored. The old safe house is compromised, we can't go there. I'm open to suggestions."

"I know where we can go," Selena said. "My place."

"Your condo? That won't work, they're bound to be watching it."

"Not the condo, not Washington. There's an island."

"What island?" Nick asked. "You never said anything about an island."

"Uncle William owned a private island in the Caribbean. It's not far from St. Lucia. He left it to me when he died. It's got everything we need, a large house, an airstrip, privacy. No one is going to look for us there."

Selena's uncle had been a rich man. It was his death that had brought Selena to the Project. When he died, some of his fortune had gone to charity. Some had been seized by foreign governments where he had held investments. Some of it had been embezzled. What was left went to Selena. She had arranged for half of it to act as ongoing investment funding for several charities. The other half was more than enough to keep her in luxury for the rest of her life.

"An island in the Caribbean." Elizabeth looked at her. "You never cease to surprise me, Selena. I don't think they'll expect us to do something like that."

"That's a great idea," Stephanie said. "At the least, it will give us some breathing room to figure out what to do next."

Lamont stroked Burps and was rewarded with a rumbling bass.

"How are we going to get there?" Ronnie asked. "We can't use our plane. They'll be watching that. We can't book a commercial flight."

Selena said, "They can't watch everything, not so soon. I know a pilot who operates a Gulfstream charter out of a private airport near Roanoke. My uncle used him all the time. He knows me, there won't be any credit checks or questions. He can fly us to the island. The airstrip there can handle a Gulfstream."

"I like it," Elizabeth said. "Call him."

They left Burps at a boarding house for cats. A few hours later, they were on their way to the Caribbean. Five hours after that, they were coming in for an approach on Selena's island. Below the wings of the Gulfstream, sunlight sparkled off the waters of the Caribbean. The ocean looked blue and inviting. A band of luminous, turquoise water stretched away from a narrow beach of white sand. Palm trees lined the shore, at the fringe of a dense thicket of jungle.

The southern end of the island featured a steep volcanic peak, covered with trees and thick green foliage. From the air, the island looked like a misshapen boot with the mountain forming the toe. Halfway up the east side of the boot, a small bay with a long wooden pier extended out into the water. A medium-sized fishing boat was docked next to the pier. At the top of the boot a large, square house with white walls and a red tile roof sat on a high promontory that looked out over the water. Beyond the house, the land fell away in a sheer cliff hundreds of feet high. Waves crashed against black rocks below. A second house, smaller than the first, sat away from the main building at the edge of the uncleared jungle.

A single runway of concrete formed the airstrip. A hangar was situated at one end of the runway. They circled the island once and landed. The Gulfstream taxied toward the hangar.

They stepped from the plane into the warm, humid air of the Windward Islands. The air smelled of salt and an explosion of green things growing.

"Welcome to St. Jeanne Island," Selena said.

Nick saw a white SUV coming toward them. "That will be Emile," Selena said. "He's been the caretaker here since before I was born. Let me take care of the plane and then we'll all go up to the house."

They walked over to the shade of the hanger. Selena had a brief conversation with the pilot and came over to join them. The pilot got back into the Gulfstream. In a moment the engines came alive and the plane turned to face the far end of the runway. They watched the Gulfstream accelerate down the strip and lift into the air.

Nick turned to Selena. "Just what I'd always dreamed of," he said. "Stranded on a tropical island with you. Only I didn't imagine we'd be here with anyone else."

She laughed. It broke the tension.

The SUV pulled up next to them. The man who got out of the vehicle was weathered with a lifetime under the Caribbean sun. It was impossible to tell how old he was. He looked like a man who had worked every day of his life. He wore a khaki colored, short sleeved shirt and trousers cut off below the knees. Well-worn brown boots protected his feet. His skin was walnut brown. He was about five feet nine inches tall, wiry and taut. The muscles on his arms and legs stood out like knotted cords under the skin.

His face broke into a grin. "Miss Selena," he said, "it has been too long since you have visited."

"Hello, Emile. It's good to see you."

"But now you are here. Things in the big house are ready for your stay. You will be here long?"

"I'm not sure. Emile, these are my friends. We all work together."

Selena made the introductions.

"Let's go up to the house," she said.

They piled into Emile's truck and followed a gravel drive from the airstrip to the top of the promontory and the house. The house was built of whitewashed stone, two stories high. A wide, shaded veranda with a sloping, tiled roof ran around the bottom of the structure. Wicker furniture with flowered cushions offered places to sit. Tall windows with wooden storm shutters painted green lined the front of the building. The view from the veranda took in the entire island and the Caribbean beyond.

Inside, the house was cool and quiet. Wooden ceiling fans turned slowly overhead. A gentle breeze coming through the open windows brought the sweet perfume of tropical flowers and honeysuckle. The floors were made of dark, polished wood, cut in wide boards. A wide, wooden staircase led up to a balcony and the second floor.

"There are six rooms on the second floor," Selena said. "Mine is the one in the front on the left. Take any of the others you like."

"Get settled in and we'll meet down here in 30 minutes," Elizabeth said. "We need to do some serious planning."

"Director," Selena said, "I need to talk with you about something."

Elizabeth was about to ask if it could wait until later. Then she saw the stress in Selena's face.

"What is it, Selena?"

"Let's sit outside."

They moved onto the porch and sat down.

"Adam gave Nick a file," Selena said. "You need to know what was in it. I was going to tell you when we got back from London but there hasn't been a good opportunity until now. "

Elizabeth gave her a curious look. "What file?"

Selena told Elizabeth about the CIA file and the accusations against her father. When she was done, Elizabeth sat without saying anything for what seemed like a long time.

"Why didn't you tell me before?" she said.

Selena took a deep breath. "I was afraid you'd throw me off the team. If my father was a traitor, you might think I was a security risk."

"Selena, you're not your father."

"That's what Nick said."

"You don't think the file is true." It was a statement, not a question.

"No, I don't. My father was an honorable man. He would never have betrayed his country. I think it was a CIA op that went wrong and somebody covered it up."

"You should've come to me sooner," Elizabeth said.

"I know. I'm sorry." Selena's eyes glistened. Elizabeth reached out and took her hand.

"There's nothing to be sorry about. It can't have been easy for you to find that out. How can I help?"

"Knowing that the people who killed my family may still be out there keeps me awake at night. I want to get into the KGB files and track down who it was. Stephanie can do that, but I need your permission."

"A lot of those files are available for anyone to study," Elizabeth said. "The really sensitive stuff has all been transferred to computers. If we hack into those, we're risking a major incident."

"I know that." Selena waited.

"What will you do if you find out the assassin is still alive?"

"I don't know. I just know that it's important to find out what happened."

Elizabeth looked out over the Caribbean. In the distance, the white sail of a private yacht cut across the deep blue of the sea.

"Let me think about it," Elizabeth said.

CHAPTER 36

The next day General Westlake and Senator Martinez were having drinks in the Senator's club in Washington. The club was designed for private conversations, with discrete groupings of high-back chairs and low tables. The politicians, lobbyists and money men all needed a place that was private and convenient to the Capitol building. If you had the money, the power and the connections, you might be invited to join.

"What the hell happened?" Martinez said. "How did they get away?"

"Someone tipped them off," Westlake said. "The place was locked down and no one was there. They chartered a plane to a private island in the Caribbean," Westlake picked up a glass of single malt and took a long drink. "I had the pilot taken into custody."

"Those people are a real pain in the ass. They know too much."

"I've arranged for a team to eliminate them. They'll go in tomorrow night."

"Good."

Westlake said, "Edmonds is an idiot."

"It wasn't Edmonds' fault," Martinez said. "He's been a good boy. He's doing exactly what we want him to do."

"And he'd better continue to do it, if he knows what's good for him."

"He wants to be President."

"He can be President," Westlake said. "We need a figurehead."

"There's still Rice," Martinez said. "Still alive."

"That is one tough son of a bitch," Westlake said. "He'll have an unfortunate relapse when it's time to make Edmonds official. Which will be soon."

Martinez said, "What is your assessment of cooperation from local commanders once we begin?"

Westlake toyed with his drink. "I've thought about that a lot. In the beginning it won't be a problem. They'll be responding to tactical situations on the ground, not thinking about national implications. That's not their job. They're trained to follow orders, and they will. Morgan is with us."

General Jeffrey Morgan commanded NORTHCOM, the Northern Army Command. All Army troops in North America were under his jurisdiction. They would be deployed as he saw fit.

"What about after, when the initial rioting has died down?"

"The key to winning the junior officers over is to convince them that they're dealing with an ongoing violent revolution, an attempt to overthrow the government."

"There could be some that see through what is happening."

"If any of them make trouble they'll be relieved of command," Westlake said. "They've all sworn an oath to protect the Constitution and the President, and they'll be acting under Presidential orders. Refusal to follow orders is a court-martial offense."

Westlake emptied his glass and signaled for another round. "I don't think it's going to be much of a problem," he said. "In fact, the civilians will probably solve it for us."

"What do you mean?"

"The diehards aren't going to turn in their guns no matter what we say," Westlake said. "Enough of them will think they can take on the Army with their hunting rifles to give us plenty of incidents we can use to prove someone is inciting revolution."

The drinks came. Westlake picked up his glass.

"The joint exercise with Homeland Security is set. We'll begin the operation in a week."

CHAPTER 37

The team gathered on the shaded veranda of the island house. Selena had put together plates of fruit, cheese and crackers. There was a large pitcher of iced tea. A tropical breeze made it feel as if they had escaped to a vacation paradise, but no one was under the illusion this was a vacation.

"Whoever is behind this has some serious clout," Elizabeth said. "Someone convinced Edmonds we were a threat."

"Edmonds must be in on it," Nick said. "Part of the plot."

"It looks that way. He may be a dupe. It doesn't really matter at this point. The question is, what do we do now?"

"Our tactical situation isn't good," Nick said. "Homeland Security has probably put our names and pictures on every computer that matters. We're isolated."

"Sooner or later, whoever is calling the shots is going to find out where we are," Harker said.

"How are we fixed for weapons?" Lamont asked. "I've got my Sig and two magazines."

Stephanie looked embarrassed. "I know we're supposed to carry them all the time," she said, "but mine is back on my desk in Virginia."

"Don't feel bad, Steph," Harker said. "So is mine."

"Selena, Ronnie and I have our pistols," Nick said.

"I know Emile has a 12 gauge shotgun and a .22 rifle," Selena said. "It's not a lot of firepower, but it's something."

"Oh that's great," Lamont said. "We can do a lot of damage with those."

"Just trying to help," Selena said. She looked annoyed.

"Let's focus," Harker said.

"I grew up on a farm in Kansas," Stephanie said. "I'm good with a .22, we had to keep the gophers down."

"Okay," Nick said. "You take the .22. Director, you get the shotgun."

"Emile will know what kind of supplies are on the island," Selena said. "There may be something we can use. I'll talk with him after we're done here."

"Stephanie, can you link into our computers in Virginia?" Elizabeth asked.

"We have the satellite uplink and I have my laptop. Unless they shut everything down, I can access them. The sat link is encrypted, they won't be able to trace it."

"I want you to look for whoever is behind this. I don't know what the timetable is, but it feels like it's set to happen soon."

"I might be able to trace the signal that went to Alaska back to its original source," Stephanie said, "the one that was supposed to trigger the attack on Riyadh. If I can do that, we'll know where their home base is located."

Nick said, "Director, even if we do find out where they are, we still have to get off this island and back into the country without getting arrested."

"The pilot will come pick us up," Selena said.

"That's fine if he can do it," Nick said. "What if he can't? We need an alternate plan."

"We could get to one of the bigger islands like Barbados and rent a plane," Selena said.

"That might not be a good idea. We need to assume Interpol is looking for us along with everyone else."

"I saw a boat docked in the bay when we were flying in," Lamont said. "It looked big enough to get us to the mainland. There are plenty of places along the coast where we could put in without being noticed."

"If we can get past the Coast Guard," Ronnie said.

"We'll worry about that if we need to," Elizabeth said. "We're not going anywhere until we find out more about what's happening."

"We should clue Emile in," Lamont said. "If things get dicey, he could get caught in the crossfire."

"I can do that," Selena said. "Don't underestimate Emile. He's one of the most resourceful men I've ever met."

"All right," Harker said. "Selena, you brief Emile. Find out if there's anything we can use for weapons."

"You mean things that go boom?" Lamont asked.

Elizabeth smiled. "That, and anything else that might help. Nick and Ronnie, once we have an inventory see what you can put together. Lamont, you go take a look at that boat and see if it will serve."

Lamont coughed. "Roger that," he said.

"Any questions?" Elizabeth asked.

"Yeah," Ronnie said. "What's for dinner?"

CHAPTER 38

Nick and Selena lay in a tangle of sheets looking out through the tall windows of Selena's bedroom, open to the warm, tropical night. The room was in the front of the house. Nick could see the dark shape of the extinct volcano rising at the other end of the island. Sheer white curtains around the windows fluttered in a light breeze. The moon was up, shedding a pale silver glow over the dark jungle interior of the island. Two tall palm trees formed silhouettes against the starlit sky outside the window. The room was warm after the heat of the day. It smelled of sex and sweat and Selena's perfume.

Selena nestled against him. She ran her fingers over the ridges of scar tissue on his body, where shrapnel from the grenade had torn into his side.

"It looks like a romantic postcard," Nick said.

"What does?"

He gestured at the open window. "That. The moon, the palm trees. All that's missing is violins playing somewhere in the background."

She laughed. "Postcards don't play music."

"Some do. You know, Happy Birthday, John Philip Sousa, things like that."

"I don't think Sousa is quite the right mood," she said.

She moved her hand across his chest, feeling the solid muscle underneath, the puckered scar on his shoulder. "I wish this could last forever," she said.

He almost said *nothing ever does* but caught himself in time.

He buried his face in her hair. "Mmm," he said. "You smell good."

"Passion flower shampoo," she said. "It's supposed to drive men wild."

"I am man, I am wild," he said. "You have driven me there. Now I must ravish you."

She laughed. "You sound like a bad line in a pirate movie."

"Isn't that what wild men do?"

"What?"

"Ravish. You know." He leered at her and pretended to stroke a mustache.

"I think you must read romance novels when nobody's looking," she said. "Nobody says ravish anymore."

"When I was a kid, I heard an actor say ravish in a movie. I thought he said radish. I couldn't figure out what he meant."

She began laughing. He grinned at her, pleased.

After she'd stopped laughing she was quiet, suddenly serious.

"Don't you get tired of this?" she said. "Doing what we do?"

"I don't know if tired is the right word. Look at what we deal with. People who don't care about anything except power and control, who'll do anything to get what they want. I don't get tired of trying to stop people like that."

"It seems like there are always people like that," she said.

She got up out of bed and walked naked to the window. Nick looked at the way the moonlight fell over her body, the way it made shadows under her breasts, the curve of her buttocks. He could make out the thin scar near her spine where the doctors had operated after she'd been shot in Mexico. There was something otherworldly about the way she looked in the moonlight, like a visitor from some magical realm. He felt his heart skip a beat.

She's so beautiful.

He wished he could keep this moment from changing, this timeless, moonlit vision. It came to him that he could no longer imagine life without her, not a life he wanted. With the thought came a touch of fear that he could lose her.

He couldn't let that happen.

Nick got up and walked over to where she stood looking out at the Caribbean. A night bird cried somewhere in the darkness. He stood behind her and wrapped his arms around her. His heart was pounding.

"Selena," he said.

She heard something in his voice. She turned to look at him.

"Selena," he said again. "I love you."

She looked up into his eyes. "I love you, too."

"Marry me. Will you marry me?"

Oh my God. He's asking me to marry him. What about children? He could get killed. A cascade of thoughts flooded her mind. She let out a deep sigh.

"Nick..."

He waited.

"Yes," she said. "Yes, I will."

He kissed her. "Come back to bed."

There was something different about the way they made love, something more intimate, more familiar.

Later, Nick fell asleep. Selena lay awake for a long time.

CHAPTER 39

It was the afternoon after they'd arrived on the island. The team met again on the veranda. Clusters of purple bougainvillea and white honeysuckle vines climbed the columns in the front of the house. Sunlight slanting through the leaves of the trees cast shadows of light and dark across the lawn in front of the house.

Selena and Nick hadn't told anyone what had happened between them. It didn't seem like the right time.

Lamont set four No. 10 cans on the table. They'd once held tomatoes. Now each one had a six inch length of cord emerging from a gray, putty-like substance that filled the cans to the top.

"This is what I came up with," he said. "I mixed fertilizer and diesel and packed it tight, with some tacks and nails thrown in. I took the powder from a few rounds and mixed it with a little kerosene to soak the fuses. I gotta warn you though, it burns quick. If you actually have to use these things, you'd better get rid of them fast."

"Will they work?" Selena asked.

"Oh, yeah, they'll work. They're nasty. You don't want to get in the way when one goes off."

"Let's hope we don't have to use them," Elizabeth said. She turned to Stephanie. "Any luck, Steph?"

"I was able to link into our computers and activate the cameras inside the house. They made a real mess of things, but they didn't get into the computers and our files. They trashed everything in the offices but they didn't find the escape hatch or get into the Armory. It's probably the best result we could have hoped for. There's nobody there now."

"What about tracking down their base?"

"I'm working on it," Stephanie said.

"All right. Selena, I want you to call the pilot and put him on standby. We'll want to get out of here as soon as we're ready."

"That's a problem," Selena said. "I tried reaching him earlier. No luck, not even an answering machine."

Nick's ear tingled. "If they grabbed him, they know where we are. If I were them, I'd send a team after us. These guys are playing for keeps."

"I checked out the boat down in the bay," Lamont said. Nick could hear the former Navy seal talking as he spoke, a man who loved the sea. "It's a 48 foot Krogen whaleback. Long range, and the tanks are more than 3/4 full. Nice boat. It's solid and the engine is in good shape. We could reach the mainland in 10 or 11 days."

"That's a long time but it's good news," Elizabeth said.

"Do you think we should leave?" Selena asked.

Harker shook her head. "Not yet. Not until we know more."

"It's better to stay here," Ronnie said. "Make them come to us. That way we have home field advantage."

"With a few pistols and some clunky, homemade bombs?" Nick shook his head. "I love your optimism."

"Hey," Lamont said, "what do you mean, clunky?"

"Don't forget the shotgun," Selena said.

They all laughed. Then Nick got serious.

"I don't think they'll wait very long to make their move. I wouldn't."

Ronnie and Lamont both nodded.

"How do you see it going down, Nick?" Ronnie asked.

"I'd come in at night. I'd time it for when the moon is down."

"When is that?" Stephanie asked.

"Around two in the morning."

"Do you think they'll use choppers?" Lamont said.

"I don't think so. Too noisy. It would alert us and it would raise questions. They'd have to come from one of the nearby islands and too many people would see them and wonder what was happening. They'll come in by sea, probably zodiacs from a boat somewhere offshore."

"Where do you think they'll land?"

"Selena, you know the island. If you were going to try and sneak in here on rafts, where would you put in?"

"There aren't many places where you can get in with a boat," she said. "There are coral reefs around the island that would tear the bottom out of a raft. Even if they got to shore, the growth is so thick that they wouldn't find it easy to make their way through. They'd probably come into the bay, where the boat is. There is only one other place that would work. It's down there, on the west side of the island."

She pointed past Emile's house.

"That looks like jungle," Lamont said.

"It is, but there's a path down to the water from the back of Emile's place. He keeps a small boat there that he takes out sometimes when he wants to catch dinner. There's a narrow gap in the reef."

"How thick is that jungle, anyway?" Nick said.

"Thick. It's not much fun. Lots of insects, mosquitoes, big spiders. The ground is rough underfoot. You have to hack your way through with a machete and there's nowhere to go except to the mountain. That's so steep there's not much point to it, unless you're a glutton for punishment."

"Okay, at least our southern flank is secure. And no one is coming up that cliff behind the house. So all we have to worry about is the two sides of the island."

"I could rig up a booby trap," Lamont said. "I could use a couple of these tomato cans."

"You could hook them up to a car battery," Ronnie said. "We did that once in Afghanistan. Surprised the hell out of a bunch of Taliban. Remember, Nick?"

"Right. We turned the tables on them with our own IED."

"We can set them up on the path in from the bay," Lamont said.

"We should use Emile's house as our command post," Nick said. "We'll leave a couple of lights on in the main house because that's where they'll expect us to be, but we can't stay here. There's no place to go. We'd be trapped. I'd rather be able to fade into the trees if we have to. Besides, the caretaker's house is right on the route from the other side of the island. It gives us good positioning."

"Makes sense," Ronnie said.

For the next half hour they worked out details.

"I'd better get working on that IED," Lamont said. He wiped sweat away from his forehead.

"I'll fill Emile in," Selena said.

"Then I guess we're ready," Nick said.

CHAPTER 40

The assassins came in two silent, black zodiacs, a little after three in the morning. Lamont and Ronnie lay concealed in a grove of trees near the shore. Ronnie watched through an old pair of binoculars he'd found in the main house. The moon was down, but there was enough light from the stars to cast a faint sheen on the water and to show the black shapes of the rafts and the men getting out of them.

"I make it twelve men," Ronnie said. "Machine pistols, no heavy weapons. Night gear, all black. Maybe pros."

His voice was quiet, little more than a whisper. Even if someone had been nearby, the soft sound of his words would have disappeared in the sound of the surf against the shore.

Next to Lamont was a car battery he'd taken from Emile's truck. A wire ran from the hot terminal down toward the shore and the path leading up from the bay. He held another wire in his right hand, the end stripped down to the copper. Two of the homemade bombs were hidden on either side of the path.

"Wait..." Ronnie said. "Wait." He kept the binoculars trained on the men coming up the path. He let the first two men go by the trap.

"Now," he said.

Lamont touched the bare end of the wire to the battery terminal. The two bombs detonated in a double thunderclap that sent startled birds screeching into the air. For an instant the night was lit with a bright, orange light. Then the light was gone. Someone began screaming.

The two men who had gotten past the IED were caught in the instant of paralyzing shock that comes before survival kicks in and turns to desperate action. It was only an instant, but it was long enough. Ronnie and Lamont stood and fired together and took them down. The rattle of automatic fire came toward them from down the trail but it was wide and high. They retreated back up the path toward Emile's house.

In the house, Stephanie, Elizabeth and Selena waited with Emile. Nick was away from the house on the path leading to the other side of the island, watching the other way in. Emile was sharpening a machete. They heard the explosion. Emile looked up from the blade.

"They are here," he said. They all went outside.

Elizabeth held a 12 gauge double-barreled shotgun with outside hammers. The finish was worn. The gun qualified as a collector's item but it was clean and tight and well oiled. Stephanie cradled an old, bolt action Western Auto .22 with a long tubular magazine under the barrel. It was a lot like the Mossberg she'd had in Kansas, if not as elegant.

A minute later Nick appeared. "Nothing on that side," he said. "Selena, let's go."

Stephanie and Elizabeth were relegated to a backup role. If someone got through Nick and the others, the plan was for Emile to take them to a hiding place in the jungle.

Selena and Nick moved down the path toward the bay. They heard someone coming. Nick held up his fist and signaled. They stepped off the path into the undergrowth. Selena held her pistol in both hands, the hammer back, her finger laid alongside the trigger. Her heart was beating hard against her ribs. Her palms were slippery with sweat. An insect buzzed close to her ear, sending a surge of adrenaline sweeping through her body. She took deep breaths, calmed the rush.

Nick whistled, a warbling bird call that Ronnie had taught him. An answering call came from down the trail. Ronnie and Lamont emerged from the gloom.

Nick kept his voice low. "How many?"

"A dozen," Ronnie said. "Not so many now, maybe five or six left. Automatic weapons. They're wearing body armor. Go for the head shots."

They have to come up the path," Lamont said. He gestured at the jungle on the sides of the trail. "No one's getting through that. They'll regroup and come after us."

Nick nodded. "You and Ronnie set up on the side of the path, a little farther down. Let the first few go by. Selena and I will stay here. When you hear us firing, take out the rest and come back."

Lamont's breathing was harsh. His face was pale and beads of sweat dotted his forehead.

"You okay, Shadow?" Nick said. It hadn't been that long since Lamont had taken a bullet through his right lung.

"Yeah. Nothing to worry about. Let's go, Ronnie."

Selena watched them trot down the trail. "He doesn't look good," she said.

"He'll deal with it. Let's get into the trees."

They settled in, a few feet apart. In the dark, with the heavy foliage all around them, it was as if Nick had disappeared. Selena couldn't see him. A dangling vine caught her hair. She reached up and pulled it away. Mosquitoes found her. She tried to brush them away without making noise. Then she saw the first man coming up the trail.

He moved with the caution of someone who had walked enemy trails before. He wore a dark colored beret. His face was smeared with green and black grease paint. *Mercenaries,* she thought. *Pros.* He held a lethal-looking submachine gun high and close to his body. His head never stopped moving, his eyes trying to see into the impenetrable jungle. She almost felt sorry for him. She reminded herself that he was here to kill her. Not far behind him, another man appeared and then another. The first man was almost past her hiding place. She took aim at the man behind him.

They were outgunned, pistols against automatic weapons. They'd only get one chance.

Somehow the point man sensed her presence. He started to turn toward her, the barrel of his weapon swinging around. The roar of Nick's pistol shattered the night silence. The man went over backward.

Selena fired, twice. Her target flailed his arms in the air and fell back off the path. She heard Nick's pistol again and then Lamont and Ronnie firing, the sound of the shots flat and deadened by the thick jungle growth. She swung toward the man who was next in line and fired at him. He went down. There was a chattering burst of automatic fire down the trail and a pistol shot. Then the night was still again.

Selena was holding her breath. She let it out, releasing the tension. On the trail, nothing moved.

"You okay?" Nick asked.

"Yes. You?"

They stepped out onto the trail. "Just mosquito bites." He walked over to the bodies, reached down and picked up two of the machine guns. He handed one to Selena.

"Czech Skorpions," he said. "They're like a .32 caliber buzz saw on full auto, rip you to pieces. A lot of mercs use them."

Selena examined the weapon. A selector switch on the left-hand side of the receiver let the shooter choose between safe, single shot or full auto. A curved magazine jutted from the front, behind a stubby barrel. The stock was a curved piece of metal that folded up over the receiver. She pulled the bolt partway open, saw the glint of a cartridge and let it slide shut. She flipped on the safety. Cocked and loaded. She hefted the gun.

"Doesn't weigh much."

"Under three pounds. It puts out about 850 rounds a minute. See if you can find some spare mags."

There were four bodies. They found a dozen loaded magazines. Nick picked up the other two guns and slung them over his shoulder. A whistle came from down trail. Nick answered. Ronnie and Lamont appeared. Lamont was limping. They each carried one of the Czech guns.

"Are you hit?" Nick asked.

"Nah. I tripped over a root and twisted my ankle."

"Any of them left?"

"No," Ronnie said. "I checked. We got all of them."

"Let's go find Harker and the others," Nick said. The adrenaline charge was fading. He felt dull, used up. His legs felt like lead. A dull ache started in the back of his head.

CHAPTER 41

Elizabeth and Stephanie moved off the porch of Emile's house into the shadows of the trees. Emile waited with them, his razor-sharp machete hanging down by his side. They listened to the sounds of the firefight down the trail. The shooting stopped and everything became quiet. The normal sounds of the jungle at night began to return, a mix of things rustling in the undergrowth, the flutter of moths and whine of insects, the occasional cry of a bird.

"I don't hear them," Stephanie said.

"That doesn't mean anything," Elizabeth said. "They're not going to come up the trail whistling Dixie."

"I hate this," Stephanie said. "This is what they do all the time, isn't it?"

"Pretty much. I don't know how Selena does it. I know I couldn't."

"I heard something," Stephanie said. "It came from that way."

She pointed at the path that led down to Emile's small boat on the west side of the island.

"Nick cleared that," Elizabeth said. "There's nobody in that direction."

Even so, Elizabeth pulled back the hammers on her shotgun. The double-click of the hammers sounded loud in the humid night.

"Careful," Emile said. "The triggers are very sensitive."

"Oh, hell," Stephanie said under her breath.

Five men dressed in black and wearing berets and body armor emerged into the clearing in front of the house. They fanned out. Two came toward the porch.

Elizabeth put her mouth next to Stephanie's ear. "The others don't know they're here." Her voice was hardly a whisper. "They'll come up here and walk into an ambush."

Stephanie looked around. "Where's Emile?" She said.

The old man was gone, vanished somewhere in the growth.

"We have to try and stop them," Elizabeth said.

"How?"

"Wait till you can't miss. I'll shoot at the ones closest to the house. Make it count."

Stephanie lifted the rifle to her shoulder and took aim. The movement caught the eye of one of the men. He shouted. His gun came up.

Elizabeth fired. The 12 gauge kicked back hard into her shoulder. A swarm of buckshot caught the first man in the chest and throat and lifted him off his feet. The tiny report of Stephanie's .22 registered somewhere in the back of Elizabeth's mind. A second man went down. Elizabeth fired the other barrel at the third man. His head vanished in a reddish cloud of blood and bone. The body stumbled and fell. Elizabeth had the shotgun open and was fumbling with shells, trying to reload.

The fourth man swung his weapon toward her. She froze, the shells motionless in her hand. Her mind stopped.

Emile appeared behind him. His machete swept across in a gleaming arc that took the man's head from his shoulders. Blood fountained high into the air. The last mercenary fired. Emile jerked and stumbled backwards and fell to the ground. As the old man's killer turned toward Elizabeth and

Stephanie, a volley of shots from the trail sent him reeling sideways. He collapsed into the undergrowth.

Nick and the others ran into the clearing.

"Jesus," Ronnie said, staring at the slaughter. Two of the bodies were headless. The ground in front of the house was wet with blood.

"Selena, you stay here," Nick said. "We need to clear that trail."

The three men disappeared down the path.

Stephanie stood holding the 22, grim faced. Elizabeth looked at the headless corpse of the man she had killed. The shotgun was still broken open in her left hand. She bent over and vomited .

Selena went over to Emile. His eyes were wide open, the front of his chest covered with blood. She knelt by him. He'd been her friend. She had always felt safe with him and now, because of her, he was dead. She had brought death with her to the island. Her eyes filled with tears. She brushed them away.

She was 14 years old, away from the island in Emile's small boat, the first time she'd gone out fishing with him. The sun was half risen, the first light of day gleaming in a golden white path along the blue Caribbean waters. Emile was showing her how to bait her hook.

"Like this, you see? The hook is very sharp. Be careful with your fingers."

"Will we see a shark?" she asked.

Emile nodded in a serious way. "It is possible. If we see a shark, we will stay inside the boat and we will be fine."

"I would like to see a shark," Selena said.

They had stayed out all morning and come back with several fish for dinner. They had not seen any sharks.

"Emile," she whispered, "I'm sorry."

She reached out and closed his eyes. She got up and went to Elizabeth and took the shotgun from her hands. "Are you all right, Director?"

Elizabeth throat was dry. She wiped her lips and swallowed. "Yes. I'm fine."

"They must've landed after Nick checked out that side."

Elizabeth's milk white skin was even whiter than usual.

"You'd better sit down," Selena said. "You look pale."

"I'm all right," Elizabeth said.

"You're sure?"

"It was his head," she said. "I wasn't ready for what it looked like when I pulled the trigger and his head disappeared. I'll never forget that."

CHAPTER 42

They buried Emile near the house where he'd spent most of his life and marked the spot with a wooden board. Selena stood at the foot of the new grave.

She looked down at the fresh earth and sighed. "I don't know what to say. He was a good man."

Nick put his hand on her shoulder. "That's as much as any man can hope for," he said. "You don't need to say anything else."

The bodies of the men they'd killed presented more of a problem. Selena showed them a deep cleft that ran like a scar across the land, a few hundred yards from shore. Nick heard a faint sound of water lapping somewhere below.

"There are old lava tubes filled with water under the island," Selena said. "This opens onto them. We can dump the bodies in here and they'll feed the sharks."

Ronnie and Lamont looked at each other. Selena's voice was cold.

They dropped the bodies into the cleft and went back to the house. The team met around the dining table.

"I've found out where those signals came from," Stephanie said. "I traced them to the Denver International Airport."

"You're joking," Nick said. "DIA? How could they be based at the airport?"

"I know a lot about DIA. It's at the heart of one of the major conspiracy theories floating around the internet. Most of them are really off the wall but I like to keep track, just in case one of them turns out to be more than a theory. I think that's what's happened here. Do you know anything about how DIA was built?"

"Why don't you enlighten me?"

"The project went way over budget, I mean *way* over, hundreds of millions, maybe a billion."

"That's a lot of over," Ronnie said.

"Where did the money go?" Selena asked.

"Part of it was ripped off, like it always is in big construction projects like that. But a big chunk went into constructing buildings that were buried under tons of earth."

"Why would they build them and then bury them?"

"The reason given at the time was that they were in the wrong location," Stephanie said. "Everyone made noises about waste, a few wrists got slapped and that was the end of it. Construction went on. What's even more interesting is that the story about the buried buildings changed."

"Changed to what?"

"Instead of buildings, the structures that had been buried never existed at all. Then the story was put out that the pictures of excavations and construction were really pictures of the underground tunnel system."

"Is there a tunnel system?" Ronnie asked.

"Yes, for the rail line that goes between concourses. There's also an abandoned baggage system that didn't work. It was supposed to be state-of-the-art but it never worked right. When they fired it up, it destroyed bags and threw them into the air. They finally gave up on it and sealed it off. It takes up a lot of space under the airport."

"Well, it was a government project," Lamont said. "Sounds like another bureaucratic screw up."

"That's just it," Stephanie said. "It wasn't a government project. The airport was privately funded. It was built by something called the New World Airport Commission."

For a moment, nobody said anything.

"Not another conspiracy," Ronnie said.

"Like I said, DIA is at the heart of a lot of conspiracy theories," Stephanie said. "There are some crazy ideas out there. But the buried buildings exist."

"You're sure the signals came from there," Nick said.

"Certain, yes. The buildings make a perfect underground bunker."

Elizabeth drummed her fingers on the table top. "It's time for us to get off this island," she said. "If they sent that signal to Alaska from DIA, that's where the control center for the weapon must be. We have to destroy it, and we have to do it without causing a lot of collateral damage."

"Let me make sure I understand you," Nick said. "You want us to find a way into secret bunkers under one of the busiest airports in the world. That's if we can get past whatever they've got for security without killing a lot of civilians. Then you want us to locate a hidden control center and blow it up. That about right?"

"Do you have a problem with that?"

Nick sighed and pulled on his ear. "We'll need equipment. Communications. Weapons, IDs, all that. DIA has a lot of security surveillance. We're going to need gear to jam it or take it out of commission."

"Langley could help," Stephanie said. "Hood isn't part of this."

"Two years ago I never would've thought of asking the CIA for anything," Elizabeth said. "It just shows how much things have changed. I can probably get Hood to give us what we need, but he needs plausible deniability. The less he knows, the better. Asking him to help us launch a raid against DIA might be a bit much."

Lamont started to laugh and broke into a fit of coughing.

"You gotta do something for that cough," Ronnie said.

"Yeah, I'm on it." Lamont held up a package of cough drops. "Menthol," he said. "Want one?"

Ronnie shook his head.

"Everyone agree it's time to go?" Nick said.

No one objected. "Let's get the boat loaded and get out of here." He turned to Selena. "What about this place?" He waved his hand in the air, taking in the house and the whole island. "With Emile gone, there's no one to look after it."

She brushed a lock of hair from her forehead. "I'll close everything up. When we get back to the mainland, I'll get somebody out here. It will be fine until then."

Lamont began coughing. He ate a cough drop.

Nick went around the house with Selena, helping her close the storm shutters. They latched the last one into place.

"That ought to do it," Nick said. "You ready for an ocean cruise?"

"I wish I could joke about it like you do," she said.

"It's the way I deal with the stress," he said.

"I know." She looked out at the ocean. "I've always loved this place," she said, "but it's different now. With Emile gone it won't be the same."

Nick took her hand. "I'm sorry about Emile," he said.

"I always thought that if I ever got married, I would come here on my honeymoon."

He kissed her. "There are plenty of islands we can go to for a honeymoon," he said, "but we probably ought to get married first."

"Jerk," she said. She was smiling.

CHAPTER 43

They sailed past Martinique and St. John's. They passed north of the British Virgin Islands and set a course for the US mainland. Four days out from Selena's island, Puerto Rico lay off the port bow, a blue-green haze in the distance.

The boat was named *Island Angel.* She was powered by a single Caterpillar diesel that drove them at a steady nine knots. The *Island Angel* was double decked, with a glassed-in bridge that provided a sweeping view. She had a raised, flush foredeck and a high, sharp prow. There were three small staterooms on the main deck. Nick and Selena were in one, Stephanie and Harker in the second and Ronnie and Lamont in the third.

Lamont's cough was worse, a racking, heavy sound. Ronnie had taken over the wheel. Lamont was in his room, lying down. The others were in the main cabin.

"He needs a doctor," Selena said.

"It's that hit he took in Jordan," Nick said. "He didn't have enough time to get over it before everything went down."

"I think he has an infection," Harker said. "Maybe pneumonia. He's running a fever."

"We're still at least a week out," Stephanie said. "Nick, what are we going to do?"

"Hope he gets better," Nick said. "There are antibiotics in the medical kit. Start feeding him pills and aspirins and soup. He'll get through it."

"What if he gets worse?"

"We'll deal with that if we have to," Nick said.

Elizabeth said, "I sent a copy of the Ajax protocol to Hood. It shook him up. He decided to take a look at the Pentagon."

"That's domestic surveillance," Nick said. "He could get in a lot of trouble for that."

"It wouldn't be the first time Langley overstepped the bounds," Stephanie said. "But at least this time there's a damn good reason to do it."

"Has Hood found anything out?" Nick asked.

She nodded. "There is a small group of senior military officers, politicians and bankers who call themselves the Augustans. They meet for drinks and conversation on an irregular basis, a few times a year. All of the members have expressed dissatisfaction at one time or another with something President Rice has done."

"That doesn't mean much. Sometimes I don't like what Rice has done."

"Yes, but Hood thinks there may be more to it. Several judges and CEOs are part of the membership as well."

"It sounds like a typical Washington power group," Nick said. "There are dozens of them."

"That's true," Elizabeth said. "Except that the chief figure in the group is a four-star general in charge of SATWEP and the station you raided in Alaska."

"What's his name?" Ronnie asked.

Elizabeth drummed her fingers on her knee. "Westlake. Louis Westlake. I want you to run a full background on him, Steph. Find out if he has any connection with Edmonds. Can you hack into the White House computers?"

"Sure. Compared to the Pentagon, it's easy. I've done it before."

"Get into the visitor records and see if Westlake has visited Edmonds recently. He could be the one who told Edmonds we were interfering with a secret military project. It would take someone with a lot of rank to put that story across."

"Will do," Stephanie said. "I'll log into the computers back in Virginia. From there I can tap into the White House and the NSA database. It shouldn't take long to find out everything about him."

Later, Selena was in her room. She lay on the narrow bed she shared with Nick, reading a dog eared paperback novel about pirates and Scotsmen she'd found in the main cabin. She across a sentence with the word ravish in it and smiled. Elizabeth knocked at the door.

"Busy?" Elizabeth said.

Selena sat up. "More like bored. Come on in."

Elizabeth entered the tiny room and sat down on one end of the bed.

"I can't stop thinking about the man I killed," Elizabeth said. "It was horrible, all that blood. Different from that man I shot in Virginia."

Selena marked the page and put the book down. "I can sympathize with how you feel," she said, "but that probably doesn't help very much."

"I remember when you came back from your first mission, you were different. I watched it all on the satellite. I saw you kill that soldier. How did you handle it, afterward?"

"Nick helped," Selena said. "He helped me see that I'd made the right choice, even though everything I'd been taught told me it was wrong. He didn't try to sugarcoat it, or come up with some platitude about defending our country, anything like that. He told me it would take time to let it in and that the best I could do was to try not to think about it and move on."

"Did it work?" Elizabeth asked. "Not thinking about it?"

Selena laughed. There was no humor in it. "No, not at all. I still think about it. But he was right about it being the right choice. Remembering that helps, that and knowing the person you killed didn't give you an option."

Elizabeth looked down at the floor.

"I was trying to reload," she said. "Emile was dead. The man I'd shot was lying on the ground with his head blown off and I couldn't get the shells into the gun. Then one of those men pointed his gun at me. I thought I was going to die. Then Nick or somebody shot him."

Selena laid a hand on Elizabeth's arm. "I shot him," she said. "Sometimes that's the only option. If you hadn't pulled the trigger on that shotgun, you'd be dead."

Elizabeth took a deep breath and let it out. "I know you're right. I guess I just needed to talk about it the someone."

"Just give it some time," Selena said. She didn't say that no matter how much time there was, it would never be enough to erase the memory.

CHAPTER 44

General Louis Westlake had become obsessed with the Project. There were factors that could disrupt any complex operation but the worst of those were rogue factors no one could predict. The Project was one of those. Their interference had screwed up the timing of his operation. It kept him awake at night.

The news from the Caribbean was bad. His assault team had disappeared. So had the Project. He'd sent another team that found the island deserted.

Where were they? The only way off the island was by air or by sea. They didn't have a plane, so they had to be somewhere on the water. There were too many boats out there to spot them from the satellites.

Sooner or later they'd have to land and when they did, he would find and eliminate them. At least they didn't know about Denver. That thought made Westlake feel better. He reached for the bottle of 25-year-old scotch next to his chair and poured himself another drink.

Anyway, he thought, *soon it won't matter*. Once the Ajax operation began, things would have gone too far for Harker and her toy soldiers to make any difference.

Westlake's mood mellowed as the whiskey took affect. After all, the Project was only six people. Six people who thought they knew better than he did what the nation really needed. They were fools. They couldn't see the path to defeat Rice had laid out by negotiating with America's enemies. He thought of Rice. The President was getting stronger, but he hadn't resumed his duties yet. He never would.

When the transition period was over, there would be a different America. Those who accepted the New Order would find themselves rewarded. Those who resisted would be brought to heel, one way or another.

Westlake got up out of his chair and went to a file cabinet next to his desk, where a false front concealed a safe. He pulled the front open, entered the combination on an electronic keypad and opened the safe. He took out a flat, red notebook that contained a coded summary for deployment of Ajax and the strategy following the takeover.

As the day neared for Ajax to go operational, Westlake found himself taking out the book more often. He was looking for flaws, making sure that he had thought of everything.

Page 8, for example, listed the primary targets and the corresponding military units that would be sent in to restore order. The coordinates for each city were already entered into the computers. Ajax would activate receivers located in each city. The result would be chaos across the entire nation.

It's too bad so many people will die. He dismissed the thought. Sacrifice was always necessary when great acts were played out on the world stage.

He looked at the list. As the riots spread across the country, the result would be terror and confusion across the nation.

The first targets were in the East. The list was like a mystical litany in his mind.

Philadelphia, Atlanta.

As the earth turned, new cities would come into range.

St. Louis, Kansas City.

The final targets were on the West Coast.

Seattle, San Francisco.

He'd considered adding Chicago and New York but had decided against it. Denver had been spared for obvious reasons. He would have liked to include the Capitol, but he needed to keep the infrastructure of government intact. It wouldn't do to have the mobs burn down the White House. As it was, major population centers would be devastated.

Homeland Security, the National Guard, and the regular troops would have their hands full. Rice would die, Edmonds would become President and then he'd panic. He'd be desperate for guidance and a clear strategy to deal with the situation. Westlake planned to be there to give it to him. New emergency regulations would be issued to control the populace. They would never be rescinded.

By the time anyone realized what had happened, it would be too late. If Edmonds presented a problem, he would be eliminated along with any other troublemakers. Westlake looked again at the list of cities, the road to power. He poured his third drink and took a long swallow of the golden liquor. It exploded with pleasant warmth in his stomach, like taking a drink of the sun.

Life was good.

CHAPTER 45

They passed Haiti on the sixth day. Cuba lay ahead off the port bow. They'd taken the shortest route home, with Cuba to the left and the chain of islands that included the Bahamas off to their right. But they had a problem.

"We have to get him to a hospital," Selena said.

They were talking about Lamont. His fever was worse. He was slipping in and out of awareness. The color had drained away from his chocolate skin. His eyes were taking on a yellowish tint.

"There are hospitals in Miami," Ronnie said.

"I don't think he'll last that long." Selena pushed away a wisp of hair from her forehead.

"There's nothing between here and Miami," Nick said.

"Yes there is."

They all turned to look at Elizabeth.

"Guantánamo isn't far from here. We can be there in a day. They have a hospital on the base."

"If we go to Guantánamo, they'll lock us up," Nick said.

"If we don't go to Guantánamo, Lamont will die," Elizabeth said.

"It could work to our advantage," Stephanie said. "If we can convince them not to hold us, we might be able to get an airlift back to the mainland."

"How do you plan to do that?" Nick asked. "Tell them we're the good guys and Edmonds is plotting to overthrow the government? That'll go over well."

"They won't believe anything we say," Elizabeth said. "Not without serious backup."

"Maybe we can get backup," Stephanie said.

"Who did you have in mind?" Elizabeth asked.

"Call Hood. They'll listen to him. Langley practically runs that place."

"I'm not sure how much he'll help us," Elizabeth said. "He's already poking his nose into the Pentagon. He'd be supporting us against the acting President. It would put his entire career on the line."

They could hear Lamont coughing in his cabin. There was something dark about the sound, something frightening.

"Listen to that," Stephanie said. "I don't think we have much of a choice."

"Give me the phone," Elizabeth said.

An hour later they had turned into the Windward Passage between Cuba and Haiti, headed for Guantánamo. Hood had agreed to clear them through. Once they got to the base, Lamont would be taken to the hospital. A plane would take the others back to the mainland.

"Hood is worried about unusual activity by Homeland Security," Elizabeth said.

"What kind of activity?" Nick asked.

"A nationwide joint exercise with the Army is planned for later this week. It's supposed to be an emergency preparedness exercise. Something to test our response in the event of terrorist attack."

"Yeah, right," Ronnie said.

"They're getting ready to deploy that weapon," Nick said, "and we're out here sailing around off Cuba."

"Maybe not for much longer," Selena said. She pointed at a low, gray shape coming fast across the water.

Nick looked grim. "That's a Cuban patrol boat. The Russians sold a few to Castro years ago. I thought they'd all been sunk or decommissioned."

"I guess not all of them," Ronnie said. They could see the Cuban flag flying from the stern of the vessel.

"We're still outside Cuba's territorial waters," Nick said. "They shouldn't be here."

"I don't think they care about that," Elizabeth said.

"Ronnie, come with me," Nick said. "We have to ditch the weapons before they get here."

They went below and took out the weapons and handed them up to Selena. She passed them to Elizabeth, who dropped them over the side. The last to go were their pistols.

They went up to the bridge to watch the Cuban vessel approach. The patrol boat was almost 200 feet long, gray and lethal. It bristled with weapons. There were deck guns fore and aft and antisubmarine missile launchers. The rail was lined with sailors armed with AK-47 carbines. As the vessel closed on them, an officer raised a bullhorn and shouted something.

"What did he say?" Nick turned to Selena. Selena spoke fluent Spanish.

"Classic," she said. "Heave to and prepare to be boarded."

"They got cutlasses, too?" Ronnie said.

Nick looked at him and shook his head. "Cut the engines," he said.

Ronnie throttled back to an idle. The *Island Angel* rode uneasily in the water, rocking in the waves.

"Selena," Nick said. "You do all the talking. See if you can talk us out of here."

She took a deep breath and went down to the main deck. A motor launch with six sailors and the officer put off from the patrol boat and came alongside. They scrambled on board, weapons at the ready. They didn't look friendly. Two of the sailors disappeared into the main cabin.

Nick watched from the bridge as Selena began speaking with the officer. It seemed to be going well. Then the Cuban began shouting at her. She backed up a step. Nick started down the steps toward them. The officer gave an order and the guns pointed toward him. The man said something. Nick didn't need to speak Spanish to know that he was being told to put his hands up.

"Selena," he said as he raised his hands. "What's happening?"

One of the sailors grasped Nick by the arm and pulled him off the steps. Another sailor went up to the bridge and prodded Ronnie and Elizabeth down with the barrel of his rifle. A sailor came out of the main cabin and said something to the officer. He had their passports in his hand.

The officer looked at the documents and then at Nick.

"Ustedes son espías norteamericanos. Si se resisten, se le disparó."

"What did he say?" Ronnie asked.

"He said we are American spies," Selena said. "If we resist, he'll shoot us. I think he means it."

"Yanquis!" the officer said with contempt. He spat on the deck. *"En el barco."* He gestured at the motor launch.

"Into the boat," Selena said.

"What about Lamont?"

Selena fired off some rapid Spanish. The officer replied and gestured again.

"He says they will bring him aboard. Now, we must get in the boat."

"I'm not going without Lamont. Tell him that."

"I'm not sure that's a good idea," she said.

"Tell him anyway."

The officer was watching the exchange. Selena told him what Nick had said. His face got red and he shouted at one of the sailors. The man brought up the butt of his rifle and slammed Nick on the side of the head. Everything went dark.

The first thing Nick was aware of when he woke was pain. He was lying on something hard and cold. The floor vibrated under him. He opened his eyes and light speared his brain like a dagger. He drifted back into unconsciousness.

The next time he woke, Ronnie was sitting next to him. He could hear Lamont coughing.

"Welcome back, amigo," Ronnie said. "You had a nice nap."

"Yeah." Nick sat up. The room spun around him. There was a metal toilet bolted to the wall. He managed to reach it before he threw up. He retched and threw up again. He choked down the bile and caught his breath and waited for the dizziness to pass. He had the mother of all headaches. He wiped his sleeve across his lips.

"Take it easy," Ronnie said. "You took a hell of a hit. Probably got a concussion."

Nick leaned back against the wall next to the toilet "How long was I out?"

"Maybe an hour."

He looked around. The front of the cell was metal bars. The rest of the room was metal, painted flaking gray. There were no windows. A bare metal cot was bolted to the wall. Lamont lay on it, delirious.

Ronnie nodded at him. "He's not doing so good."

"Where are we?"

"They took us on board and threw us in the brig." That explained the vibration in the floor.

"Where are the others?"

"Selena and Elizabeth are next to us in another cell."

"We're screwed," Nick said.

"Yeah," Ronnie said, "my thoughts exactly."

CHAPTER 46

It was going on dark by the time the boat stopped moving and the engines shut down. The Cubans brought them up to the deck. The patrol boat had docked at the waterfront of a good-sized city spread out along a broad bay. An ancient fortress of stone dominated the harbor from a high bluff. The salt air smelled of fish and diesel and wood smoke from a cooking fire. It was like being thrust into the middle of a picture postcard. It was pretty but Nick could have done without it.

Guards marched them off the boat and shoved them sprawling into a windowless van that smelled of vomit. Someone slammed the door of the van and locked it. Lamont lay on the floor of the truck, mumbling to himself. Elizabeth and Selena sat next to him.

The van began to move. Selena laid a hand on Lamont's forehead. "He's burning up," she said.

"He dies, I'm going to make someone pay for it," Nick said.

"Where are we?" Ronnie said.

"All I know is that it isn't Havana."

"It's Santiago de Cuba," Selena said. "That's the only other big city in Cuba. The fortress is a famous historical site."

"Wherever they're taking us, we're going to be interrogated," Nick said. The words came out slurred. One side of his face was swollen from the hit he'd taken on the *Island Angel.*

"We can't tell them who we are," Elizabeth said.

"They'll know who we are. They'll recognize me," Nick said.

He was right. After the incident with the President in Jerusalem, every intelligence agency in the world had his photograph. There were few places he could go without being recognized if any of them were looking.

"They might not," Elizabeth said. "It depends on who's in charge. But if it's the SDE, we're in trouble,"

"SDE?" Selena said.

"*Seguridad del Estado*, state security," Nick said. "Castro's secret police. They're bad people. The officer on that boat called us spies. We can count on SDE being in charge. They hate Americans."

"This isn't the Cold War anymore," Selena said. "It's a long time since the Bay of Pigs."

"Castro's revolutionary government has a long memory," Nick said. "The whole country is a throwback to the Cold War. Lots of things have gone wrong here and they blame us for all of it. We have to be prepared for anything."

The van came to a sudden stop. They heard doors slam. Then the back door was pulled open.

"Afuera!" a soldier yelled at them.

They started to get out. Rough hands grabbed them and pulled them from the van, threw them down on a cobbled street and tied their hands behind their backs with plastic ties. The ties cut into Nick's wrists. He was hauled to his feet and frog marched at a quick pace toward a grim stone building with barred windows and through a door held open by an unsmiling soldier.

Two men marched him down a flight of stairs and along a dim corridor. They jerked him to a stop before a metal door with a massive lock. One of the men turned a key in the lock and pulled open the door. Someone cut the ties on his hands. Before he could move, a boot in his back sent him flying. The door slammed shut.

The floor was made of rough concrete. His back spasmed from the kick. He sat up and rubbed his wrists, waiting for circulation to return to his hands.

The cell was narrow and old. The only light came from a small, dim window high up on the wall. A stinking hole in one corner was the toilet. There was no place to lie except on the cold floor. Nick listened. Faint sounds came from somewhere in the building. Someone screamed in the distance. The cry trailed off in a babbling wail.

The light faded. He was in darkness.

Something ran over his leg. He pulled back, a reflex. Something scrabbled across the floor in the dark.

Rats. There were rats. Nick made a serious effort to calm himself. *At least it isn't spiders,* he thought. *Too big to be a spider. Maybe.*

He sat for a long time in the darkness and listened to unseen things scuttle in his cell.

CHAPTER 47

When the door opened again, Nick had no idea how long he had been sitting in the darkness. They took him into a room and pushed him onto a hard wooden chair and strapped him down. Two guards stood behind him. A small man sat in front of him, behind a wooden desk that looked like something left over from a 40s movie.

The Cuban had a thin mustache that did nothing to improve his looks or hide a bad complexion. He was dressed in a cheap brown suit and brown shoes. His shirt was a yellowed white under a narrow, black tie. He wore his hair slicked back and shiny under the overhead light.

The man ignored Nick. For several minutes he studied papers on his desk, making an occasional note. When he finally looked up, his eyes were black and dead, as if they had seen things that had extinguished the light in them. They were not good eyes.

"I am Captain Ortiz," he said. "I am going to ask you some questions. You will answer me truthfully. Do you understand?"

His voice was flat and colorless His English was clear, articulate. An educated man, which as far as Nick was concerned made him more dangerous.

"Why have you brought us here?" Nick said.

Ortiz nodded at one of the guards. He began beating Nick with his fists. Nick closed his eyes and tried to make himself tight and small. He could do nothing with his arms strapped to the chair.

"Enough," Ortiz said. The beating stopped. The guard stepped back.

"I ask the questions here," Ortiz said. "Do you understand?"

So that's how it's going to be, Nick thought. He spit blood onto the floor. "I understand."

"You are Nicholas Carter, a spy for the American government." Ortiz held up a file in his hand. Nick saw his picture stapled onto it.

"I never did like that picture," he said.

"You do not deny that you are a spy," Ortiz said.

Nick said nothing. There wasn't any point.

"Why were you headed to Cuba?"

"For medical help."

"Where were you going?"

"Guantánamo."

The mention of Guantánamo seemed to trigger something in Ortiz. He nodded again at the guard. This time, the man took out a foot long length of heavy rope with a knot on the end of it and began beating Nick on his arms and legs. Each blow shuddered through his body. He grunted under the blows.

When Ortiz signaled the guard to stop, Nick felt like he was on fire. He couldn't feel anything except pain. And anger.

"That was for Guantánamo," Ortiz said.

"Guantánamo is the best thing there is on this piss ant island," Nick said.

This time both the guards beat him.

"Stand him up," Ortiz said. The guards unstrapped Nick from the chair, lifted him to his feet and gripped him by each arm. Ortiz got up from behind his desk. He came over and stood in front of Nick. His face was ugly with hatred. He shouted in Nick's face, spraying him with flecks of spittle. His breath stank of garlic and onion.

"My grandfather was killed by the Americans at the Bay of Pigs."

Ortiz reached out and grabbed Nick's left hand. "Tell me why you are here."

"For medical help." With a quick movement, Ortiz bent the last two fingers of Nick's hand backward. The bones snapped with a dull, thick sound.

Nick screamed. The pain was unlike anything he had ever felt before.

"Now you need medical help," Ortiz said. "You are a *Yanqui* spy. After I find out why you are here, I am going to send you to a place that makes your prison at Guantánamo look like a holiday resort."

Ortiz was only inches away. Nick head butted him as hard as he could. Ortiz went backward, his eyes rolling up in his head. As he went down, Nick kicked him in the groin.

The first blow from the guards knocked Nick unconscious.

When he came to, he was lying on the floor of his cell. One of his eyes was closed and swollen. His body was a symphony of pain. He moved and sharp pain shot up his left arm from his injured hand.

His hand was swollen and purple. The fourth finger and the pinky were bent to the side at a strange angle. Nick forced himself to look at it. He knew what he had to do. Before he could think much more about it, he took his right hand and pulled the damaged fingers straight.

He screamed and blacked out again from the pain. When he came back, he lay curled up on the rough floor. Then he forced himself over to a corner of the cell where dripping water had collected in a small pool. He picked a dead cockroach out of the water, cupped some in his right hand and drank it.

Weak daylight came through the filthy window. He wondered how the others were doing. He wondered if Selena was safe. He wondered how he could kill Ortiz.

At least he had gotten to the son of a bitch. He wouldn't be pleasuring his wife for awhile. If he had a wife. If any woman would have a snake like him. Nick was sure he was one *Yanqui* Ortiz would never forget, but that kick in the groin had probably signed his death warrant. There was nothing left to lose. Before Nick slipped back into oblivion, he decided that the next time the door opened he would try to overpower the guard.

CHAPTER 48

Nick heard the lock being turned in his cell door. There was light in the cell but he didn't know if it was the same day. He'd been half asleep or unconscious. Every part of his body hurt. His left hand glowed with pain. He forced himself to his feet. The door opened.

Nick launched himself at the first man into the cell, like a linebacker taking down a fullback. The man grunted as they slammed into the wall. Then something hard hit him on the back of the head. The next thing he was aware of was the sound of voices. He was lying on the floor of the cell. There was something oddly familiar about one of the voices, but he couldn't figure out what it was. He slipped back into unconsciousness.

He was sitting tilted back, a belt strapped across his waist. The seat vibrated gently. He could hear the sound of engines.

A plane. I'm in a plane.

Nick opened his eyes. He was in a private plane, a business jet elegant with accents of wood and leather. Selena was in the seat across the aisle from him. She looked worn and tired, her face strained. She smiled when she saw him looking at her.

"Nick," she said. "You had me worried."

He looked down at his injured hand. Someone had set the bones and splinted them and wrapped the fingers in tape. Under the bandage, the hand throbbed with dull, steady pain.

Selena laid her hand on his arm. Her touch felt comforting, familiar. A tiny bit of the tension from the last few days melted away. He looked at her.

"Christ, I'm glad you're all right. When this is done..."

A voice from the seat behind interrupted him before he could finish.

"You are awake, Nick? Good."

It was a familiar voice, the voice he had heard in Cuba before he blacked out. Nick turned toward the speaker. A wave of dizziness rippled through him and was gone.

Korov. What the hell is he doing here?

"Where did you come from?" Nick said.

"Moscow, of course. Where else?" Korov got up and stood in the aisle looking down at Nick. "You look like shit," he said.

"Yeah. Nice to see you, too."

Nick looked around the plane. Harker was three rows ahead of him in the front of the cabin. Ronnie lay back on the seat behind her, sleeping. In the rear of the plane was a meeting area with chairs and a table. The table had been turned into an improvised bed for Lamont. Stephanie sat nearby, watching over him. She looked worried. At the very back of the plane was a small galley. A man in civilian clothes sat there, reading a magazine.

"How are you feeling?" Korov asked.

"A little dizzy. I've been better. Where are we? Where are we going?"

"At the moment we are over the Gulf of Mexico. As to where we are going, I was waiting for you to wake up before choosing a destination."

"You want me to tell you where we're going?"

"Yes."

"I need coffee."

Korov called out something in Russian. The man in the back of the plane came forward. Korov said something. The man snapped to attention and went back to the galley. A moment later he appeared with a tray and two cups of coffee.

Nick took a sip of the strong, black liquid and sighed. His mouth hurt and his face was swollen. He tasted blood. Probed with his tongue at a loose tooth.

"How did you get us out of Cuba?" Nick said.

"Cuba has few friends," Arkady said. "We have a special relationship with them, particularly concerning intelligence about America. We have influence. They told us they had captured a boatload of American spies and that the infamous Nicholas Carter was among them."

"Infamous?"

"Like your Jesse James, no? I made it clear that giving you to me would help with trade negotiations coming up soon with Moscow. After all, I am a ranking officer in SVR. The Cubans think I am taking all of you back to Russia for interrogation. What you Americans call rendition, yes?"

"Why bail us out?"

"Your director told General Vysotsky about Ajax. Then we found out you had been forced to leave Washington. You have made powerful enemies, Nick."

"Go on."

"The General believes your director is sincere in her desire to stop these madmen from deploying Ajax. He thinks you and your team have the best chance of doing it. You can't do that from a Cuban prison. He decided to intervene."

Nick saluted Korov with the coffee cup. "Good to see you, Arkady."

"And you, Nick. Now we must finish the job."

"We?"

"Tell me where we need to go. I'm going with you. Your director wanted an entire unit, but the General decided it was too risky. All you get is me."

"This could turn ugly, real fast," Nick said. "There are going to be casualties."

"There are always casualties when it matters." Korov looked out the window of the plane.

"A Russian shooting it out with Americans on American soil won't go down well," Nick said.

"If it comes out, the politicians will deal with it," Korov said. "Probably at our expense."

"What else is new?"

"Interesting, isn't it?" Korov said. "Your country and mine, no difference. The politicians always throw the soldiers under the car."

"The bus. You throw someone under the bus."

"Ah. Yes, under the bus."

"We have to get Lamont to a hospital."

"First we must get into American airspace. Can your director arrange something?"

"I'll go talk to her," Nick said. "Lend me your phone."

Korov handed him a phone and he went forward.

Korov saw Selena follow Nick with her eyes. He sat down next to her. "You and Nick," he said. He stopped.

Selena looked at him. "Yes?" Her tone was cool. It was hard to get past the fact that Korov was Russian, even though he'd proved a friend in the past. It was the Russians who had murdered her family. She knew it was irrational, knew Korov had nothing to do with it. But it didn't change how she felt.

"You are with each other?"

"You mean, are we lovers?"

"I don't mean to be rude," Korov said. "I couldn't help noticing how you look at him."

"I guess it's obvious. Yes, we're together. Why do you ask?"

"It's good to know as much as possible about the people you fight with," Korov said. "I am glad for you." He got up and went back to his seat.

What was that about? Selena wondered.

Up front, Elizabeth called Clarence Hood.

Aside from Hood himself, Elizabeth and her team were the only ones who knew how he had become Director of Central Intelligence. The DCI owed her a very large debt. It was time to call it in.

"Clarence, it's Elizabeth."

"Elizabeth. I was beginning to wonder what had happened to you. What's your situation?" Hood's voice was cultured, with a soft hint of a Southern accent. Elizabeth pictured him in his paneled office on the seventh floor at Langley.

"Let me give you the short version," Elizabeth said.

She briefed him on Cuba. When she told him about Korov, there was a long silence at the other end of the connection.

"We seem to have a unique relationship with this officer," Hood finally said.

"That's putting it mildly," she said. Then she told him she had traced the origin of the satellite signals to DIA and that she thought the Ajax command center was concealed under the Denver airport. She told him her suspicions about General Westlake.

"I know about the complex under DIA," Hood said. "It's been abandoned for years. It was supposed to be part of the continuity of government program, but a budget decision was made to construct facilities elsewhere."

The COG program was an emergency plan to protect government leaders in the event of a catastrophic event like nuclear war.

"That confirms my suspicion," Elizabeth said. "It would make a perfect location."

"What do you intend to do?"

"I am going to put it out of action," Elizabeth said. "I intend to destroy it."

"What if it's not there?" Hood said.

"We'd better hope it is."

"The joint operation between the Army and the Department of Homeland Security is scheduled to begin the day after tomorrow," Hood said. "There is unusually tight security surrounding the exercise."

Elizabeth said, "I am certain this exercise is part of implementing Ajax. If I were planning this, I'd want the riots to really get going before the troops went in. That means they'll activate that weapon sooner than the day after tomorrow. I would guess in the next 24 hours."

"That doesn't give you much time," Hood said.

No kidding, she thought. "Whoever is running that exercise has to be part of the plot, and probably the Director of Homeland Security. There's no time to convince anyone that these people are traitors."

"This is a nightmare," Hood said.

"It will be a much worse nightmare if Ajax is deployed."

"What do you need?"

"Clearance into US airspace, for openers. We need an airport that will handle a Dassault E3. Lamont is in critical shape. He has to get to a hospital. We need fuel for the plane. Satellite phones. Weapons for my team. They need clothes. Uniforms, if there's nothing else."

"You're over the Gulf right now?"

"Yes."

"Langley has a restricted airfield near Lubbock. I'll send you the coordinates. Land there. I'll transmit an emergency code to you after this conversation that will get you through our border defenses and onto the airfield. I'll have an ambulance waiting there. It might be better if you kept Colonel Korov out of sight."

"Thank you, Clarence."

"You may not thank me if this doesn't work out," Hood said. He paused. "Elizabeth."

"Yes?"

"No one can protect you if this goes bad."

"If this goes bad, I won't be the only one without protection," Elizabeth said.

CHAPTER 49

They touched down at the CIA airfield an hour and a half later. A scorching Texas sun glinted off the windshield of an ambulance speeding toward them as they rolled to a stop.

Lamont's breathing was harsh and ragged. Nick held his hand.

"Shadow," Nick said. "You're back on US soil. We'll get you to a hospital."

"Yeah." Lamont coughed. There was blood on his lips. He turned his head away and closed his eyes.

A fuel truck rumbled up. A man in orange overalls got out of the truck and hooked up to the plane. Fuel began pumping into the tanks. A black SUV came toward them across the concrete and stopped. The man who got out wore a blue sport jacket and a white shirt open at the collar. He had on a pair of aviator Ray Bans. He didn't introduce himself.

"Are you Carter?" he said.

"That's right."

"I was told to give you what I've got in the truck."

He opened the doors of the SUV. Ronnie and Nick looked inside.

There was a box of faded uniforms that looked like they'd come from an Army-Navy surplus store. On the back seat were three M16s that had seen better days. A cardboard box held magazines, ammunition and two holstered Beretta M9 pistols. There were two satellite phones next to the pistols.

"You gotta be kidding," Ronnie said.

"That's it?" Nick said. "This is everything they sent?"

The man shrugged. "I'm only the delivery boy. You want this stuff or not?"

Nick picked up an M-16. The stock was battered and marked from use. He racked the bolt and examined the rifle. It had the old-style pronged flash suppressor on the end of the barrel. *Left over from Vietnam,* he thought. *At least it's clean and oiled.*

"Yeah, I want them. Grab the boxes Ronnie."

They carried the box and weapons to the plane. Nick said to Elizabeth, "Director, you and Stephanie get off here."

"I'm not sure that's a good idea," Elizabeth said.

"It's my decision," Nick said. "There isn't anything you and Steph can do if you go with us. If you get killed, everything goes in the crapper. I don't want you along."

"You don't mince words, do you?"

"I don't see much point to it," Nick said. "I need you to watch our back."

"What about your hand?"

"What about it? I can still handle a weapon."

Elizabeth wanted to go. The time on the island had changed something. She felt more like a part of the team, close to them, not just their boss. She wanted to stay with them, but Nick was right.

"What about communications?" she asked.

"Hood sent two phones." Nick handed her one.

"All right, Nick. Stop them." She walked away.

The attendants loaded Lamont into the ambulance. Elizabeth and Stephanie got in with him. Nick watched the ambulance drive off. It was a relief. He didn't have to think about Lamont anymore, or the two women. He felt just a twinge of guilt for feeling that way. He brushed the thought aside.

Back at the plane, Korov picked up one of the M16s. "These are old," he said.

"Yeah. Better than nothing. They only sent three," Nick said.

"I have my own."

Korov reached into an overhead compartment and took out an odd looking weapon. It was equipped with a scope and had a futuristic looking stock.

"Interesting," Ronnie said. "Can I take a look?"

"It is loaded," Korov said. "Be careful."

Ronnie found the selector switch and made sure it was on safe. He brought the weapon to his shoulder, brought it back down. It was light weight. Ronnie guessed it at around three pounds.

"Is this a spare magazine in back, like a stock?"

"Da. It holds 44 rounds. Nine millimeter. This is a PP2000. We like it, although the MP5 is perhaps better."

"Rate of fire?"

"Around 850."

Ronnie handed the weapon back. he sat down and began stripping one of the rifles.

Twenty minutes later, they were in the air.

CHAPTER 50

Flying straight into DIA didn't seem like a good idea. They landed in Colorado Springs, 70 miles South of Denver. Another anonymous agent met them and gave them the keys to a GMC Suburban. The car was several years old and spattered with mud and dirt. One of the fenders was dented.

Nick looked at the car and shook his head. "I guess Langley is getting hit with budget cuts."

"I hope this is in better shape than the guns," Ronnie said.

On the front seat was a brown envelope. It held cash and a road map, along with satellite photos of Denver International Airport. The photos were marked with the location of the buried buildings. The site was almost three miles away from the main terminal.

They settled into the car and headed for the interstate leading north to Denver.

Ronnie drove. Nick and Korov sat in back, Selena in front with Ronnie. They'd changed into the uniforms. The clean clothes felt comfortable but Nick wished he had his regular gear. Without armor he felt half naked.

"Let's look at the airport layout," he said.

Selena turned around in her seat. They studied the satellite pictures.

"Whatever's there has to be accessed from a lower level," Nick said. "There isn't going to be anything obvious, where anyone could see it."

"How about the train tunnel?" Ronnie said. "It could be like the subways in New York, where they sealed off the old stations and they're still there."

"That makes sense," Selena said. "But how are we going to find the entrance?"

"I have a better question," Korov said. "How do we get through your airport security?"

"We have to look like we belong," Nick said. "Someone with a legitimate reason to be seen away from the passenger areas. Someone with a key card. Maybe maintenance workers or baggage handlers."

Selena pointed at the map. A street called 75th Avenue split off from the main feed into the airport and passed a series of hangers and warehouses used by UPS, FedEx, and others.

"There's a cargo facility here," she said. "We could slip into one of those. There will be vehicles, clothes, IDs, everything we need."

"It will be dark soon," Ronnie said. "That will help."

"It's an idea," Selena said.

Nick shook his head. "It's an idea but it's not a plan. We're looking for something that's been well hidden. We can't go in blind and hope we stumble on it by luck."

"Why go through the airport at all?" Selena said.

"What do you mean?"

"The bunker is where those buried buildings are, right?"

"That's what we've thought all along," Nick said.

"Why don't we look for an entrance there? There has to be more than one way in. No one could bring supplies or people in and out through the train tunnels without being seen. It would defeat the whole purpose of keeping it secret."

"She's right," Ronnie said. "They have to be able to bring in equipment, whatever else they need. That means a road."

Selena shuffled through the satellite photographs and pulled out the photo with the location of the buried structures.

"There's a farmhouse and barn nearby," she said. "It's the only building in the area and its right off a paved road."

"It could be the access point to the bunker," Nick said, "but it could just be a farmhouse."

"Can Elizabeth get a real-time satellite shot, maybe a deep scan infrared reading? If it's the command center, they'll have computers in there. Computers need power and power means heat. If something's there, it should show up."

Nick took out his phone and called Elizabeth. She picked up on the first ring.

"Yes, Nick."

"Director, I need a real time satellite shot and an infrared readout. Are you set up to do that?"

"I can get it through Langley," she said. "What are the coordinates?"

Nick looked at the satellite photo and gave her the location. "It's a farmhouse and barn. It might be a camouflaged entrance to the underground complex. If there's infrared activity, that would clinch it."

"I'll call you back," Harker said. "Be careful you don't go charging into someone's living room and blow them away while they're watching *The Simpsons*." She broke the connection.

"So now we have a plan," Korov said.

"It's as good a plan as any," Nick said, "since we're winging this by the seat of our pants."

"Winging? Pants? What do you mean?" Korov said.

The three Americans laughed. "It means we don't know what the hell we're doing and we're pretending that we do," Nick said. "Making up the plan as we go along."

"You make it sound simple," Korov said. "I hope you are right."

The sun was setting behind the Rocky Mountains. The light was golden, the sky clear. The shadows on the mountain slopes were a deep purple. It made Nick think of the line in *America the Beautiful* about purple mountains' majesty. It wasn't hard to see what had inspired the song.

"It is very beautiful, the mountains," Korov said. "It reminds me of home."

They headed north toward Denver.

CHAPTER 51

It was full dark by the time they reached the objective. They parked a hundred yards away from the target, off the side of the road. Nick scanned the farmhouse through Korov's night vision binoculars.

A dirt and gravel drive led to a plain wooden house with a shingle roof and a covered porch. A single light was on over the door. The building looked rundown and tired. Rusted farm equipment was lined up in a ragged row in front of the house. A dark colored pickup was parked in the packed dirt of the yard. Light shone behind the curtained windows of a room on the first floor.

The house looked like thousands of others scattered across rural America.

Behind the house was a rundown barn. To someone passing by, the place looked like a hardscrabble farm in need of a lot of maintenance. In the green light of the night vision optics, it looked like something out of an Alfred Hitchcock film.

Nick studied the barn. "Take a look at the barn," he said, "at the doors." He handed the binoculars to Korov.

Korov focused. "The doors are closed," he said. "They look strong for a barn that needs so much repair."

"Look at the left side of the doors."

Korov shifted the lenses. He smiled. "A numbered keypad," he said.

"Doesn't that seem a little unusual for an old barn in the country?"

Nick's phone signaled a call from Harker.

"Yes."

"Nick, you were right. The satellite overpass shows infrared activity at that site, consistent with something buried underground. How far under, I can't say."

"Outstanding," Nick said. "Now all we have to do is get in. We're about to go hot, Director."

"Copy that. Good luck, Nick. Keep your head down."

Nick put the phone away and told the others what Harker had said.

"We don't know what's down there," Korov said, "but it will be defended. What are the rules of engagement?"

"If someone is armed, don't hesitate. Shoot to kill. There will be control stations for a satellite or satellites somewhere in that complex. Our mission is to destroy them."

"What if there are civilians?" Selena asked.

"These people want to destroy America," Nick said. "There are no civilians down there."

No one else had any questions.

"Lock and load," Nick said. "The house is probably a guard point. We'd better clear it first."

They crawled on all fours toward the house. The moon hadn't come up yet and the only light came from the stars, high over the Rocky Mountains. In the distance, Denver was a fairytale glow against the dark outline of the Front Range. The night smelled of grass and the dry dust of the plains. Earlier, there had been thousands of crickets chirping. Now the only sound was the quiet movement of their bodies across the ground.

They worked their way up to the rusted machinery. The front of the house was about 30 feet away. The light was still on in the window and on the porch. The curtains were drawn. It was impossible to see who or what was inside.

Nick signaled and ran forward, cradling the M-16 across his chest. The others came close behind. The old feeling came over him, the adrenaline surge rushing in his ears, a mix of fear and excitement. They reached the porch and Nick stepped onto it. A moth circled the light. He reached for the knob on the front door. Then he saw the camera.

He threw himself to the side. The roar of a shotgun came from inside the house. The front door blew off the hinges in a shower of splinters.

Big. Must be a 10 gauge, Nick thought.

Selena and Korov and Ronnie opened up at the window and door. Another blast of the shotgun sent more splinters flying. Nick reached blind around the smashed doorframe and fired a fast burst. The shotgun boomed again. Nick fired a three round burst and rolled into the house. The man with the shotgun was at the end of a long hall that stretched past a flight of stairs. Nick shot him. Someone appeared at the top of the stairs and began shooting. The rounds chopped holes in the floor behind him as Nick dove out of the line of fire. Ronnie came through the doorway and cut the shooter down. The body tumbled down the steps.

Selena and Korov came into the house and moved down the hall, fast, looking into rooms and calling out as they went.

"Clear."

"Clear."

Ronnie and Nick went up the steps. There was no one left on the top floor. They came back down.

The man Ronnie had killed wore a TSA uniform. No one would give someone in that outfit a second glance in an airport terminal.

"Only two of them here," Ronnie said.

"Spotters," Nick said. "Here to sound the alarm if someone shows up that's not supposed to."

"Like us," Selena said.

"If these two got off a signal, it means the opposition knows we're here."

"Maybe they didn't have a chance to do it," Selena said.

"We'll find out quick enough," Nick said, "once we get into that barn."

CHAPTER 52

General Westlake and Senator Martinez watched the big screen that dominated the control room of the command bunker. It showed a computerized map of the US and North America. Changing numbers on the right-hand side of the display indicated that the Ajax satellite was approaching the Eastern seaboard.

"What Caesar and the Romans could have done if they'd had this kind of technology," Westlake said.

"They did pretty well without it," Martinez said.

"But in the end, they failed. We will not. What we do here today will birth a new Empire. The glory of Rome will be nothing in comparison."

"A *Pax Americana*," Martinez said, "backed up by the most powerful military the world has ever seen."

"We don't need the entire world," Westlake said, "at least not at first."

"There will be some who try to take advantage of the transition," Martinez said. "Russia comes to mind. China."

"Let them try. They will find new strength in our foreign policy."

"You are sure that we have enough support in the Pentagon?"

Westlake gave him a hard look. "Second thoughts? It's a little late for that. "

"I've always thought Anderson could make trouble."

General Franklin Anderson was Commandant of the Marine Corps.

"I've assigned units to isolate Anderson, Admiral Kaplan and the other senior officers who won't support us. There are only a half dozen officers who could create a problem. They will be unable to affect events."

"Homeland Security?"

"Will be out in force, as soon as Edmonds announces that there has been a terrorist attack."

"Speaking of Edmonds, there's something else," Martinez said. "What about Rice? He hasn't resumed his office, but he's awake."

"I've already arranged for his, ah, relapse," Westlake said. "In any event, it's too late for anything he does to make a difference." Westlake gestured at the screen. "Ajax will be in range soon."

A red light began blinking on the wall beside the screen.

"What's that?" Martinez asked.

Westlake's lips set in a tight line. "Intruder alert. Someone has breached the security perimeter up top."

"How can that be? No one knows about this place."

"I don't know."

Westlake picked up a phone on the console and listened to it ring. He set the phone down and turned to Martinez.

"The perimeter post isn't answering. I'll send a team into the tunnels. It could be a malfunction, but if someone has breached security they won't make it past the elevator."

CHAPTER 53

Ronnie pulled the cover off the numbered keypad by the barn door and studied the wiring inside the unit. A half dozen wires of different colors ran in all directions. He pulled a red and yellow wire out of the mix and touched them together. The unit sparked. The doors stayed closed. A thin wisp of smoke rose from the keypad.

"Now what," Selena said.

"It should have been red and yellow," Ronnie said. "Let me try something else."

He raised his M-16 and put a three round burst into the keypad. There was a loud click and one of the doors slid partway open.

"When in doubt, use a bigger hammer," Ronnie said. Korov smiled.

They squeezed through the opening. The interior of the barn was in darkness. They fanned out by the doors and listened, weapons held ready. There was no one there.

Korov took a small flashlight from his pocket and turned it on. The barn was cluttered with old furniture, machinery, tools. Shadows cast by the moving light shifted as if they were alive.

"This place gives me the creeps," Selena said.

The light revealed the squat shape of a freight elevator shaft. It looked new. A metal lattice gate closed off the open shaft. A control box with two buttons was mounted on one side.

"Looks like we found the way in," Ronnie said. "I don't think they use this for moving bales of hay."

Nick's ear tingled. He scratched it.

"You're doing that thing," Ronnie said.

"What thing?"

"The ear thing."

"Yeah. Could be someone waiting for us at the bottom of this shaft."

"Is there another way down?" Selena asked.

Korov circled the barn with his light. "I don't see anything," he said.

"Here goes nothing," Nick said. He pushed the top button on the control panel. Machinery whined as the elevator rose from somewhere below. They stood to the side, rifles pointed at the opening. It seemed like a long time before the top of the cage appeared above the floor. The elevator came to a stop. There was no one on it.

Nick pulled open the gate. It moved smoothly on oiled tracks. Another two-button switch was mounted on the inside of the cage.

"We don't have much choice," Nick said. "We have to use this."

"We're sitting ducks if someone starts shooting," Ronnie said.

"Like I said, we don't have much choice. Stand close to the sides. If they're waiting for us, we'll see them through the gap when the floor of the elevator reaches the lower level. If anyone's there, shoot through the gap before the elevator stops."

"The gate's in the way," Korov said.

Nick looked at the grillwork. "There's a safety interlock where the gate shuts. If we jam it, the elevator will work with the gate open. We need something to block it."

Three empty wooden crates were stacked next to the shaft. Ronnie went to one and broke off a sliver of wood.

"How about this?"

Nick jammed the piece into the interlock.

"That'll work." He swept his hand toward the elevator. "Going down," he said.

They got on. Nick pushed the bottom button. The elevator began to descend. Nick and Selena went to one side, Ronnie and Korov to the other. They pressed up against the walls of the cage.

They descended at a snail's pace. Nick kept his M-16 pointed at the front edge of the elevator floor. A crack of light appeared, becoming wider. Nick wondered if someone was waiting.

Someone was. They fired at the elevator as it came into view.

Korov fired first through the widening gap, then the others. Bullets slammed into the bottom of the elevator floor and into the top of the cage. Whoever was below had to fire up through the gap, a disadvantage. There were three of them. By the time the elevator stopped, they were dead. They all wore the TSA uniform .

From where they stood inside the elevator, there wasn't much to see. To the left and in front were walls of gray concrete, the opposite wall a dozen feet away. They had stopped at the end of a broad corridor. The passage continued to the right, out of Nick's vision.

He held up his hand. *Wait.* There had to be more of them.

Clink!

A dark green cylinder rolled to a stop in front of the elevator.

"Grenade!" Nick shouted.

Korov moved in a blur, scooping up the grenade and hurling it back down the hallway. He landed flat on the floor and covered his head with his arms. The grenade detonated. In the enclosed space, the sound was a thunderclap. Screams came from down the hall.

Nick, Ronnie and Selena moved out of the elevator and began firing down the passage over Korov's head. At the other end, someone was still alive and shooting at them. Bullets ricocheted from the concrete walls. Selena felt the wind as they flew by. One grazed her arm, a sharp, burning pain. The passage filled with a haze of smoke and concrete dust from the explosion.

Then it was silent. Korov got to his feet.

Dust and smoke drifted through the hall. The air smelled of burnt gunpowder and spent brass and hot blood. Down the passage, six men in TSA uniforms lay dead on the floor. There was a lot of blood, pools of it. What a grenade did to the human body wasn't pretty.

The corridor ended in a T. The bodies lay in the junction.

Nick turned to Korov. "Nice move with the grenade. You ought to try out for the Yankees."

"Yankees?"

Ronnie stifled a laugh.

Nick said, "Never mind, Arkady."

"It's clear up to that T," Ronnie said.

They ran to the junction. The crackle of static froze them in place.

"Echo team, report."

Ronnie bent down and took a radio from the belt of one of the dead men. It was a standard military issue.

"Echo team, report," someone said again.

Nick nodded. Ronnie pressed send.

"Echo," he said. He muffled his voice.

"That you, Jack? What the hell's happening?"

"Four intruders. All dead."

"You sound funny," the voice said.

Ronnie coughed into the radio. "Lot of dust. Hadda use a grenade."

"All right. Come in. Out."

"Copy," Ronnie said. He turned the radio off.

"You should have been an actor," Nick said. He glanced around the corner. The passage was empty in both directions.

"Which way?" Korov said.

"Damned if I know," Nick said.

"Left," Selena said. She pointed at a layer of dust covering the floor in the right hand passage. "No footprints." She looked at the bodies lying by her feet. "These men didn't come that way."

"You're bleeding," Korov said.

Selena's sleeve was red with blood.

"Only a scratch."

Korov took out his knife and cut the fabric away from her arm. She winced as he pulled the cloth away.

"It's not serious. A flesh wound," he said. He cut a strip from his shirt and used it to wrap the injury. His touch was gentle as he did it.

Selena gave him an odd look. "Thanks," she said.

Nick inserted a fresh 30 round magazine into his M-16. "Let's go," he said.

They moved into the left-hand corridor. Light bulbs lined the walls at regular intervals, each one protected by a metal grill. The tunnel was big, at least two dozen feet across and almost as high.

"You could drive a truck through here," Ronnie said. "What were they thinking of?"

"It was supposed to be part of the train system," Selena said. "At least that's the story."

They walked along the deserted tunnel. Nick felt fatigue setting in as the adrenaline wore off. He forced himself to stay alert.

"Someone spent a lot of money to build this," Korov said.

"If it was meant to be an emergency hideout for the big shots, they wouldn't have cared about how much it cost."

"But they never used it," Selena said. "Why build it and then walk away?"

"Who knows?" Nick said. "I gave up trying to understand how Washington spends our money a long time ago."

Ahead, the corridor turned left around a blind corner. They moved single file along the wall until Nick signaled a halt. He glanced around the corner.

The corridor ended in a wall and a steel door painted gray.

They moved to the door. Nick tugged on his ear. It itched.

"Maybe they think we're dead. Maybe they don't. My guess is were going to find out when we go through that door," Nick said. "The door opens toward us. Ronnie, you and Korov take the left side and Selena and I will take the right."

They took up positions on either side of the door. Nick pulled it open. Nothing happened.

The door led to a large storeroom filled with old office furniture and odds and ends from the airport. Everything was stacked in haphazard piles. The place looked like a junk shop organized by a schizophrenic. On the far side of the room was another door.

"I don't see anyone," Ronnie said. His voice was quiet.

They started into the room.

"Look out!"

Korov jumped in front of Selena and pushed her aside. A burst of automatic fire came from behind a stack of boxes. The bullets hurled the Russian backward. Nick had time to see a dark object hurtling through the air before the world vanished in a wave of light and sound.

CHAPTER 54

Nick came to his senses and retched. He was lying on the floor. A man in a TSA uniform stood over him. The muzzle of a rifle was pressed into his neck.

"Don't move, asshole."

The voice was muffled. Something was wrong with Nick's hearing. *Flashbang,* he thought.

Another man grabbed Nick and bound his hands behind his back with zip ties. Nick clenched his teeth against a jolt of pain from his broken fingers. The man pulled him to his feet. For Nick, it felt like his arms were going to come out of their sockets. He was dizzy. He stumbled and retched again. The other man kept a harsh grip on his arm. Then he saw Korov.

The Russian lay on his side, his eyes open, unblinking. His face had a look of childlike surprise. The front of his shirt was soaked with blood. Blood spread in a slow, red stain around him.

Aw, hell, Nick thought. Then, *Selena!*

He looked to his right. Selena was being hauled to her feet. A little ways past her, Ronnie lay on the floor as someone tied his hands.

Selena looked over at him and he felt relief that she was still alive. She looked at Korov's body and her face set. Nick knew the look. You didn't want to be on the wrong side of that look.

"You all right?" he said.

"Yes."

"Shut up. No talking." Nick's guard poked him hard in the back with his rifle.

One of their captors was on his radio. He had three gold stripes on his shoulders. He listened for a moment, acknowledged and put the radio away.

"We're going to the control room," he said to the man standing next to Nick. "The General wants to see them."

"Wants to ask them a few questions, I'll bet. They won't like that."

"I wouldn't mind asking *her* a few questions," one of the men said. He walked over and stood about six feet away from Selena.

"What do you say, honey bunch? Be nice, and I can make things a lot easier for you."

"I can't be nice to you if you're way over there," Selena said.

The man grinned and stepped close. Selena kneed him in the groin. He doubled over in pain, grabbing his crotch.

After a moment he straightened up. "Bitch," he said, and punched her in the stomach. She went down on her knees, gasping for breath.

"That's enough," the man with the stripes said. "The General's waiting." Selena struggled to her feet. Stripes went over to her. He stood well out of her reach.

"You try anything else, I'll put a bullet in your head. Understand?"

She said nothing.

"I'll take that as a yes," Stripes said.

As the men prodded them forward, Nick thought about Korov. They had been under fire together in Texas and Russia, gotten drunk together, sung songs together. Nick didn't let many people into his life, but Korov had been one of them. Nick felt rage stirring, the kind of rage that had erupted on the day he almost killed his father, all those years ago. He took a deep breath to get himself under control. Blind rage wasn't going to get them out of this. He looked over at Ronnie, then at Selena. Something passed between them. It wasn't over yet.

The guards marched them through the door at the end of the storage space and into another passage. It led to a big room where a half dozen technicians tended computers and watched their monitors. Everyone wore the TSA uniform except for two men standing in front of a huge display screen mounted on one wall. The men turned to look as the guards herded them into the room. One was dressed in the green uniform of a full general in the U.S. Army.

Westlake, Nick thought. The other man looked familiar. Then it clicked. *It's Martinez, the Senate Majority Leader. What's he doing here?*

"Bring them here," Westlake said.

"Sir, be careful of the woman," Stripes said.

"You heard me."

"Yes, sir."

The guards stopped them about six feet away from Westlake.

He looked at Nick. "I recognize you," he said. "You were the one with Rice in Jerusalem. You should have stayed in Washington."

"I'm not the only one who should have stayed there," Nick said. "How does it feel to be a traitor, General? Your country has given you everything. Why are you doing this?"

"The victors decide who is a patriot and who is a traitor," Westlake said. "George Washington was a traitor, as far as England was concerned. Everything I do is for the good of the country. Someone has to take action. Fortunately, there are several of us who have decided that enough is enough."

"Ten minutes, General." The man speaking sat at a console in front of the big screen. It looked like a fancy gaming console, with a joystick and keyboard. "On schedule."

"Very well, Abingdon," Westlake said over his shoulder. He kept his eyes on Nick. "Do you understand what's about to happen, Major Carter?"

"It's not Major anymore," Nick said. "I'm a civilian, now."

Westlake said. "You can serve again, if you like."

"Are you offering me a job?"

"I need competent commanders. You're a patriot like me. You know what's been happening to our country. Come over to me and you'll have an important role to play in the new military."

"What rank?"

"Full Colonel, to start. I'll give you a Battalion. How about it?"

"I don't think so," Nick said, "I've had enough of tin pot generals like you."

"Why are you Marines always so damn stubborn?" Westlake said. "You call yourself a civilian, but there are no civilians in a war."

"We're not at war."

"No?" Westlake said. "We have been at war for some years. Are you aware of the storms that just ravaged the Mid West?"

"The twisters?" Nick said. "Those were acts of nature."

"No, Carter, they were not. They are the result of interference in the ionosphere by our enemies. Do you know what SATWEP is?"

"I know it's a secret satellite weapons program and that you're in charge of it."

"Our primary mission is to develop satellite weaponry that can manipulate weather over enemy territory. Beijing and Moscow have similar programs. The Chinese are developing new technology that could tip the balance. We need a firm hand in Washington to do something about it."

"By starting riots? Killing American citizens, non-combatants? I know about Ajax and what you intend to do."

"My," Westlake said. "You have been busy. It's unfortunate, but there are always casualties in war. Do you know the story of Ajax?"

"The Greek hero in Homer's Iliad?" Nick said.

Westlake nodded in approval. "I'm glad to see that your education was adequate. Ajax was the strongest of the Greek warriors. Strength is what we lack now, thanks to Rice and his ilk. That ends today."

"This isn't a Greek poem," Nick said. "What's Ajax got to do with it?"

Talking about Ajax seemed to infuse Westlake with energy. He sucked on his cheeks. His eyes gleamed.

He's nuts. Crazy as a loon, Nick thought.

"Ajax was a hero and a credit to his nation," Westlake said. "He carried a massive shield to protect him and his comrades. I am building a shield for our country. Then no one will dare challenge us."

"It didn't protect Ajax from himself," Nick said. "If I remember the story right, he threw a temper tantrum over who would get Achilles' armor and killed himself. Doesn't sound very heroic to me."

Westlake studied him. "That was because Homer was biased in favor of Achilles. Ajax was a greater warrior than Achilles, but he never got the credit he deserved. He was cheated by Homer out of his rightful due."

"The way you were passed over for the Joint Chiefs?" Nick said.

Westlake's face flushed. "You are an insolent bastard," he said.

"Five minutes, General," Abingdon said.

Senator Martinez said, "These people are a distraction. What are you going to do with them?"

Nick looked at him. "It's people like you that give democracy a bad name," he said. "You're a disgrace. All that crap about protecting the little guy, jobs for minorities. I always knew you were a phony."

Ronnie laughed.

Martinez gave him a look of contempt. "You won't be laughing soon, Tonto."

"You asked what I'm going to do?" Westlake said. "I'm going to let them watch. It's only fitting for them to witness their failure."

"Four minutes," Abingdon said.

"Bring up a live view."

"Yes, sir."

The wall monitor displayed a computerized map of the Eastern seaboard. Changing numbers scrolled on the right side of the screen as the satellite neared the coast. Abingdon entered a string of commands. The view changed to a live shot of the Northeastern Seaboard. Boston, New York and Philadelphia were clearly visible.

Westlake said, "When I give the command, Ajax will transmit ultra high frequency radio waves and trigger the amplifiers at the target sites. The amplified waves affect everyone within several square miles. The result is a total loss of impulse control and stimulation of the reptilian brain. You get primal rage. Survival instincts are activated. Riots will begin in the targeted cities. Edmonds will have to declare martial law."

His tone was conversational. He might have been discussing the weather.

"The numbers you see on the screen tell us time to target, range, velocity relative to the Earth's surface, everything else we need to know. In another two minutes or so, Ajax will be in range."

"Sir, I've detected a deviation of almost two degrees," Abingdon said.

"Don't bother me with that sort of thing, Abingdon. Correct it."

"Yes, sir."

Abingdon moved the joystick on his console. On screen, the live picture of the US altered slightly as the satellite changed position. Selena watched him, then glanced at the readout indicating time to target. The numbers were in bright red. They descended in numbing indifference.

1:19.

1:18.

1:17.

"This satellite is something we developed at DARPA," Westlake said. "It uses an experimental nuclear propulsion system that generates a stream of ionized gases. It never runs out of fuel. I can move it anywhere I like. It does require monitoring and careful control, however."

Selena and her guard stood near the control console. Nick saw her edge a fraction closer to the panel. Their eyes met. He nodded, the movement almost undetectable.

"I don't understand something, General," Nick said. He needed to keep Westlake's attention. "What do you hope to gain by this? You'll never be able to follow through. The Army will stop you."

Westlake laughed. "Oh, really, Carter. You don't think I would do this without the support of the Army, do you? Senior officers who are not with us are being isolated as we speak. The troops follow orders. They'll be told terrorists are behind the riots, domestic agitators. There are plenty of angry groups out there we can blame. Once martial law is in place nation-wide, there won't be anything anyone can do."

Selena edged closer.

"One minute," Abingdon said.

"The President will stop you," Nick said.

"The President is about to have a fatal relapse," Westlake said. "Edmonds will be sworn in. He'll do what I say."

"He's part of this?"

Before Westlake could answer, Selena made her move. She couldn't use her arms, bound behind her. Her guard was looking at Westlake. She pivoted on one foot and swept the man's legs from under him. As he fell, she slammed her body into Abingdon and knocked him aside. She butted the joystick with her head.

On screen, the picture spun in a crazy arc as the satellite went out of control.

"NO!" Westlake shouted.

Nick body checked Westlake against the computer bench and the two of them went down. Someone was shouting. Abingdon got to his feet and started for the console. Ronnie launched himself at him and sent him flying.

On screen, the picture was a dizzying swirl. The red numbers cascaded in a blur on the right of the screen as the satellite tumbled toward the planet's surface. It entered the atmosphere. The cameras registered a brief, orange glow. Then the screen went dark.

The guards had Nick and the others pinned to the floor.

Westlake got to his feet. His face was flushed, the skin pulled tight. A vein throbbed on the side of his forehead.

"Stand them up," he said. His voice had a strangled sound. "STAND THEM UP!"

The guards pulled Nick, Selena and Ronnie to their feet. Abingdon looked shaken. Martinez seemed stunned by what had happened.

"Good job, Selena," Nick said.

"Give me your rifle," Westlake said to the man with the three stripes. A name stenciled on his shirt identified him as *Miller.*

"Sir..." he hesitated.

Westlake's voice was filled with menace. "I said give me your rifle." Miller handed him the assault rifle.

"Stand them against that wall," Westlake said.

The guards moved Nick, Selena and Ronnie over to the wall and backed away.

Westlake looked at Nick. "You have no idea what you've done."

"I know exactly what I've done. You're missing a few cards in the deck, General. Like all the other assholes who think they can decide how the world ought to be run and who should run it."

"Ajax would have made America supreme. Secure. We would have taken back our rightful place in the world. It would have initiated a New

World Order that would have lasted a thousand years."

"Where have I heard that before? We don't need a New World Order. Much less someone like you running it."

"Enough talk," Westlake said. He pulled back the bolt on the rifle, checked to see if a round was chambered. He let the bolt slide home.

Nick turned to Selena. "I love you," he said.

"I love you, too," she said.

"How touching," Westlake said. He raised the rifle.

One of the technicians called out. "Sir, we have a security breach."

"What? Where?"

"Terminal entrance, sir."

On the large screen, images appeared from cameras placed around the complex. Most of the cameras showed empty hallways and rooms. Two showed men moving down the hallways. They were in full tactical gear, black uniforms, vests, helmets. They carried MP-5s and a breaching ram.

"Looks like the cavalry's here, General," Nick said. "That makes us worth more alive than dead. You need hostages."

Westlake considered and lowered the rifle. Nick let out his breath. He hadn't realized he was holding it.

"You'll stay alive for now," Westlake said.

"What do we do?" Martinez asked.

"We evacuate and fight another day." Westlake turned to Miller. "You watch these. Bring up the rear with them. Any more trouble, kill them."

"Sir."

Westlake went to the computer console and pressed a sequence of keys. A door opened in one wall in the bunker. Nick saw a passage beyond.

"This way. Hurry up," Westlake said.

Westlake and Martinez went into the passage beyond the door, followed by Abingdon and the rest of the technicians. There were two other guards besides Miller.

"You go ahead," he said to them. "I'll bring up the rear with the prisoners."

"You sure?"

"Go. Protect the General."

The two men entered the passage. Miller looked at Nick. "You were a Marine?" he said.

"Yes. What about it?"

"So was I."

"What do you expect me to say? Semper Fi?"

"Westlake was going to shoot you. It's not right."

"He's crazy," Nick said. "He'll take you and everyone else down with him."

"I heard everything he said, about Ajax and what it would do. I didn't know that. I thought it just caused trouble."

"He used it against a city in Russia," Nick said. "Thousands of people died. The city was left in ruins. He was going to do the same to Riyadh and London, but we stopped him."

"Riyadh *and* London?" Miller said. "That doesn't make sense."

"It does if you're crazy," Nick said.

Miller looked at the screen. The black-clad shock troops were close.

"It's not right," he said again, "shooting unarmed prisoners. I cut you loose, you put in a word for me?"

"You cut us loose, they'll probably give you a medal," Nick said.

Miller set his rifle down. He took out a knife and cut the ties on Nick's wrists, then Selena's and Ronnie's. Nick rubbed his hands together, getting circulation back.

Ronnie bent down and picked up the rifle. "What about Westlake?" he said.

"He's long gone by now. Let the others go after him." He turned to Miller. "You did the right thing."

Miller said, "Westlake has some kind of backup plan."

"What plan?" Nick said.

Miller shrugged. "I don't know. I heard him talking with Martinez. Something with a Greek name like Ajax, only different. A second satellite."

"Drop your weapons!" Nick looked at the doorway. It bristled with rifles pointing in their direction.

"Better set it down, Ronnie." Nick raised his hands.

Ronnie raised one hand and held the rifle away from his body. He bent over in slow motion and set the rifle on the floor.

Selena raised her hands.

"That was sweet," she said to Nick, "what you said when Westlake was about to shoot us."

CHAPTER 55

The tactical unit in black was part of an FBI SWAT team. Once things got sorted out, Nick called Harker.

"Nick. Are you all right?"

"Yes. Westlake and Martinez got away. Korov is dead."

"What?" she said, "Martinez? Who's Martinez? Korov is dead? You'd better start at the beginning."

Nick ran it down. When he was done, there was silence at the other end of the connection.

"You still there, Director?"

"I'm here. What's happening where you are now?"

"The team leader sent men after Westlake and the others, but I don't think they'll have much luck. How did the FBI know about this place?"

"Hood sent them. He gambled that the Bureau wasn't part of whatever was going on. He went to see Rice. Hood briefed him and got full authority. He knew where the underground entrances were and told the Feds where to go."

"They got here just in time. Westlake had us lined up against a wall and was going to shoot us. He's crazy, Director. When he escaped, one of his men kept us back and freed us. He thinks there's a back up plan. Selena brought down the satellite, but there might be another one, with a Greek code name. If there is, and Westlake gets to somewhere that lets him control it, he could still make a lot of trouble."

"Hood and the Bureau are tracking down officers who may have been involved. The DOJ is trying to sort it out but it's a snake pit. Rice has reassumed the duties of the Presidency. When Hood told him about the Ajax Protocol, he almost blew a gasket. He's pissed."

"I'll bet."

"He ordered Hood and the FBI to pull out all the stops. The Director of Homeland Security is under arrest, though it's not being called that. Officially, she's on administrative leave until it can be determined what role she played."

"What about Edmonds?"

"There's no evidence against him, but Rice has isolated him. He has no power. He couldn't order a cheeseburger in a fast food joint. We didn't know about Senator Martinez. I don't think Rice is going to like that when I tell him. The DOJ will follow up."

"There have to be other politicians involved," Nick said. "Look at all the preparations they made to take over. They've been getting ready for a long time. The new FEMA centers, the AFVs for Homeland Security, all that. It took political clout to do that and it can't be a coincidence. It's a long-standing conspiracy."

"The Ajax Protocol," Harker said. "They were really going to implement it."

"We have to find Westlake," Nick said.

"I'm still in Texas with Stephanie, but we're going back to Virginia. I want you and the others back as well," Harker said. "We can't do anything without more intel. You might as well be where we have resources."

"All right."

"I'm sorry about Korov," Harker said.

"Yeah," Nick said.

"I'll make the arrangements to send him home. I'll talk to Vysotsky after we're done here."

Selena saw him put his phone away.

"What did Elizabeth say?"

"She wants us back East. Nothing we can do until we get an idea of where Westlake went, or what he might do."

"I'll be glad to get back," she said. She paused. "What about Korov?"

"Harker is taking care of it."

"He saved my life, Nick. He jumped in front of me."

"I know."

"Why did he do that?" her eyes were moist.

"I don't know," Nick said. "I don't know why he did that. I don't mean this to sound cold, but I'm glad it's not you lying back there."

She put her arms around him. "Let's go home," she said.

CHAPTER 56

Hood had someone from the Agency waiting for Elizabeth and Stephanie at Andrews. He gave them the keys to a black suburban, Ashley if there was anything else he could do for them and left them to it.

They stopped on the way and retrieved Burps from the cat boarding house. They parked in front of Project HQ. When they went into the building, they both stopped short. Stephanie set the cat down. He seemed nervous and uncertain. It was easy to see why.

Elizabeth looked at the mess left behind by the Homeland Security agents sent by Edmonds and swore under her breath. She tried to tell herself that they were under orders, doing their job. She wondered if that's what people said in Germany in the 30s, when they saw thugs destroying shops and breaking into homes.

"Those bastards," Stephanie said. "They didn't have to do this."

Elizabeth's office looked like it had been looted. The desk drawers had been pulled out and dumped on the floor. The desk itself had been tipped on its side. The locked drawers had been smashed open. Her computer monitor was trashed. Her chair was slashed, the guts of the cushion spilling out where someone had cut it open, searching for God knew what. Half a dozen plants in pots had been ripped out and strewn around the room.

The rest of the floor wasn't much better. Stephanie's office had been searched, but her monitor still functioned. Downstairs, the room where Lamont had been staying was torn apart.

The armory was still locked. It took serious electronic savvy to breach the security for that room. The computers were untouched. They were big, taking up an entire room, not the kind of thing you could throw in the back of a truck.

"Do you think they got into them?" Elizabeth asked. She stood with Stephanie looking at the Crays.

"I doubt it," Stephanie said. "My firewalls are better than NSA's or the Pentagon's. There aren't more than two or three people in the world who might be able to get past them. None of them work for the government."

"Edmonds really makes me angry," Elizabeth said. "I knew he was an ass, but I didn't think he'd do something like this."

"Do you think he's part of the plot?"

"I don't know, but somehow I don't think so. Would you trust a man like that to keep a secret?"

"Not a chance," Stephanie said.

"I think it will turn out that Westlake manipulated him, had him thinking we were a threat to national security, something like that."

"I don't think Edmonds will be a problem in the future. The President will force him to resign."

"At least Rice is all right. I'm worried about Lamont."

"So am I," Stephanie said.

"I talked to his doctor earlier, while you were asleep on the plane. He has a staph infection. They haven't got it under control. He's weak, barely hanging on."

Stephanie sighed. "When do Nick and the others get back?"

"Later today," Elizabeth said.

They went back upstairs to Elizabeth's office.

"Ajax was developed by DARPA under Westlake's oversight," Elizabeth said. "I want you to look at everything else he did with them. See if you can find anything besides Ajax with a Greek name."

"That's a long shot."

"I know, but we have to figure out what Westlake has in mind. It could be something DARPA developed. Whatever it is, it can't be good. While you're doing that, I'm going to call Vysotsky. He needs to know about Korov."

"Better you than me," Stephanie said.

"Let's get this desk up," Elizabeth said.

They set the desk back on its feet.

"I'll get started," Stephanie said. She went to her office while Elizabeth called Vysotsky.

Rice had talked with Harker and given her access to the Pentagon's computers. *If only they knew,* Stephanie thought as she entered the access codes. She couldn't remember how many times she'd hacked into the Pentagon servers to find out something the Pentagon or DARPA didn't want anyone to know about. It felt strange to go in with official blessings.

She gained entry to the DARPA servers. She began looking at weapons recently developed or under development, anything with a Greek code name. She'd found Ajax. If there was anything there, she'd find it.

The heart of DARPA was a hundred of the most brilliant technological minds in America. Originally conceived by Eisenhower as a brain tank and technological development group for both civilian and military projects, DARPA's mission had been subverted in the 70s. Now it focused only on the military applications.

Stephanie worked her way through a list of current and past projects that read like scenes from a Terminator movie or pages from an H.G. Wells novel. An hour later, she still hadn't found anything with a Greek name or the suggestion of one. Something nagged at her about the list. She couldn't pin it down. What was it?

Stephanie got up and made a fresh pot of coffee. She pored a cup and sat back down at her computer. Then she realized what was bothering her. Ajax wasn't on the list. Where was it? Why not there with the others?

Ajax was a hero in Homer's poem about the siege of Troy, she thought. *Maybe Westlake used another name like that.* She tried to remember what she'd learned about Homer's Iliad in school. It wasn't much.

The Greek hero was Achilles.

She entered a new command path combining Westlake's name and Achilles. The screen gave her a familiar message:

ACCESS DENIED

Yes! So much for official access codes and Pentagon co-operation, she thought.

As she'd done with Ajax, she called up the program she'd written to get through encrypted firewalls. While she waited for the computer to sort through possibilities, she thought about Lamont. He'd survived enemy fire and years of combat, only to finally be brought down by a lousy bug. Sometimes Stephanie wondered how anyone could think they knew what the day would bring.

It made her think of Lucas. She was looking forward to seeing him later. If she could get away. If there wasn't another damn crisis.

The screen cleared. She'd expected to find a single file. Instead, she'd accessed a list.

ACHILLES
AJAX
CYCLOPS
PROMETHEUS
SIREN
ZEUS

Plenty of Greek names, each from Homer's Iliad. She clicked on Achilles and began reading. It was the code name for an EMP weapon that wiped out the grid in an entire country without the need for a messy nuclear explosion. Stephanie made a note. Maybe Westlake was planning on taking down the American grid. That would create chaos, as Ajax would have. But how would that help him now? The Ajax plot was blown. She'd bring it to Elizabeth and the others.

The Ajax file told her what she already knew, that there was a satellite with a weapon capable of disrupting human brainwaves and sending people into frenzied rage. There were technical drawings and specifications. She moved to Cyclops.

Cyclops was an extensive upgrade to the satellite surveillance programs already in place. It didn't seem like Westlake would be concerned about that as a backup. She went to the next name on the list.

Prometheus was a satellite, like Ajax. As she read, she shivered. Prometheus was armed with six 20 megaton hydrogen bombs on the tips of missiles packed with experimental evasion technology that made them all but impossible to intercept. Without thinking, Steph glanced up at the ceiling. Somewhere high overhead, Prometheus circled the globe. If this was Westlake's backup...she left the thought unfinished.

What else is on this damn list? she thought.

Siren was a sonic weapon that vibrated solids at a high frequency, causing the molecular bonding to break down. Structures like bridges and buildings would literally disintegrate. Siren could be used on people, with unpleasant effects.

Last on the list was Zeus. Zeus was an ongoing development of the SATWEP program, with the goal of creating super storms at will over an enemy's homeland.

Her coffee was cold. Stephanie got up and headed for Elizabeth's office.

CHAPTER 57

Alexei Vysotsky set the phone down and sat for a moment, thinking of Korov, dead in America. He cursed and slammed his fist down on his desk. The door to his office opened and his aide looked in.

"Sir? Is everything all right?"

Vysotsky picked up an ashtray and hurled it at the startled man. It shattered against the wall.

"Out! Get out, now!"

The aide closed the door. Quickly.

Korov! Damn the day he had listened to Harker. Damn the Americans.

Vysotsky took a deep breath, another. He reached into his desk drawer and took out a bottle of vodka and a glass. He poured four fingers of the clear liquid into the glass and downed it. He poured another. The vodka ignited inside him. The warmth spread through his body, calmed him. He took out a *papirosa*, a long tube of paper and harsh, Russian tobacco. It was a peasant's cigarette, a habit left over from the old days when luxuries like American cigarettes were impossible to obtain. He pinched the end together and lit up, exhaled a stream of blue smoke toward the ceiling.

He thought about the Americans. Everything to do with America had always been a problem. He'd thought that he could work with Harker, even though she was the enemy.

Now my best officer is dead. That's what I get for trusting Americans. Lie down with dogs, get fleas.

He thought about Harker and her Project team. It was a good thing she didn't know about California.

In 1988 he'd been an ambitious young officer in the KGB, back in the days when the Russian security apparatus was far flung and almost invincible. Before *Glasnost* and the shame that followed. He had been adept at wet work, targeted assassinations carried out for the glory of the Motherland. A traitor had been discovered, an American recruited years before, supposedly a disgruntled CIA agent. The man had fooled them. He was a double, taking his orders from Langley and feeding Moscow false information. Who knew how many Russian lives had been lost, what damage had been done because of his betrayal? Alexei hadn't needed to think much about killing him.

It hadn't been hard to arrange the car accident. It was simple bad luck that the target had his family with him when the car went over a cliff. All except his daughter Selena, who now worked for Harker.

Vysotsky scuffed out his cigarette on the edge of Beria's desk. The irony did not escape him. The daughter of one of his assignments, now a key part of Harker's elite team. A dangerous woman. If she ever found out that he was responsible for her family's deaths, she'd come after him. But she never would. There was no way she would ever find out.

No way.

Vysotsky poured another vodka.

CHAPTER 58

Stephanie told the team about the DARPA weapons in Westlake's encrypted files.

"He could go after the grid" Ronnie said. "You take it down, out come the lowlifes looking for a free TV and you get troops on the corner. Martial law, like he wanted."

"That's what I thought at first," Stephanie said. "But things have changed. Before, Westlake had Homeland Security lined up and support from some key generals and politicians. That's gone. Taking the grid down would cause a lot of disruption, but it wouldn't have the same result."

"What's left for him to do?" Ronnie asked. "Like you say, his support is gone. He can't pull off his plan. I was him, I'd disappear. Get a new identity and go underground. Someplace like Brazil."

"Yeah, but you're not him," Nick said, "and Miller said he heard Westlake mention a backup plan to Martinez."

"We need to look at this differently," Selena said.

"What do you mean?" Elizabeth picked up her pen and began tapping it on her desk.

Tap. Tap. Taptaptap.

"We've been trying to figure out what he might do but we haven't thought about why he would do it."

"Go on."

"We need to get inside his mind if we want to predict his actions, or try to. He's finished as far as starting a government takeover. So what's left?"

Elizabeth set her pen down. "I guess that depends on who he is. What makes him tick."

"There ought to be a psych profile in his jacket," Nick said.

"It probably wouldn't tell us much," Stephanie said. "This man reached the highest rank possible in a world of psych testing and rigid structure. He fooled everyone. I don't think we're going to learn anything from it."

"We haven't been asking the right questions," Selena said. "So far we've been asking ourselves what he's going to do and where he might have gone. A better question might be why did he want to take over the government in the first place?"

"Why would anyone?" Nick said. "He wanted power."

"More than that," Selena said. "He thought he was going to make America strong."

"We're already strong," Stephanie said.

"But Westlake saw attempts to gain peaceful solutions on the world stage as a sign of weakness."

"Some would say he had a point," Ronnie said. "I wouldn't trust any of the so-called world leaders out there, no matter what treaties they signed. Treaties are only pieces of paper. My people know all about treaties."

Elizabeth said, "Let's stick to his motivation. Nick, you said he wanted power. That seems obvious, but it doesn't tell us anything we didn't know."

"It's not so much that he wanted it," Nick said, "it's what he was prepared to do to get it. That puts him in the company of the psychopaths. People like Caligula and Pol Pot."

"You think he's a psychopath?" Selena said.

"What else would you call someone who's ready to kill thousands of people so he can get what he wants?"

"Westlake believed in what he was doing," Stephanie said. "That tells us something."

"People like that always have a good reason for murdering everyone."

"I can guess what he might do," Selena said.

"What?" Ronnie said.

"He's finished, right? I mean, there isn't any way he can gain what he wanted."

"Of course not. What are you thinking, Selena?" Elizabeth asked.

"Westlake is a megalomaniac. A narcissist. He thinks the world revolves around him. He wants to be remembered. When people like him have nothing left to lose, the only thing left is revenge."

"Oh, my God," Stephanie said.

"Steph?" Harker looked at her.

"He's going to use Prometheus," Stephanie said. She began twisting bracelets on her arm. "It's armed with heavy nukes. If he can control it, he could start a world war.."

"There have to be safeguards on it," Selena said. "Fail safes."

"He'd have to know the codes," Nick said.

"He was in charge of the weaponized satellites," Elizabeth said. "He must know the codes." Elizabeth set her pen down. "You could be right, Steph. Westlake has nothing to lose and sooner or later he's going down. He could try and take everyone with him."

"He could use Prometheus as a negotiating point," Nick said.

"It wouldn't work. The Pentagon would just change the firing codes. They should change them anyway. I'd better call the President," Elizabeth said.

CHAPTER 59

A half hour later, Elizabeth's worst fears were confirmed.

"The President didn't know about Prometheus."

"That figures," Nick said. "Someone thought it was need to know and Rice wasn't on the list."

"That's not all. He got the Joint Chiefs on the line and told them what we thought. After they got over their surprise that anyone knew about Prometheus except them, they assured him it couldn't happen. Ten minutes later they called back. They can't access the satellite. Normal control procedures have been locked out. No one knows when that happened, or how. The satellite sends regular status reports and nothing indicated any change."

"Westlake," Nick said.

"It certainly looks like it."

"Now what, Director?" Ronnie said.

"We might be in better shape than we think," Elizabeth said. "I don't see how Westlake can access the satellite. He'd need to get on one of the bases where they have the right equipment. Everyone is looking for him. He'll never get close. You can't call that satellite up on a CB."

"Maybe not a CB, but he doesn't have to be on a military base," Selena said.

"What do you mean?" Elizabeth looked at her.

"All he needs is a powerful enough radio and the right frequency. If he's got a transmitter and an antenna hidden somewhere, he can reach the satellite when it's in the right position."

"If that's the case, we're screwed," Nick said. "We'll never find a hidden location in time."

Elizabeth's phone rang.

"Harker. Yes, Clarence."

She looked at them. *Hood*, she mouthed. She listened. "Thank you, Clarence. I'll keep you updated."

She set the phone down. "The FBI found Senator Martinez."

"He knows where Westlake is," Nick said. "Let's ask him."

"We can't. Martinez went home and shot himself."

"Uh, oh," Ronnie said.

"It gets worse. Martinez left a note. He said he didn't want to be part of what was coming."

"That's all?"

"That's all."

"That doesn't sound good," Ronnie said.

"We have to assume Westlake has gone over the edge," Elizabeth said, "and that he intends to launch those missiles."

"What are the targets?" Nick asked.

"Programmable. They could go anywhere."

"Can we knock down the satellite?" Selena asked. "Missiles? Some secret plane that can get up there? Anything?"

"No. Only a missile could reach it and Prometheus is programmed to defend itself against missile attack. The Pentagon says the missiles wouldn't get through."

"The Pentagon could be wrong, or maybe they don't want to blow up their billion dollar toy on our say so."

"Even if we could blow it up, those are hydrogen bombs up there," Elizabeth said. "They'll go off and they're loaded with plutonium. The explosion would poison the atmosphere for generations. It would create an EMP burst that would blanket half the globe and take out electrical power everywhere. The results would be catastrophic."

"Didn't anyone think about stuff like that before they put it up there?" Ronnie said.

"Apparently not."

Ronnie shook his head.

"Westlake would need a place to keep a transmitter," Nick said, "someplace no one would think of. Has anyone checked to see if he owns property somewhere, like a vacation home? Somewhere he could put up an antenna without attracting attention?"

"They did," Elizabeth said. "He doesn't own any property aside from his house. They searched that. They didn't find anything."

"Is he married?" Selena asked. "His wife might know something."

"He was married, but she died a few years ago," Elizabeth said.

"Another dead end," Ronnie said.

Nick rolled his eyes. "Come on, Ronnie."

"Maybe not," Selena said. "What was the wife's name?"

CHAPTER 60

Westlake parked the rental car on the steep slope leading up to the cabin. In winter, the driveway was impassable. When his wife had been alive, they'd tried to come here at least once a year during the good months. The cabin had belonged to her father. The county records still had it listed in her name. It had been the perfect place to install the transmitter.

The cabin sat below the tree line at 9,000 feet. The antenna was unnoticeable unless you were looking for it. No one ever came this way, except for an occasional hunter. Alice's father had liked the privacy of the wilderness.

He climbed onto the porch and unlocked the front door. The front room smelled of dust and closed space and stale mouse urine. Mice had always been a problem up here. But now it didn't matter. He wouldn't be coming here again.

Westlake opened a window. He went out through the kitchen to the generator shed in back. The generator was solar powered, running off energy stored in deep cycle batteries connected to an inverter. It was silent and provided enough power for the refrigerator, the lights, the radio. Pure sine wave power that wouldn't fry the transceiver in the bedroom. The system panel showed full charge and a green light. Westlake turned on the power.

The afternoon was bright and sunny, but he could feel the chill of the high country. He went back into the cabin, where a fire was already laid in the fireplace. He lit the kindling and watched it spread until the logs caught. He felt detached, as if someone else stood there, watching the orange and yellow flames.

Westlake went into the back room, where a large radio transceiver sat on a wooden table next to a computer monitor and keyboard. He turned everything on. The display lit with an orange glow, locked onto the frequency for Prometheus. Once the satellite was in range, all he needed to do was to transmit one preprogrammed signal and Prometheus would launch its nuclear spawn.

The missiles had been programmed months ago, targeted on China, Russia and Iran. The Pentagon had to point them somewhere, and the Pentagon technicians were sure they could always re-program the missiles for different targets as needed.

The Pentagon technicians were wrong. Westlake had used Phil Abingdon's expertise to alter the command codes. Prometheus answered only to him. Like the god himself, Westlake would bring the fires of heaven to earth.

He entered a new string of commands on the computer, re-programming one of the missiles with a new target.

Washington.

Westlake had never believed in surrender. Like Ajax, he planned to kill himself in protest. Unlike Ajax, he would take those who had been the instruments of his humiliation with him. It was only right.

He walked from the radio room to the front of the cabin and went to a wooden cabinet. He took out a bottle of whiskey and a glass. There were mouse droppings in the cabinet. He took the bottle and the glass and sat down in a chair in front of the fire. He poured a drink, held it up to the firelight and downed it. He poured another.

Westlake looked at the fire blazing in the stone fireplace. A picture taken in happier days of Westlake, his wife and his son rested on the mantle. Alice would have appreciated the fire. She'd always liked it up here in the mountains. She'd liked a fire on a chilly evening.

His thoughts drifted in a random haze. If only his son hadn't died. If only Alice had lived, things might have been different. In a few hours all those who had opposed him would find out what a mistake they had made. The satellite would come into range early in the morning.

For now, he could relax and enjoy the warmth of the fire and the whiskey. In the morning, the world would change forever. Westlake knew he would always be remembered.

He would be immortal, like Homer's heroes.

It was a satisfying feeling.

CHAPTER 61

"We've got it," Elizabeth said. "Westlake's wife owned a cabin in Colorado. It's still listed in her name. It's up in the high country, on the Western Slope. I'm sending you to find out if he's there."

"I know that part of the country," Selena said. "I grew up on the Western Slope."

"Why not call in the Feds?" Nick asked. "They've got a big presence in Colorado. Or SOCOM?"

"I talked it over with Rice," Elizabeth said. "He wants us to do it. He doesn't trust the military at the moment. It's not certain all of the plotters have been identified. Someone could know where Westlake is and tip him off. That leaves out SOCOM."

"What about the Feds?"

"The Bureau can get clumsy. Remember Ruby Ridge and Waco? If Westlake saw them coming, he'd launch. You have a better chance of getting to him before he can launch. Assuming he's there, of course."

"We'd have spotted him if he'd tried to leave the country," Nick said. "It makes sense he'd go to ground where he thought no one could find him."

"You're wheels up as soon as you can get to Andrews," Elizabeth said. "The Air Force will get you to Colorado Springs and from there to Aspen. There's no place to set a chopper down near the cabin without Westlake hearing it. From Aspen, you'll have to drive."

"How far?"

"It's around seventy miles or so. He's in a remote area. Mostly only hunters go up that way.

I've already tasked a satellite. Steph, can you bring up the shot?"

Stephanie entered the commands. The wall monitor lit with a live satellite view of the area where Westlake's father-in-law had built his getaway cabin. It was rugged country. A winding dirt road led to a tiny dot Nick assumed was the cabin. It was almost invisible among the trees.

"The satellite will be out of range soon," Elizabeth said. "Zoom in, please, Steph."

The picture grew large. Now they could make out more details. A dark colored truck was parked under the trees near the cabin. The picture was good enough to see smoke rising from the chimney. There was a shed in the back of the cabin.

"Someone's there," Nick said.

"It has to be him," Selena said.

"No power lines."

"He's got solar panels on that shed," Ronnie said. "Probably runs everything on batteries."

"There's the antenna," Selena said. She pointed at a mast on the roof of the building, topped with something that looked like a TV dish.

"Bingo," Ronnie said.

"You'd better get your gear together," Elizabeth said.

Down in the armory they sorted out what they wanted to take with them. This wasn't a long term engagement. They could keep it light. Pistols and MP5s. Flashbangs. Comm gear. Armor. Ammo. Night vision optics. They'd drive close to the cabin and go in on foot.

Ronnie finished what he was doing and went upstairs. Nick's ear itched. He scratched it. Selena saw him.

"What's the matter?"

"Nothing. Just an itch."

"Why don't I believe you?" she said.

"I don't have a good feeling about this," he said. "It seems straight forward enough, but something feels off."

"Maybe it's anticipation. You know, like pre-game jitters."

"Maybe." He pulled the straps tight on his pack. "I've been thinking."

Selena looked at him.

"We need to set a date for the wedding." The words were rushed. "When Westlake was going to kill us, all I could think about was you. I don't want to waste any more time. I'll say what I said before. Will you marry me?"

"Nick." Selena had been checking her MP-5. She set it down on a table and took his hand. "This has got to be a first," she said.

"What is?"

"Getting proposed to in an armory."

"I asked you before, remember?"

"Yes, but this is different."

"So?"

"Yes, I'll marry you."

"Hey." Ronnie called down the stairs. "Get a move on down there."

Nick kissed her. "Come on," he said, "lets go get the son of a bitch."

CHAPTER 62

They'd made it to Aspen and up into the mountains in record time, but it was still past midnight by the time they reached the cabin. The moon cast enough light to see the building in the dark shadows of the trees. A thin, damp mist rose from the forest floor. Nick studied the scene through his binoculars. His breath made little clouds of condensation in the night air. At this altitude, the temperatures dropped fast after dark.

They lay under tall evergreens on sloping ground, less than a hundred feet away from Westlake's mountain retreat. Selena was on Nick's right, Ronnie on his left. The cabin had a wide, covered porch. Light shone through a window in the front. Smoke from the chimney gave the night a pleasant, familiar scent. Nick had always loved the smell of wood burning in a fireplace. It reminded him of his place in California, before it had burned to the ground.

Maybe I should rebuild it.

The thought annoyed him. He pushed it away.

"I don't see anyone," Nick said. He handed the binoculars to Ronnie.

"Not a good angle to see in," Ronnie said. "We need to get closer."

He pressed a button on his wristwatch. A faint glow illuminated the dial. It was a little before two in the morning.

"Maybe he's asleep," Ronnie said.

"Not likely, with that light on." Selena scratched her nose.

"Watch out for trip wires," Nick said. "He may have set something, just in case."

They got up and moved toward the cabin in a crouch until they reached level ground. Silent as the moonlight, they stepped onto the porch. Nick held up his hand. From where he was, he could see through the window.

A cheerful fire burned in a stone fireplace. There was a leather arm chair and a rocker on either side of a circular rug laid down on the floor in front of the fire. Nick could see the kitchen area and a wooden dining table and four chairs. It looked like a scene painted by Norman Rockwell. He half expected a kindly old lady with spectacles and a gingham dress to come into the room, carrying a steaming apple pie.

There was another room in the back. Westlake came out of it and walked across the room. He was halfway across when the porch window shattered and the sound of a high powered rifle echoed hard and flat through the trees. Westlake dove for the floor.

"What the hell," Ronnie said

They scrambled off the porch and ran for the trees. Three more shots came out of the darkness. Ronnie stumbled and went down. Nick and Selena made it to the trees,

"Ronnie," Nick called. "How bad?"

There was no answer. Ronnie lay without moving.

Nick said, "We have to get the shooter."

"Who is it?" Selena said. "A sentry?"

"I don't think so. That first shot was aimed at Westlake."

"I saw muzzle flashes over there." She pointed at a tight packed cluster of trees.

"Lay down fire. I'll flank them. Ready?"

She nodded.

"Now."

Selena opened up with her MP-5 on full auto, spraying quick bursts at the trees where she'd seen the flashes of a rifle. Nick got to his feet and ran to his left. Selena could see dark bits and branches flying off the trees as she raked the stand. She used up the magazine, ejected, rammed in another, fired again.

Whoever was in the trees let loose a volley. She could see the flashes in the dark. Bullets whined off the ground near her. She tried to press herself into the earth. She heard Nick's MP-5. Then the night was still.

"Clear," Nick called.

The man he'd shot lay on his back. He was dressed in green and black camouflage. A scoped assault rifle lay beside him on the ground. Blood ran from his mouth. He coughed, said something. Nick bent down to hear.

"Kill him," the man said. "You will...rewarded." He choked. Blood bubbled out of his mouth. He died.

Selena got up and ran over to Ronnie. He stirred as she got to him. She helped him sit up. "Come on. We're exposed." She cast a nervous look at the building. The lights were still out. They moved to the side of the cabin. There was only a small bathroom window there, high up. They stopped behind a large rock outcrop. It gave good cover.

Ronnie had a deep gash on his forehead. Selena could see a lump forming. When he'd gone down, he'd hit his head on a rock.

"Stupid," he said. "Tripped and knocked myself out." he said. He felt his head. His hand came away bloody.

"Probably a good thing," she said. "We thought you took a hit. The shooter must have thought the same thing."

Nick came over to them, crouched low. "There was only one shooter," he said. "He said something odd before he died."

"What?" Selena asked.

"He said, *kill him.* He meant Westlake. Then he said I'd be rewarded. At least I think that's what he meant. "

"That is odd," Selena said.

Nick turned to Ronnie. "How are you, amigo?"

"Just a bad headache. I'm all right."

"What now?" Selena asked. "After that, Westlake knows we're here."

"That's for sure," Nick said. "Maybe we can reason with him."

"He's a psycho, Nick. How are you going to reason with him?" Ronnie rubbed his forehead.

"We won't know unless we try. If we go through that door, he'll launch."

"You expect him to open the door and invite us in?"

"Let's find out."

Nick stood up. It was a safe bet. The bath room window was frosted glass and closed. He couldn't be seen from the cabin.

"General Westlake," Nick called. "Let's talk."

There was no answer.

"Appeal to his vanity," Selena said. "Make him feel important."

Nick thought for a moment.

"Sir, this is a historic moment," he called. "The fate of the world is in your hands. Generations to come will want to know what you were thinking tonight."

Ronnie pointed his finger at his throat and pantomimed gagging.

They heard the sound of a door opening. "Is that you, Carter?" Westlake's voice came from the darkened cabin. "How did you find me?"

"It wasn't easy, sir. You covered your trail well."

Ronnie rolled his eyes.

"I know you want to stop me, Carter. But you can't. You want to talk, come out where I can see you, in front of the cabin. Leave your weapon. The satellite is overhead. I have a dead man's switch in my hand that keys the transmitter. If you shoot me, the missiles will launch. There's nothing you can do about it."

Nick kept his voice low. "Ronnie, are you all right?"

"Yeah."

"Selena, there has to be a back door. You and Ronnie go in. Be quiet. Disable that transmitter. I'll keep him busy."

"What about that switch?" Selena said.

"I'll figure something out. Try not to let him know you're there."

"I'm waiting, Carter." Westlake's voice had an odd lilt to it, as if he were amused about something. His voice sounded a little slurred.

"Yes, sir," Nick called. "I'm putting down my weapon. I'm coming out."

"Nick, he could shoot you," Selena said.

"His ego won't let him, at least not right away. Go."

They got up and faded into the dark. Nick stood up, raised his hands and walked out in front of the cabin. Westlake stood on the porch, pointing a Colt .45 at Nick with his right hand. His left hand was clenched around a silver cylinder. His thumb was pressed down on the top.

Dead man's switch.

"That was clever of you, Carter, escaping back in Denver."

"Thank you, sir." *Careful. Don't overdo it.*

"I know what you're doing. Flattery isn't going to make me change my mind."

"I wouldn't dream of it, General."

"Was that you that shot at me?"

"No, sir. It was someone waiting in the trees."

"You eliminated him?"

"Yes, sir."

"My former colleagues are unhappy with me," Westlake said. "They probably sent him. Too bad they won't have any time to reflect on their mistake."

I don't like the sound of that, Nick thought. He moved closer. The muzzle of the .45 was pointed straight at him. Nick had never noticed how large a Model 1911 looked from the wrong end.

"That's far enough, Carter." Nick stopped moving and kept his hands where Westlake could see them.

"Why are you doing this, General? If you launch those missiles, millions of people will die. You'll be vilified as a mass murderer."

Where are Selena and Ronnie? Nick thought.

Now that he was closer, Nick could see that Westlake was unstable. *The shrink would have a word for it*, Nick thought. *Whatever it is, it's not good.*

Westlake was unshaven. He had the hand with the switch pressed against his chest, as if he needed to hold it steady. His cheek twitched. The hand with the gun trembled. It was almost imperceptible. It wasn't enough to spoil his aim. His eyes had a strange gleam, an unnatural wetness.

A voice in his mind said *He's going to do it.*

Up until that moment, he'd held out the hope that Westlake could be made to change his mind. Looking at him, Nick knew it wasn't going to happen. Westlake already had the look of a walking dead man, someone who had nothing left to lose.

Keep him talking, the voice in his head said. "Why did you start all this?" Nick said.

"You really have to ask? The world thinks we're a laughing stock. Congress is a collection of self-serving fools who can't see past the next election and the money they need to keep their job. We've gotten weak. America needs a strong leader, someone who backs up policy with action, someone who won't tolerate dissent."

"It's a democracy, General. Dissent is part of how we got to be a nation."

"We're not a democracy, Carter. We never were. We're a republic, like Rome once was. In more ways than one. Like Rome, the system has become corrupted, dysfunctional. It must be transformed. Prometheus is the instrument of transformation."

He's completely nuts, Nick thought.

Behind Westlake, Nick saw Selena. She moved with a graceful slowness, like a cat pacing toward a mouse, one step at a time. If she could clamp down on the switch before he knew she was there, maybe they could stop this. Maybe Ronnie could shut down the transmitter before Westlake released the switch.

Maybe.

Ronnie stood in the doorway of the back bedroom. He saw the computer and transmitter on a table next to the back wall. The radio was about the size of a desk top printer. It was painted olive drab. The face bristled with black knobs and white calibrating marks. There was a rectangular window in the center with a digital readout. The readout glowed in the darkened room with black numbers dialed to Armageddon against an orange background. A black cable ran from the back of the radio and up through the ceiling.

Must be the antenna, he thought.

All he had to do was turn it off. Or disconnect the antenna. Ronnie went into the room. He couldn't see how to shut the radio down. There were a lot of switches and no time to figure it out. He looked for a plug. The unit was hardwired into the wall.

A black coaxial cable for the antenna ended at a screw-on connection on the back of the transmitter. Something had been gnawing on the cable. Bare copper and torn white insulation showed through the black sheathing. *Mice have been at this,* Ronnie thought. He reached down and tried to unscrew the antenna connection. It was tight. He felt it begin to turn.

Out front, Nick saw Selena move. Westlake sensed her step. He smiled at Nick.

"Don't do it!" Nick shouted.

Westlake took his thumb off the switch.

Ronnie pulled the cable away as the knurled fitting of the antenna came free. A bright arc of electricity jumped from the transmitter to the cable and crackled around the spots where the insulation was eaten through. It felt like grabbing a hot poker. Blue, electric light danced over the transmitter and around Ronnie's hand as he grasped the cable. His muscles spasmed and he went down on the floor. Flame started where the antenna cable was fastened to the wall.

Unaware of what was happening in the cabin, Westlake laughed. It had the sound of insanity in it. "Too late, Carter."

Selena brought the edge of her palm down hard down on Westlake's collar bone. He dropped the switch. The big .45 went off. The slug slammed Nick in his armor and knocked him down. Selena hit Westlake in the neck with a vicious swipe of her elbow. He crumpled to the porch. She kicked him in the head, kicked the Colt off the porch and ran to Nick, gasping on his back.

"Nick."

"S'all right." He struggled for breath. "Good armor."

"Nick, he used the switch."

"I know."

Nick's breath was coming back. Getting hit by a .45 was a new experience. The front of his armor was flattened, the plate dented.

Nick sat up. "Where's Ronnie?"

"Inside."

Selena helped him to his feet. Westlake lay unconscious.

"You kill him?" Nick asked.

"No. We'll let someone else do that."

"We were too late," Nick said. "Selena, damn it, we were too late." His voice was resigned.

"I smell smoke," she said. As she said it, a cloud of black smoke roiled out of the open front door. Nick got to his feet. It was hard to breathe. He felt like he'd been kicked by a mule. They looked at each other. Ronnie hadn't come out of the cabin.

They ran inside. Flickering, orange light lit the back room. Smoke poured through the doorway. Inside the room, Ronnie lay on the floor, dazed by the electric shock. The room was burning. Flames clawed at the wooden ceiling.

Nick coughed, every cough a stab of pain from his injured ribs. His eyes stung from the acrid smoke. They dragged Ronnie out of the room and outside. They kept going until they were away from the cabin.

The fire spread through the building. Westlake still lay on the wooden porch. The flames reached the front room and pushed out through the broken window. A red spot appeared on the roof as the fire broke through. Even though they were many yards away the heat felt intense, like standing near a blast furnace.

"Westlake," Selena said. "We should get him."

She started toward the cabin. Nick grasped her arm and held her back. "Too late," he said.

The fire roared over the porch. General Westlake stirred. His clothes smoldered and burst into flame. He screamed, a horrible sound, unlike anything Nick had ever heard. He knew it would echo in his mind for the rest of his life.

Westlake got to his hands and knees and tried to stand, surrounded by flames. Then he fell back on the burning planks and stopped moving. The dry wood of the porch turned into an inferno. A faint odor of roasting flesh mixed with the smell of the fire.

"Jesus," Nick said.

Ronnie was conscious. "Burned my hand," he said. A vivid, red wound crossed his palm where he'd grasped the antenna cable.

"I'd better call Harker and tell her we couldn't stop him," Nick said.

He punched in her code. She answered on the first ring.

"Yes, Nick."

"Director, Westlake is dead but he fired those missiles."

"What do you mean? Everyone has been monitoring Prometheus. There hasn't been any change. The Pentagon can read system status, but they still can't get control. It's just sitting up there in orbit."

"But Westlake pushed the button. I saw him do it. The bastard was smiling."

"Then the signal didn't go through. The missiles didn't launch."

"Harker says the missiles didn't launch," Nick said to the others.

"Mice," Ronnie said.

"What?"

"Mice. Mice chewed up the antenna."

"Mice? The world got saved by mice?"

Ronnie coughed and nodded.

"Kind of puts things in perspective, doesn't it?" Selena said.

"I'll never set a mousetrap again," Nick said.

CHAPTER 63

Two days had passed since Westlake's death. Everyone except Lamont was in Elizabeth's office to mark the end of the mission. Lamont was in the ICU at Bethesda, with visitors restricted. His absence hung over them. Stephanie opened a bottle of champagne and filled the glasses.

"This has been a hard one," Selena said.

"They're all hard," Ronnie said. He had a soda in his hand instead of instead of alcohol.

Nick picked up the champagne and refilled his glass. "Westlake said his colleagues were unhappy. Someone sent that sniper after him."

"Westlake had backing from some powerful people," Elizabeth said. "We don't know who all of them are. If Westlake hadn't died, we would have interrogated him. Someone didn't want anyone else to know who was behind this. I think whoever it was wanted Westlake out of the way."

"It would explain why the sniper was there," Nick said.

"Lousy shot, though," Ronnie said.

"He rushed it. We were on the porch, he didn't know what was going on. Maybe he thought we were there to help Westlake. So he took the shot."

"The question is, who are they?" Nick said.

"The FBI is making a lot of arrests," Elizabeth said. "We may find out. What's interesting is that the plotters are from all over the political spectrum. There's no common political ideology."

"If people like that have an ideology, it's one of power and greed. Everything else is a smokescreen," Nick said. "Politics is just a tool to help them advance their agenda."

There was one of those pauses that comes when no one has anything to say. Nick broke the silence.

"I want to propose a toast," he said. They all looked at him. "Arkady Korov." Nick held his glass up. "An enemy who became a friend. He'll be missed."

"Arkady Korov," the others echoed. They drank.

Selena looked at Nick. He nodded.

"We have something to tell you," Selena said. She took a deep breath. "Nick and I are getting married."

No one said anything for several heartbeats. Ronnie's face was unreadable. Stephanie's mouth dropped open.

Then Elizabeth stood. "Selena, that's wonderful. Congratulations, both of you." She went to Selena and hugged her.

"When's the wedding?" Stephanie said.

"We haven't set a date," Selena said. "Sometime soon if nothing comes up."

Elizabeth thought *something always comes up.*

But she didn't say it.

Acknowledgements

My Wife and First Reader, Gayle. She always has excellent comments and sees things in the story I don't think of. She also puts up with my mood swings while I'm writing, no easy task.

Many thanks to Cathy Nobles, Valerie Miller, Gloria Lakritz, Penny Nichols and Kathleen Orescan for wading through an earlier version and giving me their constructive feedback. It makes for a better story.

Special thanks to Emma Sweeney. Her excellent editorial comments have made this a much better story.

Another awesome cover from Neil Jackson. I love what he does with layer upon layer of subtle images and color. Thanks, Neil.

New Releases...

Be among the first to know when I have a new book coming out by subscribing to my newsletter. No spam or busy emails, only a brief announcement now and then. Just click on the link below. You can unsubscribe at any time...

http://alexlukeman.com/contact.html#newsletter

The Project Series

White Jade
The Lance
The Seventh Pillar
Black Harvest
The Tesla Secret
The Nostradamus File
The Ajax Protocol

Reviews by readers are welcome!